**Nick Brownlee** is a former Fleet Street journalist who now lives in Cumbria with his wife, daughter and dog. Following the success of *Bait, Burn* and *Machete*, *Snakepit* is the fourth in the acclaimed Kenya-based series featuring maverick crimebusting duo Jake Moore and Daniel Jouma.

Visit Nick's website at www.nickbrownlee.com

*Praise for Nick Brownlee's previous novels*:

'Fast-moving and thought-provoking, with a nail-biting climax, *Bait* is a vivid and intense read'

*Guardian*, Laura Wilson's Choice

'A captivating debut'

*Daily Mirror*

'*Bait* will have you hooked'

Mark Billingham

'*Bait* is an intriguing debut, brimming with action, memorable characters, and a fascinating Kenyan setting. Jouma and Jake are a pair to watch'

Jeff Abbott

'*Bait* is a fresh debut by a writer of exceptional promise who brings a confident and vibrant slant to the crime genre. Set in the shadowy world of expatriate Kenya ... if you thought that African detective novels are all about bush tea, gossiping and large women, think again as the violent opening sets the scene for a tale that will disturb and haunt. People are murdered brutally with no apparent motive, but it will take all of Jouma and Jake's survival instincts not to become one of the fallen. I have no fear that this is the start of a powerful new series from a new and vibrant voice'

Ali Karim, *Shots Magazine*

'Gripping and action-packed'

*Company*

'A winning combination of high-octane drama and sympathetically likeable heroes ... Highly recommended to those looking for cliff-hangers, ruthless megalomaniacs'

*Big Issue*

'A cast of characters who could have come straight from an Ian Fleming novel. The dialogue is crisp, the settings vivid and the pace swift'

*CNN Traveller*

'Excellent opener from Mr Brownlee'

*Daily Sport*

'Nick Brownlee's debut novel is a pacy thriller set under the searing African sun ... sensational plot twists and hard-boiled narrative make this unputdownable'
*Newcastle Evening Chronicle*

'It's action-packed and keeps you guessing and looks to be the first in a great new series'
*Love Reading – November 2008 Book of the Month*

'Offers a different take on the continuing assault on civilisation ... It speaks volumes for the issues currently facing contemporary society'
*Irish Sunday Independent*

'Executed with an energy and vigour lacking in much crime fiction. Vividly depicting a society on the verge of collapse and the struggle of the few to hold on to decent values amidst mayhem, it's a brutal but undeniably thrilling ride ... A fresh spin on the African crime novel'
*The List*

'As a resident of Kenya myself, the locations and the various references, for example to the post-election violence that swept across the country in late 2007 and early 2008, were things with which I could easily identify and made the novel all the more real. Mixing violence, glamour, wealth and poverty, *Bait* is an extremely interesting novel and makes a welcome change to the libraries of thrillers set in the United Kingdom or the United States'
*ReviewingTheEvidence.com*

'This lively debut thriller is set in Kenya, and I'm hoping that we will see an increasing number of crime novels that give an insight into contemporary Africa. Nick Brownlee's people inhabit a very different world from that familiar to readers of Alexander McCall Smith or the late Elspeth Huxley ... The various strands are pulled together neatly at the end and the final scenes, in which Jake takes centre stage, are very well done – something you often don't find in a first book'
Martin Edwards, *Shots Magazine*

'If you are a fan of this style of fiction this should definitely be on your reading list. Brownlee's writing is accessible and communicates immediacy and a sense of urgency that makes it difficult to stop reading'
*Good Reading Magazine* (AUS)

'Engaging and authentically-staged crime thriller'
*Your Choice*

'*Bait* is an example of how settings for works of crime fiction have turned increasingly exotic, and to a certain extent have become something of a platform'
*The Rap Sheet*

'A rollicking adventure'
*Tangled Web*

'A lively page-turner'
*Esquire Magazine*

'Nick Brownlee is on terrific form in his second thriller as he ratchets up the tension. In boiling Kenya, former British bobby Jake Moore teams up with local cop Daniel Jouma to face a ruthless developer as bodies start piling up in the morgue. Unearthed in the process are the remains of a deadly inferno and an even deadlier secret'
*Daily Mirror*

'In Daniel Jouma and Jake Moore, Brownlee has created a team so different – so compelling – those who pick this novel up will be delighted at how reluctant they will be to put it down again. Deftly crafted prose with a superb range of characters and these vivid descriptions all help to create an electrifying pace in a second novel that is sure to follow up the success the author enjoyed with his Mombasa-based debut. Without question, Nick Brownlee is fast establishing himself as one to watch'
Chris High, *Tangled Web/Shots*

'Once again, Brownlee has produced an intriguing story, brimming with action and memorable characters in a fascinating Kenyan setting ... A stream of hidden secrets throughout the book keeps Jouma and Jake on their toes and the reader totally hooked. If you enjoy being constantly at the edge of your seat, then get your hands on this!'
*RTE Guide*

'*Burn* is a fast-paced and exciting novel that brings the dark and dirty streets of Mombasa alive. Brownlee has succeeded in establishing the same sense of place that was so powerful in *Bait*. There is no doubt in my mind that, with each successive novel, Nick Brownlee's stock is rising'
Luke Croll, *Reviewing the Evidence*

'Superb ... a fast-paced thriller that brings the real Kenya to life'
*www.bookbag.co.uk*

'Absorbing and entertaining'
*The Times*

*Also by Nick Brownlee*

Bait
Burn
Machete

# SNAKEPIT

*Nick Brownlee*

PIATKUS

First published in Great Britain as a paperback original in 2011 by Piatkus



*All characters and events in this publication, other than those clearly in the public domain, are fictitious and any resemblance to real persons, living or dead, is purely coincidental.*



A CIP catalogue record for this book is available from the British Library.

ISBN 978-0-7499-4266-3

Typeset in Times by
Action Publishing Technology Ltd, Gloucester
Printed and bound by Clays Ltd, Bungay, Suffolk

Piatkus
An imprint of
Little, Brown Book Group
100 Victoria Embankment
London EC4Y 0DY

An Hachette UK Company
www.hachette.co.uk

www.piatkus.co.uk

To A.W.C. and J.H.B.
The original storytellers.

I would like to thank Ed Jardine, aka The Scotby Assassin, for his invaluable assistance with all things weapon-related and for sharing his shady contacts in the world of international maritime security. Proof indeed that old soldiers never die.

*When the crack of the gunshot had faded, and the dead man had finally stopped twitching on the deck, his executioner hawked with a noise like bubbling tar and spat contemptuously into his startled face. Now there were just two men on their knees waiting to die in the broiling midday sun: the men from the fishing boat – and from his perch high on the superstructure of the ship the boy called Jalil waited to see which of them the great Omar Abdulle would choose to kill first.*

*Others were waiting, too. The crew of the* Kanshish *had emerged like rats from the vessel's hold and the tarpaulin shanties on deck to watch the executions, and a frantic exchange of dollar bills had already begun. Jalil could hear their excited jabbering, had been deafened by the firing of their weapons, and he knew that the smart money was on the Kenyan policeman. He shifted uncomfortably on the baking asphalt roof. It was all very strange. Not for the first time, he wondered what had gone so terribly wrong that morning that meant they had to die.*

*Below him on the blood-soaked deck, Omar stood in front of the two men, his face impassive, moving his gun from one hand to the other as he decided who to kill first. The crew began agitating excitedly, and Jalil, no stranger to violence in the short time he had been aboard the* Kanshish, *felt his heart thudding in his chest.*

*He was eight years old and short for his age, with a palsied left leg that he'd had from birth. Normally he would wear a calliper, but he hated the unwieldy leather and metal contraption and took it off at every opportunity. Not only was it uncomfortable to wear, it drew unwelcome attention to his disability. Jalil knew he could not walk unaided without it, yet when he wore it he felt like a cripple. Up here, on the highest point of the ship's superstructure, fifty feet above the freighter's deck, was the one place he felt free from constraint.*

*He looked down at the two men again. How different they were, the white-skinned English skipper and the quietly-spoken little detective from Mombasa. It seemed strange that they should be friends when they appeared to have so little in common, and Jalil wondered how they had met.*

*One thing they shared was courage. Neither man had been reduced to begging for their lives. Their eyes were fixed defiantly on the deck as they waited to die; and as the crowd began to bay and the great Omar Abdulle levelled his gun Jalil hoped that, when his time came, he would face death in the same way.*

# The First Day

# 1

Early morning – nine-fifteen to be precise – and Captain Stelios Aristophenedes, master of the 300,000-tonne North Korean-registered freighter *Arturet*, had already downed one bottle of ouzo and was well into his second. But this was in no way unusual. In fact the fifteen-man crew of the rusting vessel would have found it odd if their Greek skipper had been sober, because Aristophenedes was drunk pretty much all of the time. It was, quite simply, how he functioned.

The second man on the freighter's bridge was trying to put this out of his mind. It was easier to label Aristophenedes as an alcoholic and, in doing so, despise him for it. Trey Stewart was a former US Marine lieutenant who was now in command of a four-man team of ex-military personnel working for a private security company called Yellow Canyon Global Inc. Furthermore he was a Mormon who did not drink alcohol, and found even the smell of it to be offensive – which was bad news for him, because booze fumes were emanating in thick, sour waves from every pore of Aristophenedes' body.

'Whereabouts you come from in America?' the Greek said, suppressing a belch.

'Santa Barbara, California, sir,' Stewart said crisply. He

was staring with a fixed expression through the rattling window, because even the sight of Aristophenedes was an abomination of everything his religion stood for. Ahead of him, the *Arturet* stretched for a quarter of a mile to its blunted bows. The ship was low in the water, its upper cargo deck laden with neatly stacked rectangular metal containers. Inside the containers were automobile parts from the Far East bound for Cape Town.

'Santa Barbara – nice place?'

'Extremely.'

'And the women? They nice too, I bet.'

'Yes, sir.'

The Greek smiled ruefully. 'You know, I was great friends with your Jackie Kennedy when she was fucking that pig Onassis.'

'That's interesting, sir,' Stewart said through gritted teeth.

'Yes. I worked on his yacht for two years.'

Aristophenedes did not tell him that he had been sacked for drunkenly goosing JFK's widow during a cruise of the Dodecanese.

'She was a beautiful woman.'

'She was indeed, sir,' Stewart said. The thought of the overweight Greek, with his sweat-stained vest and hair-matted shoulders, coming within a hundred feet of the former First Lady of the United States made him shudder.

Through his Ray-Bans he saw his own features reflected in the pitted glass of the bridge window. He was thirty years old, lean and clear-skinned thanks to a regimented daily fitness regime and a lifetime of clean living. Beneath his baseball cap his hair was straw-coloured and thick, and although he had not been a serving officer for eight months he still wore it in a military-issue buzz cut. He was wearing neatly pressed khaki combat pants and a crimson polo shirt with the Yellow Canyon Global Inc logo stitched unobtrusively to the left breast. There was a Glock 9mm handgun in a holster fixed to his belt.

'You think they will come?' Aristophenedes said, scanning the empty expanse of the Indian Ocean through red-veined eyes. 'You really think these thieving niggers give a damn about car parts? I thought they preferred oil tankers.'

Stewart clenched his jaw again. 'They don't care what the cargo is as long as they think someone is prepared to pay a ransom for it, and as long as the ship is easy to board.'

'Then they will have no worries here,' the Greek snorted. 'It will be like taking candy from a baby.'

Perhaps, Stewart thought. But the *Arturet* was now approaching the relative safety of Kenyan waters and her scheduled stop-off at Mombasa, and it looked like her long trip south from the Gulf of Aden through the pirate-infested waters of the Indian Ocean would be drama-free. It was mission accomplished as far as the company was concerned, of course – but Stewart couldn't help feeling a twinge of disappointment that there had been no action.

Aristophenedes muttered something indistinct and went across to the map table. He glanced momentarily at the sea chart, which showed the ship's position twenty nautical miles north of Kenyan waters; but he was more interested in the bottle of ouzo positioned over the vast teardrop of Madagascar. He poured himself a measure into a shot glass and fired it down in one. *Dah, this was nonsense*, he thought. Car parts? What self-respecting nigger pirate would hijack a ship full of car parts, for God's sake? They were cutthroats, not motor mechanics. He poured himself another drink. Earlier he had offered Stewart a glass, but the look the American had given him had made him break out in a cold sweat. What was it with this new breed of Yankee? Whatever happened to hard-drinking heroes like John Wayne and Ernest Borgnine? Clark Gable and William Holden? Those guys were *real* men.

The walkie-talkie on Stewart's right hip crackled.

'What is it, Chief?' Stewart said into the receiver.

'Bogeys approaching, sir,' a voice replied.

Stewart's eyes glittered. 'Profile?'

'Two small vessels. Look like skiffs.'

'Speed?'

'I'd say thirty-five knots.'

Stewart nodded and tried to remain aloof despite the fizz of excitement in his veins. 'I'm on my way.'

'Roger that, sir.'

Stewart looked across at the Greek and there was a grim smile on his face. 'Looks like somebody is interested in your cargo after all, Captain Aristophenedes. I suggest you and your crew stay out of sight until this is all over.'

He left the bridge, and Aristophenedes, alone now with his bottle of ouzo, found himself fuming at the arrogance of these so-called *security advisors*. Who did they think they were, strutting around *his* ship as if they owned it, looking down their noses at *him* as if he was an unsightly stain on the deck? Could any of them pilot a 300,000-ton freighter? Could they hell! In fact this whole Yellow Canyon Global Inc scenario was an irritation that was rapidly turning into a full-blown sore as far as the Greek was concerned. Had *he* been consulted about their presence on board the *Arturet*? Had he hell! This was an arrangement that had been imposed upon him by the ship's owners in Pyongyang. Fucking slant-eyed communist bastards. Redistribution of the wealth was all very well until you landed a contract to transport thirty million dollars' worth of cargo four thousand miles through one of the world's most treacherous shipping routes. Then it was every man for himself, and fuck the rest.

Well, to hell with them, Aristophenedes thought, swilling directly from the bottle now as he staggered towards the staircase leading to his cabin on the floor below. He would show *them* who was master of this ship.

# 2

For several years now the pickings had been rich for the pirates who operated off the Somali coast. Oil tankers and goods freighters were ponderous beasts, their crews unarmed, and their owners seemingly all too happy to fork out a couple of million dollars to anyone with the inclination to take their vessels by force. There were, of course, naval patrols – at the last count more than twenty countries had contributed ships to an international protective convoy, operating mainly in the Gulf of Aden – but the Indian Ocean was a million square miles in area, the pirates knew most of it like the backs of their hands, and even if they struck lucky the warships were hamstrung by international maritime law that forbade them from opening fire unless they happened to catch the pirates in the act of actually boarding a ship.

Trey Stewart was well aware of this loophole, and of the supine attitude of the majority of ship owners, and privately he thought it was a goddamned disgrace. He was not alone in that opinion and, as hijacks increased and insurance premiums rocketed, a number of frustrated ship owners had started employing private security firms to guard their vessels.

Yellow Canyon Global Inc was one such outfit. Like

most so-called private security companies it was essentially a government-sanctioned paramilitary organisation, employing ex-service personnel tempted by huge, tax-free wage packets, state-of-the-art weaponry, and, in hot zones like Iraq and Afghanistan, virtual carte blanche to operate outside the law. And, like the others, it had enjoyed a boom time courtesy of 9/11 and the War On Terror.

Stewart had first become aware of the private security phenomenon in Iraq. As a young Marine he had watched with a mixture of contempt and envy as teams of highly-paid mercenaries, cool and aloof in their shades and bullet-proof vests, cruised the streets of Baghdad in armour-plated SUVs while he scraped the sand out of his assault rifle and glued the soles back on to his combat boots. And as firms with names like Blackwater, ArmorGroup, Meteoric Tactical Solutions, and Diligence Middle East flooded into the city in the aftermath of Saddam Hussein's overthrow, Stewart heard talk that there were more private soldiers on the ground than regular military personnel.

His buddies called them Hollywood Heroes, but one by one he watched them quit and join their ranks. Stewart had despised them for it, because as far as he was concerned the Corps was life itself, an honour that no amount of money could buy. Never in a million years could he imagine the day when he would become one of them.

Yet eight years down the line from Operation Iraqi Freedom here he was, pimping his experience for thirty thousand dollars a month to an organisation with its headquarters in Boulder, Colorado, while the Corps were still getting their butts kicked by the Taliban.

Stewart didn't like to think about that too hard,

because it made him queasy. The motto of the Marines was *Semper Fi*, Latin for *always faithful*, and there wasn't a day went by when Stewart didn't feel it burning on his brain. But when your youngest boy had leukaemia and the medical bills were ten thousand dollars a month, principle came a distant second in any man's list of priorities.

From the *Arturet*'s quarterdeck he observed the approaching skiffs through a pair of high-resolution Zeiss binoculars. He'd pretty much given up all hope that they would be targeted on this run – they were too far south of the usual pirate hunting grounds – but now that he had them in his sights the sheer effrontery of these sons-of-bitches was truly something to behold. There were two open boats, each carrying up to a dozen men. They were all armed – AK-47s and rocket launchers mainly – and they were making no attempt to disguise their approach, or even their intentions. As they came within five hundred yards of the *Arturet*'s rust-streaked hull some of the bastards were even *laughing*, as if they were out for a day trip.

Then again, Stewart thought, that's what hijacking had been for these guys up until now.

'Howdy, boys,' said the man beside him at the rail, emitting a low chuckle as he peered through his binoculars. 'What kept you?'

Chief Wojcek was a veteran Navy Seal warrant officer who, at forty-three, thought his day had been and gone. Unlike younger men, who had followed the money without a second thought, the Chief saw his new job as a second chance, and a hell of a better alternative to stacking shelves in his local Seven Eleven back in Chicago.

Above him, positioned on a steel container, were two men manning a .50 calibre general purpose machine gun trained at the approaching vessels.

'You know, Chief, I almost feel sorry for those poor bastards,' one of them said, chewing gum with a bovine relentlessness as he gazed out through wraparound shades. 'I heard most of 'em are fishermen without two beans to rub together.'

'My heart bleeds for them, Slocombe,' the Chief said matter-of-factly. 'But my daddy always told me stealing was a sin.'

'Amen to that,' Slocombe said.

The skiffs were less than two hundred yards away and slowing fast. The pirates were studying the *Arturet*, checking for potential opposition and obstacles before preparing to board the vessel at its lowest point using rudimentary grappling hooks and rope ladders. Through his binoculars Stewart could see that their boats were made of flimsy wood and fibreglass, but propelled by heavy outboards that had clearly been scavenged from more powerful craft. They had been built for speed and manoeuvrability, but little else. A single burst from the .50 Cal would turn either one into confetti in the blink of an eye.

'What I don't understand,' Slocombe said, 'is why we can't just kick their butts? Make an example of them. As a warning to the others, so to speak.'

'You mean blow 'em out of the water?' the Chief said.

'Well – yeah, Chief. I mean, you let the thieving sons of bitches know you mean business, word soon gets round. As it is they know damn well we ain't going to shoot at 'em. Soon as they see us, they'll just bid us good day and move on to a ship that don't have protection.'

'I agree,' Stewart said. 'But I didn't write the Rules of Engagement.'

It did indeed strike Stewart as perverse that even though he and his men had nothing to do with the international maritime force patrolling the Indian Ocean, they were still bound by the same rules that made the gunboats so ineffective.

Several minutes passed. The pirates were clearly taking time to fully scrutinise the freighter for its weak points. By now they would have spotted Stewart and his men. The hefty .50 Cal was unmistakable.

'OK,' Stewart said. 'Time to let them know we're here.'

'Yes, sir,' Slocombe said. A moment later there was a deafening *chugga-chugga-chugga* noise as the .50 Cal opened up. The rounds were aimed way over the skiffs and exploded into the sea more than a quarter of a mile beyond them, but the Chief chuckled as the pirates flung themselves into the bottom of their boats in a tangle of arms and legs.

'And when the music stops, you gotta freeze,' he said.

Stewart raised his hand to signal ceasefire, then went to the rail. He was holding a loudhailer, which he brought to his mouth.

'Vessels off the starboard side,' he said carefully, his amplified voice leaping back off the surface of the ocean. 'Be advised this ship is protected and any attempt to board her will be resisted. Do you understand?'

Presently a head popped up over the side of one of the skiffs and looked around suspiciously. It was followed by more as the pirates realised they had not been the target of the .50 Cal.

'They look like fuckin' meerkats,' Slocombe chuckled.

'Do you understand?' Stewart repeated into the loud-hailer.

'What's a fuckin' meerkat?' said the second man at the gun, whose name was Earlie.

There was a pause, then one of the pirates stood, placed

his foot on the bow of his skiff and, with a smile that could have been seen from space, bowed theatrically at the freighter.

This time even Stewart could not help smiling. In that single action, the pirate had summed up this whole crazy situation.

'I think they get the message,' he said.

But then the damnedest thing happened: from somewhere off to his right, Stewart heard the unmistakable chatter of small-arms fire – and two hundred yards away, the bowing pirate flung himself back into the boat as bullets began peppering the water around both skiffs.

'What the hell?' the Chief said.

Stewart turned and stared open-mouthed at the ship's superstructure where Aristophenedes was standing unsteadily on the observation gantry of the bridge, blasting away at the skiffs with what looked like an Armalite assault rifle. He was yelling and laughing, the bullets spraying indiscriminately as he staggered drunkenly along the walkway.

'God*dammit*!' Stewart exclaimed, but now the startled pirates were beginning to manoeuvre their boats away from the killing zone.

'They're moving out, sir,' Earlie said.

'No, they ain't,' the Chief said ominously.

He was right. To Stewart's horror he saw that they were merely repositioning. And now they were aiming their own weapons at the ship. A moment later a volley of AK-47 bullets peppered the superstructure close to where Aristophenedes was standing, and the Greek skipper hurriedly ducked down out of sight.

'RPG,' the Chief reported calmly. 'I think they're pissed at us.'

In the bow of one of the skiffs was a man with a

shoulder-mounted grenade launcher, the bulbous missile aimed directly at the *Arturet*'s fat, inviting flanks.

'Take him out, Slocombe,' Stewart barked without hesitation.

'Yes, sir.'

There was a roar as the .50 Cal opened up, and in the blink of an eye the skiff was chewed up by heavy-duty shells, then ripped apart as the drums of fuel it was carrying exploded.

'I got another, two o'clock!' the Chief yelled. 'Oh, these boys are mad all right.'

Slocombe swung the machine gun's long barrel towards the second skiff, which had executed a sharp one-eighty degree turn and was speeding away from the *Arturet*, using the roiling black smoke as cover as the sea around it boiled with ordnance. One of the pirates was drawing a bead on the gun emplacement with his RPG launcher. Shells from the .50 Cal chased them, biting a hole in the side of the boat and turning three of the men on board into red mist. But the man on the rudder was good, and the skiff was designed for manoeuvrability. Weaving the vessel left and right, all the while keeping its engines at full throttle, he was somehow able to dodge the incoming fusillade long enough for the smoke from the burning skiff to completely obliterate the vision of the gunner.

'*Incoming!*' Earlie screamed as a flaming object suddenly ripped from the smoke pall.

The RPG, travelling at nearly 1,000 feet per second, fizzed over their heads and struck the container. It was a glancing blow and barely dented the sturdy metal exterior – but the missile exploded in mid-air and the next thing Stewart knew he was face down on the deck, feeling like he'd just been kicked in the back by a mule. He lifted his head and the Chief appeared in his vision. There was an urgent expression on his face and his mouth was moving, but all Stewart could hear was a dull whine in his ears.

'I'm OK, I'm OK,' he muttered. He staggered to his feet and, looking up, saw Slocombe and Earlie wrestling with the .50 Cal, which had been knocked off its stand by the force of the airburst.

'Goddammit,' Wojcek said.

He was looking out to sea, at a roiling cloud of oily black smoke and at the second skiff, which had performed a tight U-turn and was now speeding back to the ship. Then, when it was no more than a hundred metres from the side, the vessel slowed and turned again – and, as Stewart watched impotently, his gaze was met by a tall African with a streak of orange dye running through his tight black curls. The man's eyes burned with hatred and they remained locked on Stewart's as the bullet-riddled, bloodstained skiff once again moved away from the *Arturet* and was swallowed up by the smoke.

# 3

On the flying bridge of the game fishing boat *Yellowfin*, Jake Moore was laughing. The reason for his amusement was Detective Inspector Daniel Jouma's legs, which poked from a pair of oversized khaki shorts like a pair of black pipe cleaners.

Jouma himself was putting a brave face on matters. He knew that his appearance could be construed as faintly comical – but what did his friend expect? A suit? He stared glumly at the ocean and reflected, not for the first time that day, that this cruise was a bad idea. He had, after all, quite happily spent almost all of his fifty-plus years on dry land, nurturing a healthy mistrust of the sea. That he should find himself, of his own volition, so far from the mainland that it was no longer visible on the horizon seemed now even more ludicrous than his appearance.

There were certain people who were born to be on the water, he reflected glumly. Jake, six foot tall, 210 pounds, and with all the languid confidence of a natural sailor, was one of them – but Jouma, who was five-feet-five, built like a jockey, and who had spent the trip desperately trying to keep his breakfast down, was most definitely not.

It had seemed such a good idea at the time, the detective

sighed. With his wife Winifred away visiting her sister at Lake Turkana, and with four days' leave courtesy of Superintendent Simba, Jouma had been determined that now was the perfect opportunity to conquer his fear of the ocean.

And Jake, with whom he had been through more in the last few months than could reasonably be expected in a lifetime, had been more than willing to help him. After everything that had happened lately, both men felt they were owed some downtime, safe in the knowledge that at least out here on the ocean there was nobody who wanted to kill them.

They had set off from Flamingo Creek at dawn and were now heading north along the Kenyan coast towards the Lamu archipelago, where Jake said he knew a good place for lunch. All Jouma knew of Lamu was that it was the last outpost of civilisation before the swampy badlands of the Somali border; a tourist paradise just a few short miles from lawless purgatory. The thought was a sobering one, although Jake didn't seem to care. In fact his friend seemed supremely confident in the sanctity of Kenyan waters – to the extent that Jouma felt ashamed at his own squeamishness. Maybe his nerves had been rubbed raw by recent events.

'I didn't think you'd want a beer, Inspector,' Jake said. 'So I brought you some tea.'

Jouma momentarily brightened as he saw Jake waving a large tartan thermos flask.

'I'm afraid it's just Typhoo bags – but the dealer in Kilindi didn't stock the fancy loose-leaf stuff you like.'

'It will be fine, thank you.'

Jake glanced down at the Inspector's legs and stifled another giggle. 'I'm sorry,' he said.

'I should have gone to Lake Turkana with Winifred,'

Jouma grumbled. 'Then at least I could have worn trousers.'

'Listen, I promise you that when we get to Lamu it will all be worth it,' Jake said. 'The restaurant is right on the beach, and Gunther does the best lobster in east Africa.'

Jouma put a straw hat on his head. 'Then perhaps I will forgive your impudence,' he said. 'And then I should thank you for taking me out for the day. I know you have a business to run.'

'To hell with the business. We've earned a little R&R after everything we've been through. And after Harry nearly lost her in a card game, I'm not letting this boat out my sight.'

'An eminently sensible precaution,' Jouma said. He had heard how Harry Philliskirk, Jake's business partner, had very nearly allowed his own brother to use, and lose, *Yellowfin* as collateral in a poker game.

Beside him in the captain's chair Jake smiled and pushed the throttles forward, relishing the kick from *Yellowfin*'s diesels. It was good to be out here, and it was good to have Jouma for company.

But best of all it was good to be alive.

The two men had known each other for an indecently short period – but in that time they had run up against sex traffickers, professional killers, and a psychopath with a penchant for beheading people with a machete. Death had stalked them relentlessly: Jake had barely survived his encounter with the assassin known only as the Ghost, while Jouma had been so close to the Headhunter's swishing blade he could still taste the serial killer's fetid breath.

*And of course others had not been so lucky.*

Jouma, he knew, had been deeply scarred by the death of his young detective sergeant, David Mwangi, at the hands of the Headhunter. Scars like those, he knew, would take more than a pleasure cruise to heal.

'Jake.'

Jouma was gazing out towards the eastern horizon where a small white fleck had appeared. It was a boat, intermittently visible on the swell, and it was travelling at speed towards them. Jake grabbed a pair of binoculars from the dashboard – and as he fixed the vessel in his sights his blood chilled. It was a skiff, pimped with a powerful outboard. There were men in the boat. Eight, nine Africans in sun-bleached T-shirts, bandanas, head-scarves and baseball caps.

And they were carrying guns.

'Inspector.'

'I see them,' Jouma said, peering across from under the straw brim of his hat.

Jake turned for the mainland, gripping the throttles, trying to squeeze some more speed out of the thirty-footer. But the skiff was faster and more nimble. In only a moment, it seemed, it had cut across *Yellowfin*'s bows, forcing Jake to veer sharply, sacrificing valuable momentum. He looked behind him and saw the skiff arcing round in his wake, then straightening so that it was speeding on a parallel course. As it drew alongside Jake yanked *Yellowfin*'s wheel in an attempt to ram it; there was a dull crunch and for a moment the skiff looked as if it might tip over. But then a pair of grappling hooks clattered onto the cockpit deck and held fast against the gunwale. With both vessels travelling at breakneck speed the skiff thumped against *Yellowfin*'s hull and four men leapt aboard.

'Grab hold and keep her steady,' Jake yelled, planting Jouma's hands on the wheel. He reached down and ripped the portable fire extinguisher from its mounting beneath the dashboard, then moved to the top of the connecting ladder bolted to the side of the bridge superstructure. Two of the Africans were already clambering up it, AK-47s slung across their shoulders. With a mighty swing, Jake caught the first man full in the face with the metal canister. He yelped and fell back into the cockpit, but the second man was too fast and too agile. Springing up from the last rung of the ladder, he wrapped his arms around Jake's waist and toppled him sideways. Jake reached out and grabbed the awning stanchion, but he was already hopelessly unbalanced. Dangling over the cockpit he felt more hands grabbing from below and the next thing he knew he had crashed down onto the deck. Punches and kicks rained down on him, and then the butt of an assault rifle thudded against the side of his head and his vision exploded.

Up on the flying deck, clinging to the wheel for dear life, Jouma looked up to see a man approaching. The man had a crude slash of orange dye running across his hair, and there was an assault rifle in his hands.

'I am a police officer with Kenya CID!' Jouma exclaimed, rising to his feet with one hand outstretched as if he was directing traffic on Nyali Bridge in Mombasa. 'Piracy is a criminal act and I must warn you that—'

The pirate looked at him irritably, as if he was a buzzing horsefly, and then swatted him aside with one sweep of the hand, grabbed the wheel and eased back the throttle to kill *Yellowfin*'s speed.

'I will warn you again,' Jouma protested. 'This is an act of piracy and the penalty for—'

'Shut up, old man,' Orange Flash said, without bothering to look up this time. 'Or I will kill you.'

# 4

'*Poor little cripple boy*,' the girl sang. '*Stupid little metal leg.*'

'Stop it, Sheba.'

'*His mother was a whore and his father was a goat.*'

'Please, Sheba.'

The girl emitted a trill of laughter and dropped another date into her open mouth. She was eleven years old, of Arab extraction, with honey-coloured skin and thick black hair folded up onto the top of her head and held in position with four bone chopsticks. She might have been pretty were it not for the fact she weighed 190 pounds, double the average weight of a girl her age, almost all of it translated into vast rolls of fat that bulged beneath her white cotton robe and distorted her face so her features looked like they had been stuck in a ball of honey-coloured dough. She was lounging on a coil of rope in the shade of the *Kanshish*'s superstructure. A few yards away Jalil limped with as much purpose as he could muster, his eyes fixed on the wooden aft deck.

'You'd better find it, little cripple boy,' Sheba cooed. 'It was a gift from my father.'

'Then you shouldn't have dropped it,' Jalil muttered.

'What did you say?'

'Nothing.'

'You'd better not have,' she warned.

Jalil bit his tongue and kept looking for the amber pendant, even though he knew it could be anywhere. Down a crack. Overboard. Anywhere.

'Yes, my father gave it to me, metal leg,' she called, stressing the point. 'For my birthday.'

'I know.'

'And you know that Omar is my father's brother.'

'I know, I know.'

The boy had been searching for nearly half an hour in the hot sun, hobbling up and down every inch of the deck until his withered leg ached, while she just sat there like some bloated lizard on a rock.

'Would you like a drink, Jalil?'

He looked up and saw that Sheba was holding a canteen of water in one plump hand.

'Yes, please.'

'Then keep looking and I might give you a sip,' she snapped.

Jalil looked up at the roof of the ship's superstructure and he wished he was up there with the cool sea breeze against his skin.

'Are you sure this is where you dropped it?'

'I did *not* drop it,' Sheba corrected him. 'It fell from my neck when I was throwing those metal rivets from the back of the ship. And don't you forget whose idea it was to throw metal rivets, cripple boy.'

'Don't call me that!'

'I will call you anything I like.'

Again Jalil said nothing, even though he was almost bursting with the injustice of it all. *She* had spotted the oily cardboard box of rivets down in the engine room. It had been *her* idea to throw them over the side. They weren't even supposed to *be* in the engine room. Only the Nigerians were allowed down there – Omar had expressly forbidden them to go anywhere near it.

No doubt *he* would get the blame for that as well, the boy thought miserably.

'Hey, cripple boy. Look what I found.'

Jalil looked up and saw Sheba twirling something on her outstretched finger.

It was the amber pendant.

Fury pulsed through the boy's body and it was all he could do to stop himself from picking up one of the few remaining rivets and bashing in her grinning face with it.

'*Sheba?*'

The voice belonged to an old Somali woman, her impossibly wrinkled face poking out of a Muslim hijab. She was standing on the narrow quarterdeck jutting from the rear of the superstructure overlooking the stern of the ship.

'What is it, Maira?' the girl called out irritably.

'The Imam is waiting for you.'

Sheba pulled a face. 'Tell him I'm busy.'

'You know I can't do that.'

'Then what *can* you do?' the girl snapped, heaving herself to her feet and glaring up at the old woman with her balled fists jammed into her hips. 'What is the point of your useless life?'

'Please, Sheba,' the old woman said, her voice so soft it was almost whipped away by the sea breeze. 'Your uncle has ordered it.'

Sheba emitted a shriek of annoyance. 'Very well, very well,' she said, shaking her head. 'I'm coming.'

She stomped towards the aft door in high dudgeon, but paused to flash a wicked smile at Jalil.

'Don't forget to take that box back where you got them,' she cooed. 'And you'd better hope that my uncle

Omar doesn't find out there are some missing – or you're in *big* trouble.'

Jalil winced as the door slammed behind her, but he was relieved that she was gone. The boy loved Omar more than anyone else in the world, but Sheba drove him to distraction. How could such a great man have such a monster as a niece? It was only three weeks since the girl had flounced onto the ship, full of airs and graces, but not one day had passed without Jalil wishing she was back on the mainland.

*Why was she here?* Sheba said it was because her father – a very important man, naturally, and no doubt the most important man in Mogadishu – was in great danger.

But Sheba made up stories like that all the time. Most of the time Jalil didn't believe a word she said.

He stared despondently out towards the horizon. The ship was at anchor, the roar of its mighty engines reduced to an insignificant hum. It would not have been so bad if Sheba actually treated him with respect, he reflected. But no, she treated him like dirt. To her, Jalil was a dogsbody to humiliate at will.

# 5

Held at gunpoint in the pirate skiff Jake had no way of knowing where they were heading – but they'd been travelling at full throttle for the best part of an hour now, which was enough to confirm his worst fears.

They were in Somali waters, and all bets were off.

*Kidnapped by pirates.* Jesus! It was scarcely believable, the kind of thing that happened to dimwit amateur yachtsmen unaware that they were pleasure-boating in the most treacherous waters in the world. Yet in his defence, Jake and Jouma had been a good thirty miles inside supposedly safe Kenyan waters, heading for a convivial lunch date in Lamu, when *Yellowfin* had been boarded. These pirates were way, way out of their natural hunting ground.

But what worried him more was the demeanour of the pirates themselves – silent, seething, almost *distracted.* There was nothing in their manner to suggest they had achieved some calculated objective by taking Jake and Jouma prisoner; in fact Jake got the distinct impression that the hijacking had been *forced* on them, that it was a desperate measure by desperate men.

His suspicions were reinforced by the condition of the skiff. There were ragged holes in the fibreglass hull that could only have been caused by bullets, and mingled in with the water and diesel oil by his feet were threads of fresh red blood that had also splashed against the sides and onto the clothes of some of the pirates. These men had been involved in some sort of shoot-out, and every indication was that it had been recent.

And that, Jake surmised, was why he and Jouma had been taken and *Yellowfin* left adrift. This was no opportunist kidnapping and they were not simply ransom fodder. They were hostages, pure and simple; human shields to be used to secure a desperate getaway.

*But from who?*

He glanced at Jouma, sitting opposite him in front of the boat. The Inspector looked hollow-eyed and stunned, and Jake wondered what was going through the little detective's mind. He wanted to reach out, to reassure his friend that everything was going to be fine. But what was the point, when he couldn't even convince himself?

In fact Jouma was thinking about his wife and how she would react when she learned he was missing. He and Winifred had been married over thirty years, and in that time they had been apart so rarely that her visit to Turkana was, upon reflection, almost inconceivable. In fact it surprised him how it had taken until this moment to realise how unusual it was. He had often thought it curious, even *unnatural*, that two people could become so inextricably linked to the extent that, after a while, they could no longer function independently of each other. His profession had turned him into a student of human nature, and over the last thirty years what he had learned was that mankind had few if any redeeming features and that, given a choice between brotherhood and venality, the latter won out every time.

Yet how did that explain Daniel and Winifred Jouma? Were they an anomaly? A freak of nature like the two-headed calves sometimes born into his father's cattle herd? They had no children, and no money to speak of – nothing but themselves. Perhaps that was it. But then even for a man as resolutely unromantic as himself this struck Jouma as an unduly prosaic explanation. The truth was that, over the years, their love for one another had blossomed, flowered, and been diligently nurtured. And until now Jouma had always assumed that it would continue until, like them, it simply ceased to exist.

The thought that he might be about to die at the hands of pirates – that he would never see Winifred again – filled him with sorrow and, even more than that, it filled him with rage.

*Pirates!* It was an incongruously romantic term for ruthless oceanbound hijackers armed with machine guns and rocket launchers. Oh, he had heard the familiar tale of woe, how they were just ordinary fishermen driven to desperate measures to feed their families – and quite frankly it made him sick. There were millions of ordinary men in Africa who had mouths to feed, but did *they* turn to crime? No, they got off their sorry backsides and found work. Jouma's own father, a simple cattle farmer from Mount Kenya, had walked his herd three hundred miles one year when the rains failed. That was because he understood his responsibilities in life. The men in this skiff could be working in the fields, or in the cities, or even – God forbid – striving to rebuild their shattered country. But instead they preferred crime because it was easier, because it made them big men, but mostly because they were cowards.

The Inspector's sense of outrage seemed to transmit itself to Jake, and when their eyes met across the shallow boat any bewilderment or fear they might have felt in the minutes after their capture had gone, replaced instead by indignant anger that they had been deprived of their liberty. Nothing was said between the two friends, because their set expressions said it all: *whatever happened now, whatever the pirates did to them, they would be dealing with a united front – one that would live or die together.*

# 6

On the main deck of the *Kanshish* a knife fight was taking place between two crewmen in a chalked-out circle. Such contests were strictly forbidden on board ship, largely because able-bodied men were in such short supply; but boredom and the almost impulsive need to gamble meant that such rules were bound to be broken. The fight had lasted the best part of ten minutes and had been evenly matched; then one of the combatants hooked the tip of his blade into his opponent's eye socket and, with a dextrous flick of his wrist, flopped the eyeball onto the screaming man's cheek. As the spectators began to ululate their approval, the two men watching from the bridge turned away.

Omar Abdulle was forty years old – which in a country where few men lived past thirty was an achievement in itself. Of Ugandan extraction, he did not share the wiry physical genetics of the true-born Somali: he was short, barrel-chested, with a gleaming bald head like polished ebony. There was an arrogance to his movements, a martial swagger that was reflected in his olive-green combat fatigues and US Army-issue desert boots, although he had never served in any army and had spent his entire life avoiding military service.

Following him was a huge bear of a man, with the looks and appearance of a heavyweight boxer only just beginning to go to seed. His name was Rafael, and he was Omar's bodyguard, a position he had once held for General Aidid, the notorious Somali warlord gunned down in a CIA-sponsored ambush in 1996. During the shoot-out Rafael had killed fifteen men, two of them with his bare hands. The reward for his loyalty was a fist-sized tear in the tissues of his throat, as if he'd been swiped by a wild animal. It had been caused by one of the bullets that had killed Aidid and it had cost him his larynx.

Omar strode across the bridge and through a door into an adjoining wardroom. When the *Kanshish* had been a Nigerian-registered commercial coaster plying its trade up and down the east African seaboard this wood-panelled room had been used as a dining room for its officers. Since the hijacking of the ship and the murder of her master and senior officers eighteen months ago, Omar had put his own particular stamp on the wardroom. Where once it had been a sparse, functional affair, now it was filled with furniture, equipment and trinkets ransacked from other vessels – sea charts, cabin lamps, life rings, porthole windows, a pair of nautical clocks, an ornamental sextant, a brass spyglass. Omar himself sat in a fine hickory and leather captain's chair behind an equally grand oak desk, stolen from a crate of handmade furniture bound for the home of a wealthy Yemeni businessman.

Indeed the only items in the room that seemed incongruous were the laptop computer on the desk and the state-of-the-art satellite phone beside it. The clash was unfortunate but necessary. In the technological age, such devices were a pirate's tools of the trade.

A man was waiting patiently in a high-backed Shaker

chair, his hands neatly folded in his lap. His name was Moses Bani, and he was nominally Omar's second-in-command. He was twenty-eight years old, although he looked much older, and possessed the tight, almost feral features of the Hawiye, the most populous of the Somali clans.

'Who won the fight?' he asked as Omar swept into the room and flung himself into his chair.

Omar shrugged disinterestedly. 'I don't know his name, but the other one lost an eye.'

Rafael raised his meaty hands and communicated with a series of gestures, punctuated by strangely pathetic gasps from his ruined throat. It was a language that nobody except Omar understood. To everyone else on the ship, Rafael made himself understood with the increasing hostility of his stares.

'His name is Karim?' Omar said, and the big man nodded. 'Well, he is Half-Blind Karim now, and no good to me. When we reach Kismaayo get rid of him. In fact, don't bother. Throw him in the brig and I will deal with him myself. He knew the rules.'

Rafael nodded obediently and left the room. Now Omar turned to Moses. 'What news of your brother?'

'Nothing yet.'

He glanced at one of the nautical clocks. 'We should have heard something by now.'

'Perhaps the Korean ship's radio is not working,' Moses suggested.

Omar grunted and went across to one of the sea charts, which had been crudely pinned to a wooden board on the wall. It showed Somalia perched on Kenya's left shoulder like some grotesque rat, with its huge upturned snout – the Horn of Africa – separating the Indian Ocean in the south from the Gulf of Aden above.

'The ship was on this heading,' he said, tracing a perpendicular route south with his finger. 'Julius should have intercepted it *here* two hours ago.' He rapped an expanse of blue just north of the Kenyan border. 'He should have been in contact.'

'He will be,' Moses soothed. 'Have patience.'

Omar grunted and was about to say something when Rafael returned, propelling a small, squealing Arab into the wardroom by the scruff of the neck. The man stumbled forward and then fell onto his knees at Omar's feet. He was dressed in a shabby cotton *dishdasha* stained with sweat and food.

'*Salaam alaikum*, cousin,' he bleated. 'May Allah smile upon you this day.'

The pirate leader looked disdainfully at his visitor. 'Hafiz. I thought I saw your rat-infested dhow moored alongside. If you have come to sell me some more of your mouldy vegetables then I am not interested. I would rather my men died of starvation than dysentery.'

'May I be forgiven for my incursion, *inshallah*!' Hafiz said, his head bowed respectfully as he stood before the pirate leader's desk. 'And a thousand thanks for allowing me the singular honour of granting me an audience.' He rummaged frantically in the folds of his filthy robe, then held up a bulging A4 manila envelope thickly bound with tape. 'Believe me, cousin, I brought it to you personally because I did not trust it with anyone else. Open, open!'

Omar examined the envelope, then sliced open the tape with an antique silver letter opener. Inside was a wad of hundred dollar bills.

'Three thousand US dollars, cousin,' Hafiz said, his lips wet with anticipation.

Attached to the bills with a paperclip was an embossed business card.

'*Nancy Griswold, Channel Seven,*' Omar read. 'What does this mean?'

'She is a journalist. From a television company.'

'And she gave you this money?'

'To give to *you*, cousin,' Hafiz slavered. 'She says she will pay you another five thousand US dollars if you agree to be interviewed by her.'

Omar's eyes narrowed. 'Interviewed?'

'You have been misrepresented in the eyes of the world. She wishes to give you the opportunity to give your side of the story. The lies that have been told must be answered.'

Omar got to his feet and idly flipped through the money. 'Three thousand US dollars, eh?'

'With the promise of another five, cousin,' Hafiz said, and then he squawked as Omar suddenly grasped him in a headlock, pulled back his chin, and pressed the point of the letter opener against his jugular vein.

'I would not wipe my backside with three thousand dollars! Three thousand dollars is an insult. But the greatest insult of all, Hafiz, is that you presume to barter the name of Omar Abdulle with some journalist whore.'

'Believe me, cousin!' Hafiz squeaked. 'Your name was not mentioned in negotiations. She wants to interview a Somali pirate leader for her television channel. She was in Malindi, looking for a guide to take her across the border – I heard from my friends at the market.'

'And you suggested *me*, eh?'

'Not by name, I swear. I said I might know of *someone*. Please, cousin – I swear I said nothing of you or your whereabouts. Such is my respect for you, I felt obliged to offer you first refusal of the whore's money.'

Omar pushed the blade to the cutting point. 'Where is this woman now?'

'She is still in Malindi. Believe me when I tell you I acted only with your best interests in mind. I hear what they say about you and the others, cousin. The lies the infidels tell about the noble Somali seafarers, it grieves my heart.'

'You always were a terrible liar, Hafiz,' Omar said. 'I ought to kill you for it.'

Just then came the sound of an alarm bell being rung urgently from the bridge roof. Omar raised an eyebrow, because the bell was the signal that an unidentified boat was approaching.

'Are you expecting anyone?' Moses asked.

'No,' Omar said, throwing the cowering Hafiz across the room into Rafael's arms. 'Get the men ready on deck.'

# 7

'I'll be damned,' breathed Jake – and while he had no truck with the profanity, Jouma had to admit that sentiment pretty much summed up his own feelings at that moment.

The sight that greeted them a few hundred yards off the pirate skiff's bow was nothing like what they had expected, because it was nothing like the teeming mainland lairs where most pirate gangs were holed up.

Instead it was a ship, maybe three hundred feet long, with a three-storey superstructure to the stern and a stumpy cargo crane amidships. They were near enough to see its name, *KANSHISH*, *LAGOS*, in faded white paint across its stern, and the figures of gesticulating men on deck. Some of them were clambering down cargo netting to where a small flotilla of skiffs nuzzled against the rust-streaked hull. Two of the boats had already detached from the mother ship and were speeding towards them.

At the prow of the skiff Orange Flash signalled once with his hand and the rudderman tamed the engine. Jake and Jouma watched warily as the boats circled and then came alongside. Words were exchanged between the hijackers and the men from the *Kanshish*, and then the new arrivals broke away and headed back towards the freighter, followed by Orange Flash's vessel.

Up on the roof of the ship's superstructure Jalil had kept ringing the alarm bell until the approaching boat was less than two hundred yards off the starboard side.

This was his job on board the *Kanshish* – when he was not keeping Sheba company, of course – and he was good at it. His leg may have been crippled, but there was nothing wrong with his eyesight; and while the unexpected arrival had whipped the crew into a frenzy, Jalil had known almost immediately that it was not a navy vessel. But then he had been brought up in a one-room shack overlooking the harbour at Kismaayo, and while his mother was selling her body to any man with a couple of shillings spare, he had spent his days watching the boats. He could identify a vessel from three miles away just from its profile.

Until it came alongside, however, Jalil could not identify who the men in the lone skiff were – until, to his astonishment, he saw that one of them had a tell-tale orange strip in his hair.

*Julius Bani*?

But Moses's younger brother had left that morning in two boats and with twenty men. Jalil knew this because he had helped them load up with provisions and fuel the previous evening, and jealously watched them depart in the gloom of first light.

Now there were just eight men and only one skiff.

Something was wrong. Something was *very* wrong.

Jake had already identified the *Kanshish* as the sort of workhorse he saw every day toiling up and down the coast of Kenya laden with lightweight domestic cargo. He had no idea when this particular bucket had last seen active service, but as he stepped onto its grimy wooden deck it was clear it had not been for some time. Merchant seamen may have been mercenaries, content to fly under whichever flag of convenience paid the most, but they damned well looked after their ships when they were at sea. When you lived cheek by jowl for six months at a time in some of the most treacherous conditions on the planet it paid to scrub decks, paint rusting panels, repair leaking seams, store and maintain equipment, and crew hygiene was a priority.

The *Kanshish*, by contrast, had been allowed to slide into a state of ruinous neglect. Her scabrous exterior was merely an indication of the conditions on board. The deck was like a refugee camp, littered with tarpaulin shelters, washing lines, discarded bottles and bowsers, and weapons, lots of weapons; guns and RPGs lying about, propped up or slung carelessly in boxes. The men who lived here ranged from crazy-eyed teenagers to toothless old men, some of them missing arms or legs, others with terrible scars where bullets had torn away their flesh. The sense of menace was palpable. The pall of greasy smoke coming from an open cooking range situated in the bows only added to the apocalyptic scenario.

But worse, far worse, than the charnel house on deck was the realisation that this was the equivalent of first-class accommodation aboard the *Kanshish*. It was reserved for the fifty or so men who made up the fighting force of this pirate gang. The other occupants of this godforsaken ship – the women and children, the elderly and the crippled – lived in the cargo hold. God alone knew how many were down there; the stench of unwashed bodies, human waste and decay that emanated from the vast open hatch was sickening.

He looked at Jouma, but the Inspector's gaze was fixed

on the stained white edifice of the vessel's superstructure where, from his vantage point high up on the bridge gantry, the man he assumed was the pirate leader surveyed his apocalyptic kingdom. Then he turned away and the two men were bundled through a door into a place that, after the dazzling sunlight outside, seemed almost obscenely dark.

In his wardroom lair, Omar Abdulle listened impassively as Julius Bani, leader of the ill-fated hijacking expedition, described how a dozen of his men had been wiped out that morning.

'They did not stand a chance,' the orange-haired pirate said. 'The men on the ship were using a .50 calibre weapon.'

His elder brother sat forward. 'They were *military*?' Moses said. 'On a merchant vessel?'

Julius shrugged. 'I suspect they were private security.'

'But these private security firms are bound by the same laws as the foreign navies. They gave you no warning?'

'They fired over our heads.'

'Then what?'

'Then they opened fire on us.'

'And you returned fire?'

'Things got out of control,' Julius said irritably. 'The men in Salim's skiff panicked.'

Moses nodded grimly. 'And they paid for it with their lives.'

Omar, who had been listening with almost reptilian disinterest, abruptly smashed the desk with his fist. 'But to fire first is against their rules of engagement. *Their own laws!*'

'Perhaps they have changed the rules,' Moses said thoughtfully.

'So they can shoot us in the water now, like fish in a

barrel?' A vein pulsed in Omar's forehead. He glared at Julius. 'Tell me about the men from the fishing boat.'

'The skipper is English,' Julius said. 'His passenger says he is a Kenyan policeman.'

'A *policeman*? And you brought him *here*?'

'I thought it would be wise to have some sort of security. Just in case we were being pursued.'

'Did you see anyone chasing you?'

Julius shook his head.

'Their boat will soon be found,' Moses said. 'We must dispose of them while we have the chance. While nobody knows we have them. They have no value as hostages, and the longer they are alive the more we are vulnerable. We cannot allow ourselves to be compromised.'

It seemed that Omar, staring into space, was not listening to them.

'Omar?'

Omar shook his head irritably, as if the question was a fly buzzing in front of his nose. He went across to the other side of the room and tapped the thick glass frontpiece of a vintage barometer. 'You say they have no value as hostages, Moses – but are you so sure?'

'The Kenyans will not pay. And neither will the British government. It is their policy.'

Julius nodded. 'They will send their SAS to kill us all.'

'The crew are restless,' Moses continued. 'They must be appeased.'

'I will kill them myself,' Julius said with feeling.

Omar turned and looked at his advisors. 'Sometimes, my brothers, you must look to the bigger picture.' He smiled crookedly. 'The crew will get their entertainment – but sometimes you must look beyond the pursuit of money.'

# 8

The brig of the *Kanshish* was a long-defunct cold storage room attached to the crew's galley on the ground floor of the superstructure. It was metal-panelled with a mesh floor, and the only light came from a small aperture set high in the heavy door. It was big enough to hold two men in reasonable comfort, but only if they were prepared to squeeze together in the sweaty, oppressive gloom. Jake was over six foot and tipped the scales at 210lbs – so it was just as well that Jouma was five feet five inches and weighed a little over 150.

'Well,' Jouma said. 'Do you have any suggestions?'

Jake thought for a moment. 'Just one,' he said presently.

'I am all ears.'

'Next time the guards come, you distract them and I'll break their necks. Then we'll overpower the crew on deck, dive over the side, and swim for the mainland.'

'A good plan,' Jouma nodded. 'But with one small flaw.'

'Which is?'

'I can't swim.'

'Damn. Then I guess we'll just have to wait and see what happens.' Jake shifted uncomfortably in the restricted space. 'Who are these guys anyway? Pirates?'

'Undoubtedly.'

'I thought the days of pirates living on ships was long gone.'

'I too assumed we would be taken to the mainland,' Jouma said. 'But then I don't think our abduction was planned.'

'Me neither. And that skiff was shot to pieces. I think those guys were on the run from someone – the question is, who? Did you recognise the man on the bridge?'

'I assume he is their leader. But my field of expertise is Mombasa gangsters, not Somali pirates. Not that there is any intrinsic difference, of course.'

There was a deep rumble and the steel walls of the cell began to vibrate.

'She's on the move,' Jake said. 'Makes sense. Pretty soon someone is going to find *Yellowfin*, and then they'll come looking for us.'

'Except they will be looking on the mainland,' Jouma pointed out.

'Either way we're hostages. Presumably the pirates will issue a ransom demand?'

Jouma shrugged. 'You are assuming our respective governments will pay for our release, my friend.'

'You're kidding me. A Kenyan cop and a British citizen? They're hardly going to leave us to rot here, are they? What *is* the going rate for a hostage these days? One million? Two? Christ – that's a piss in the ocean compared to the trillions they paid to bail out the banks a couple of years back.'

'You surprise me, Jake. I thought you would know that it is the policy of the British government *not* to pay ransoms, because it encourages others.'

'What about you?'

The little detective shrugged again. 'It is the policy of

the Kenyan government not to pay ransoms because, unless you are the President, you are worthless.'

Jake blew out his cheeks. 'Well, that's just fucking brilliant.'

'I suspect the reason we were taken was to provide the men in the skiff with protection in case they were caught. Now we are here, I cannot see that we have any worth. In fact, I would suggest that we present them with something of a headache.'

Nothing was said, but in the half-light both men understood the implication of what Jouma had said.

They came thirty minutes later. Rafael and three wild-eyed henchmen pulled the two men into the harsh artificial light of the galley, and beat them down with their rifle butts and kept beating them as they lay in a foetal position on the filthy linoleum floor. Neither man resisted, but it didn't stop the beating. Heavy, meaningful blows to the torso and the legs. Kicks to the unprotected kidneys. And as they were pulled to their feet and frogmarched from the galley and out on deck, Jouma looked at Jake – and suddenly, after all the confusion about what was going to happen to them, it all seemed blindingly clear to him.

They were going to die, and he would never see his wife again.

*I'm sorry, Winifred*, he thought sadly. *I am so very sorry.*

# 9

In one of the cabins on the first floor, the old woman called Maira was brushing Sheba's hair and surreptitiously picking lice from her scalp. Most of the tiny insects were deftly crushed between her fingertips; but Maira was not a fool. She knew about the importance of protein and how, when one's diet consisted largely of rice and fish scraps, it was necessary to supplement one's intake whenever possible. That was why she took great care to separate the plumper, juicer specimens she found crawling on the girl's scalp and keep them stored in a small polythene bag in her pocket.

The cabin was small. Along one wall was a narrow cot surrounded with built-in shelves and a wardrobe space. Sheba sat at a small antique dresser, staring at the reflection of her own scowling face in its yellowed mirror.

'How much longer, old woman?'

'Almost done, almost done,' Maira said, plucking another tempting morsel from the lank strands. This one was impossible to resist and she discreetly popped it into her toothless mouth.

Jalil was sitting on the floor by the door and watched with distaste as the toothless hag used her gums to render the louse into a paste before swallowing it.

'So tell me about the prisoners,' the girl said. 'I hear one of them is an Englishman.'

Jalil nodded.

'I have never seen an Englishman before. Is he handsome?'

'I don't know.'

Sheba tutted derisively. 'Of course. You're too stupid to know anything.' She glanced at Maira in the mirror. 'Have you ever done it with an Englishman, old woman?'

Maira looked aghast. '*Sheba!*'

Sheba cackled. 'Oh, come on. It might have dried up now, but I bet it saw some service in its time.'

The old woman averted her gaze and instead began to draw up Sheba's hair into a bun. She took one of the four bone chopsticks from the dresser and began deftly to pin the unruly locks into position.

'Anyway, perhaps I will ask my Uncle Omar to give him to me,' Sheba announced airily. Then she squawked as one of the chopsticks nipped the fine hairs on the back of her neck. 'Enough!' she bellowed. 'Get out! I am sick of looking at you.'

Maira backed away respectfully, her head bowed.

Was this how *he* was destined to end up, Jalil thought disconsolately? Lately he had begun to think that it was. It was not how he had expected things to be. Four months ago his whore of a mother had marched him to the harbour at Kismaayo, demanding payment from the crewman she claimed was his father. When Omar heard about it he gave the woman a hundred dollars and said he would take the boy on his ship. He needed a reliable watch boy, he told her.

Later that day, when he saw the whip marks on Jalil's back, he had gone back and put a bullet through the whore's pockmarked face and fed her corpse to the wild dogs. It was the happiest day of Jalil's young life, and as he stepped onto the deck of the *Kanshish* he was so proud to be a member of the great Omar Abdulle's crew. At that moment, as the ship left port for another six months at sea, Jalil would have gladly followed him through the fires of hell and back.

But was this what Omar wanted from him? To be his precious niece's slave? Sheba kept talking about her own father, Omar's brother, and how, once his business in the Yemen was completed, she would be returning to her palatial home in Mogadishu to live with him once again. Jalil could not wait for that day to arrive. The three weeks she had been on board the *Kanshish* had been horrendous.

Sheba was examining her face in the mirror. 'Do you think I am beautiful, Jalil?' she cooed.

The boy fidgeted awkwardly. 'Very,' he mumbled.

'Perhaps you would like to marry me.'

'I—'

She cackled. 'Don't worry. My father would *never* marry me to a cripple. He would sooner see me wed to Rafael.' She laughed again and then began to sing the song he hated. '*Poor little cripple boy. Stupid little metal leg.*'

Rage pulsed through him – and with it came a sudden frosting of his vision, a dizziness in which the walls of the cabin seemed to slide away into a dislocating vortex. It was not a new experience; he had suffered attacks like this as long as he could remember, triggered by his mother's beatings or more likely an escape from them.

He forced himself to take several deep breaths and slowly his vision cleared and his heart rate began to even. And it was then he realised there was something in his hand. It was a gutting knife with a four-inch carved wooden handle and a two-inch blade. Omar had given it to him that first day when he had come aboard the

*Kanshish*. 'No man should be without a knife,' he had said. It was Jalil's most treasured possession.

*But what was it doing in his hand?* Normally it was kept for safekeeping down the bindings of his calliper, because he knew that if Sheba saw it she would take it for herself for no other reason than sheer spite.

*Had she seen it?* No – she was still staring at herself in the mirror. Quickly Jalil hid it away, and as he did so he realised that he had wet himself. He stared with horror at the tell-tale stain on his cheap cotton trousers, and when he looked up again he saw that this time Sheba *was* staring at him. Her lips were twisted into a triumphant smile and her small, sharp teeth hung there like needles.

'Oh dear,' she crowed. 'Have we had an accident, cripple boy?'

'I – I'm sorry,' Jalil blubbed.

'Too late for that now. My uncle will have you whipped to within an inch of your life,' she hissed. 'And then he will feed you to the sharks.'

But now, over the rumble of the engines, a bell was ringing.

'Oh, *good*!' Sheba squealed, springing from her seat. 'It must be time to kill the prisoners.'

# 10

There was quite a crowd for the execution. The rats had spilled from the hold and the deck was choked with bodies, every vantage point taken. The sun seared the eyes as Jake and Jouma were jostled through the baying crowd. They felt warm, sour phlegm on their faces, the tug of grabbing hands at their clothes, slaps, punches, the relentless screams of abuse in their ears.

Then there was a gunshot and the mob suddenly melted away.

A thick-set black man in military garb and silvered Ray-Bans stood in front of the superstructure, a handgun raised above his shaven head. It was the man they had seen on the bridge gantry. Already on his knees before him, hands tied and head bowed, was Karim, the loser of the knife fight, abject, bloodied, the bones of his spine and ribs sticking out against the dark skin of his bare, emaciated torso.

Rafael forced Jake and Jouma to their knees on the deck beside him, and Karim looked across for a split second, long enough for them to see where his left eye had been inexpertly pushed back into the raw socket so that loops of tendon and optic nerve still protruded.

'My name is Omar Raghib Abdulle,' the pirate leader

told them in a portentous voice. He lowered the gun and pointed it at Jake. 'You are the Englishman, yes?'

Jake nodded.

'Then you must be the policeman.'

Jouma fixed him with an acid stare. 'I am Detective Inspector Daniel Jouma of Kenya Police,' he said through split lips that were already beginning to swell up.

'Maybe so,' the pirate leader said, a thin smile playing at the corner of his mouth. 'But on this ship *I* am the law. Which is why you are on your knees, Inspector Daniel Jouma.'

'Listen,' Jake said. 'I don't know who you are or why your men brought us here. But we're no use to you as hostages. Nobody will pay a ransom. So you might as well let us go.'

Omar raised an eyebrow. 'Is that so? How nice of you to tell me my business, Mr – ?'

'The name's Moore.'

'*Moo-ah.*' He rolled it round in his mouth as if sampling a new delicacy. Then his face twisted in disgust, as if the morsel had turned to ashes against his tongue. 'You think we have brought you here to sell you off like cheap cuts of meat, Mr *Moore*?' he hissed. 'You think my men are nothing better than filthy *kidnappers*?'

'They hijacked my boat,' Jake said. 'They took me and Jouma from it, against our will. Sounds like kidnapping to me, Mr *Abdulle*.'

The pirate's eyes bulged. 'Look around you. Look at the faces of my men. Do you see the sorrow in their eyes? The *anger*? Twelve of their brothers have been taken from them this day. Twelve of my men.' As he spoke his voice grew in volume, and flecks of spittle formed at the corners of his mouth. It was clearly a carefully considered and choreographed speech, and even if the majority of his crew spoke no English the tone left them in no doubt what was being said.

'I'm very sorry about that,' Jake said calmly. 'But it has nothing to do with us.'

Omar bent down so his face was barely an inch away. 'Your governments treat our people like slaves. They lay waste to our land and poison our oceans, and then hunt *us* down like vermin. It has *everything* to do with you, Englishman.'

Jouma groaned. 'For pity's sake – spare me the sanctimonious lecture, Mr Abdulle. I'd rather you put a bullet in my brain right now than force me to listen to your pathetic excuses. People like you – *criminals* like you – are all the same. You would rather blame anyone else but yourself for your problems. You make me sick!'

Omar's right hand moved in the blink of an eye, and there was a crunch as the barrel of the handgun made contact with Jouma's nose. The Inspector toppled sideways onto the deck, blood bubbling from his nostrils. Jake made to lunge for the pirate leader – but Rafael, standing behind, floored him with an expert rabbit punch to the kidneys.

The crowd, already in a state of barely contained frenzy, erupted with yells and deafening bursts of AK-47 fire.

'You want death, Inspector?' Omar screamed, dragging Jouma up by his hair and jamming the gun against the top of his skull. '*I will give you death!*'

And even as Jouma closed his eyes and waited for his life to end, Omar turned the handgun at the kneeling Karim and fired a single shot at close range into the side of his head.

'Let this be a lesson to you, my brothers and sisters,' the pirate said, dropping Jouma and wheeling away to address the stunned crowd as the Somali's body slumped to the deck. 'I do not condone knife fights.' He hawked and spat in what remained of the dead man's face. 'People get hurt.'

Then he stepped casually over the body and glared down at Jake and Jouma.

'Now get these dogs out of my sight,' he said to Rafael.

# 11

In a rented room in a warehouse complex overlooking the northern end of Kilindini harbour, Mombasa's main freight port, a silver-haired man drew on his pipe, leaned across a chipboard desk, and blew smoke with precision just above the head of the man sitting opposite.

'Bit of a balls-up, all in all, wouldn't you say, Mr Stewart?' There was the faintest hint of a West Country lilt in his otherwise plain English accent.

Former Marine lieutenant Trey Stewart blinked once as the foul-smelling fug settled about his ears. 'I take full responsibility, sir,' he said.

'Very admirable – but it hardly solves the problem, does it?'

The older man's name was Pottinger. He was fifty-three and a time-served veteran of the SBS, the British Navy's elite special forces unit, with whom he had served with distinction in the Gulf, East Timor and Afghanistan. He was now the man in overall command of Yellow Canyon Global Inc's operations in east Africa. What Stewart had just told him would have put most commanders into apoplexy, but Pottinger had never been the ranting and raving sort.

'This Greek skipper, Aristophenedes – where is he now?'

'Under supervision on board the ship, sir.'

Pottinger tamped down the smouldering tobacco in the bowl of his pipe. He said nothing for a long time. Then he relit the pipe and, when he spoke, it was through a billowing cloud of blue smoke.

'I know what you're thinking, Mr Stewart.'

'Really, sir?'

'You're thinking, "So we shot a bunch of pirates today – what's the problem?" The problem is you're not in the Marine Corps any more. We're all private sector employees, now.'

'I understand that, sir,' Stewart said, pushing back his shoulders slightly.

Pottinger's eyes narrowed. The only sound was the rhythmic *tik-tik* as the former SBS man tapped his bottom teeth with the stem of his pipe.

'*Do you*, Mr Stewart?'

'Absolutely, sir.'

'I hope so – because for an ex-military man, used to seeing the world in black and white, the complexities of the corporate world can often appear baffling. I know, because I've been in your position. The fact is, it doesn't matter if you killed ten pirates today or ten thousand. It's all a question of liability. More accurately, it's a case of *deniability*.'

'I'm not sure I follow, sir.'

Pottinger sighed. 'All private security firms take their public image very seriously. We all remember what happened to Blackwater in Baghdad.'

Stewart nodded. In 2007 a security detail from Blackwater, one of the world's biggest private military contractors, opened fire on a group of Iraqis, killing seventeen of them. The resulting furore ended with the firm having its licence to operate in Iraq revoked, costing them millions in lost contracts.

'The suits in Boulder don't give a damn about dead pirates,' Pottinger said. 'What *would* concern them is a compensation claim from the Koreans for damage to their ship. And what would *really* get their goat is a reputation for hiring gung-ho employees. That, as I'm sure you understand, Mr Stewart, would be very bad for business. They say Blackwater never recovered from what happened in Baghdad. Now, you say Aristophenedes fired first?'

'That is correct, sir. The superstructure and cargo deck were fitted with security cameras, as per standard operating procedure. The footage shows clearly what happened.'

Pottinger nodded. 'Good. Then as the captain is an employee of the client, I don't think the suits in Boulder will be overly concerned. In fact if there's a claim for compensation I'm sure the lawyers will have good grounds for a counterclaim.'

'A counterclaim?'

'For personal injury and psychological trauma suffered by you and your men.'

'But we were fine,' Stewart said.

Pottinger smiled faintly. 'Welcome to the corporate beanfeast, Mr Stewart. I guarantee it is unlike anything you have ever experienced.'

'I see.'

'I'll take a look at the footage and the damage to the ship. In the meantime you will not mention anything about today's incident and you will instruct your men to do the same. Any inquiries are to be referred to me. Understand?'

'And Aristophenedes?'

'When he sobers up I will remind him of the ramifications to both himself and his employers should he choose to jeopardise our mission further.' Pottinger checked his watch. 'Now, we are contracted to accompany the *Arturet* as far as Cape Town – so as soon as the ship is refuelled and resupplied, you and your men will be on your way on the next available tide.'

Since the *Arturet* had docked at Kilindini that morning her crew had been confined below deck and her master locked in his cabin. Officially this was due to irregularities in the cargo manifest – but Stelios Aristophenedes, who had spent the day drinking from his supply of ouzo, knew that was horseshit. He was a prisoner on his own ship, the victim of a disgusting conspiracy between the slant-eyed communists and their American security consultants. But as he drank he chuckled to himself about how the fucking slants and the fucking Yanks thought they were so fucking clever, when in fact they knew fucking *nothing*.

*They thought they could keep Stelios Aristophenedes caged on his own ship like an animal?*

The cabin was a typically condensed affair, with a cot, sink, toilet and seating area all within reach of each other. The walls were made of laminated chipboard, and against one of them was a desk and chair. There were no decorations or photographs or seascapes. Aristophenedes used it only to sleep and ablute, because as far as he was concerned the bridge was his home. The only item that could be considered superfluous, or even homely, was a small short-wave radio on the nightstand. Sometimes, when the drink had made him maudlin, Aristophenedes liked to listen to the Voice Of Greece and think about the day when he finally made enough money to open that bar in Skiathos.

The radio was on now, the crackly lyra music of Alekos Karavitis filling the room. Aristophenedes drained the bottle, kissed it, and placed it on his pillow. Then, with surprising delicacy for a big man who had been drinking hard liquor for the best part of six hours, he knelt before the stainless steel bowl of the toilet and began carefully removing the screws that secured it to the floor of the cabin. When he was done, all it took was a sharp yank to the left and the entire unit shifted to reveal a hole beneath. Aristophenedes had created the space for use in emergencies, like if the ship was boarded by gun-toting Somali niggers.

But it was much more than a hiding place, and now it was going to be used for another purpose.

Aristophenedes turned the music up a notch and squeezed into the hole. He was now in one of the freighter's air ducts. A few feet along the duct was an access hatch that led by means of a metal ladder into a storage bulkhead. A few moments later, having crawled along the duct, he landed with a thump in the storeroom. Outside the door he took the stairs down to the cargo deck. Once there he crossed to a maintenance hatch, opened it, and casually stepped out onto one of the service walkways that extended from the ship to the wharf.

In the chaos of the wharf, nobody saw him leave. Thirty minutes later he was in Mombasa Old Town, in a matelot's bar called The Bosun's Chair.

'Stelios!' the barman grinned, sliding the ouzo bottle across the counter. 'As I live and breathe, I didn't know you were in town.'

'You can call it a flying visit,' Aristophenedes said. 'I can't stay too long. Just a couple of drinks.'

As the harsh aniseed liquor sloshed against the back of his throat, the Greek permitted himself another smile of satisfaction. Just a couple of drinks, he thought, then back to the ship. The clueless fucking Americans wouldn't even suspect he'd been gone.

# 12

The *Kanshish* had been on the move for a couple of hours now. Deep in its belly its turbines hummed and vibrated, and a thin skein of black diesel smoke had penetrated the storeroom where Jake and Jouma were once again prisoners.

They didn't mind: they were still alive.

They had said little since being bundled back into the metal-walled cell. Both men were engaged in their own thoughts, replaying in their minds the moment when they thought they were going to die. Sometimes it seemed as if it was all a bad dream – but the darkening spatters of Karim's blood on their clothes and skin was real enough.

Presently Jake said: 'Why didn't he kill us?'

'Presumably he has other plans for us.'

'Like what?'

'I have no idea.'

The cell door opened. Rafael entered and, with an ugly-looking serrated blade, slashed through the ropes binding the two men. Then he grunted and signalled for them to follow him.

This time there was no violence. Instead of the main deck

they were taken to the aft of the ship where they were led onto a small quarterdeck overlooking the stern. A man appeared carrying two metal buckets full of water. He was followed by a second man with a bulging polythene grocery bag. The men placed their loads on the deck beside Rafael and waited expectantly. The bodyguard grinned and signalled to Jake and Jouma to remove their bloodied clothes, after which he doused them both in freezing seawater from the buckets. He then folded his arms expectantly and waited for the prisoners to wash Karim's blood from their bodies. When they were finished, his assistant reached into the grocery bag for two sets of clothes – cheap cotton T-shirts and shapeless trousers that, judging by the powerful stink of sweat, were neither new nor clean.

'Good day, gentlemen,' a now familiar voice said. 'I trust you enjoyed your shower.'

Omar stood at the doorway to the quarterdeck, flanked by the Bani brothers. There was an amused look on his face.

'It is always nice to get another man's blood out of your hair,' Jouma said.

'And the clothes are the height of fashion,' Jake said.

Omar laughed, an unpleasant bark. 'Well Karim won't be needing them any more. Now – I understand you have already met my chief of staff, Julius Bani.' He gestured to the younger brother. 'And this is his brother, Moses, my chief strategist.'

The Banis regarded Jake and Jouma with cold, hooded eyes.

'Sounds like you've got a regular junta here, Abdulle,' Jake said. He looked at Rafael. 'So who's he? Head of the Secret Police?'

'Rafael helps with the smooth running of the ship,'

Omar said. 'Disciplinary matters are his speciality.'

Jouma sensed a bristling antagonism between the two men. 'May I ask, Mr Abdulle, what you intend to do with us?' he said, changing the subject.

'*Do* with you?'

'Considering you were going to kill us earlier on.'

Another laugh. 'I had no intention of killing you.'

'You had Jake and me convinced. And your crew. I think they were disappointed that you spared our lives.'

Omar shrugged. 'Bread and circuses, Inspector, bread and circuses. I know how the Roman emperors must have felt. It is a constant struggle to keep them entertained.'

'I can't imagine Karim will keep them pacified for long.'

'I imagine you are right. The crew are most aggrieved that so many of their brothers were slaughtered today.'

'Let me assure you once again, Mr Abdulle – we had no involvement in what happened.'

'We don't even *know* what happened,' Jake pointed out.

'I know, I know,' Omar said, raising his hands defensively. 'Julius has explained precisely the circumstances of your . . . unplanned visit to my ship.'

'So why don't you let us go?' Jouma said softly. 'You know there will be no ransom paid for our release.'

'All in good time, Inspector, all in good time. First, though, I feel I must redeem myself for any inconvenience caused to yourselves.' He grinned munificently. 'You must be hungry, gentlemen. Eat now – we will talk later.'

# 13

Jake had never tasted salt beef stew before, and he vowed that, if he ever got out of this shit alive, he never would again. But he was hungry, ravenous even – so he spooned the slop gratefully into his mouth and tried to ignore the fact there was a dead man's blood under his fingernails, his battered body was aching, and his host was a cold-blooded killer who, despite his apparent hospitality, probably had it mind to execute him.

They were seated around a table in the crew canteen, although the large room – which must have once buzzed with the laughter and profanity of twenty or so merchant seamen – was pointedly lacking in anyone other than Omar and his entourage. The dividing line between the elite of the *Kanshish* and the ship's underclass was stark.

The pirate leader was holding court at one end, the sullen-faced Bani brothers sitting opposite Jake and Jouma. The table was covered with a thick linen cloth, and the stew was ladled into china bowls by an orderly who materialised like a ghost from the small adjoining galley. There was silver cutlery, and crystal glasses for the claret, a 1986 Chateau de Beaucastel. To the casual observer, it could have been five friends enjoying a cordial luncheon at a gentlemen's club in Mombasa –

which was clearly the illusion the pirate leader intended to create.

'You clearly appreciate the finer things in life, Mr Abdulle,' Jouma said, without enthusiasm. In fact the whole charade sickened him. It reminded him of the sewer rats of Mombasa, who dined like kings on discarded morsels from five-star hotels and expensive restaurants.

'You might say it is one of the perks of the job,' Omar smiled, gesturing at the table.

'I take it that when you hijack a ship you help yourself to whatever you choose from its cargo? Was this cutlery part of a bulk export, or was it someone's personal property?'

'You don't like me, do you, Inspector?' Omar said diffidently, chewing on a cube of rubbery flesh. Across the table Moses Bani's eyes bored into the little detective.

Jouma shrugged. 'I have nothing against you personally, Mr Abdulle. It is what you stand for that I find abhorrent.'

Omar smiled thinly. 'And you, Mr Moore?'

'Well, your stew sucks.' Jake raised his glass. 'But the wine is excellent.'

There was a moment of suspended silence, then Omar threw back his head and roared with laughter.

'How true, Mr Moore,' he said. He gestured at the orderly in the galley. 'Suleiman does his best with limited resources, but we are coming to the end of a long stint at sea and our supplies are low. Only the wine cellar is well stocked. How is your face, by the way? It looks very sore.'

'I'll live.' Jake looked directly at Julius and grinned. 'How's the guy I hit with the fire extinguisher?'

'Disappointed that Omar did not kill you,' Julius said matter-of-factly.

'Julius, please!' Omar scolded. 'We are friends now.'

'You've got a funny way of making friends, Abdulle. I'll be pissing blood for a week – assuming I live that long.'

The pirate looked sheepish. 'I apologise if Rafael was a little overzealous. However, it is important to establish house rules whenever new guests arrive.'

Jouma cleared his throat. 'This ship – I assume you acquired it in the same way as you took *Yellowfin*? By force.'

'I have seventy men,' Omar shrugged. 'Forty women and children. I have to house them somewhere, Inspector. *Kanshish* is not exactly the *QE2*, but it suits our purposes.'

'I was under the impression most pirates were based on the mainland.'

'Most are. But you are assuming I am a pirate.'

Jake choked on his stew. 'Then what are you? A wandering band of minstrels?'

'*Pirate* is a very lazy term,' Omar said. 'Very – what is the word? – *pejorative*.'

Jouma raised an eyebrow. 'So you are an educated man, Mr Abdulle. What, then, is the nature of your business?'

'I don't deny that my business is the acquisition of vessels. But I prefer to think of myself as a businessman providing a service for interested third parties.'

Jouma thought about this for a moment. Then he blinked as realisation dawned on him. 'You mean you hijack ships to *order*?'

'For a prearranged fee,' Omar nodded. 'Dependent on the risk involved and the potential ransom to be gained by my clients.'

'And who are your clients?'

‘There are many of them on the mainland.’

‘So you do the donkey work for the pirate gangs – for a healthy percentage, I imagine?’

‘I like to think we provide value for money.’

‘An ingenious arrangement.’

‘I find it a lot less stressful than having to bargain with ship owners and government negotiators. In the west I believe they call it procurement.’

‘Of course. But then comparing their activities to those in the west is how most African criminals justify their actions.’

Omar shrugged. ‘At least I do not compare myself to a shipping magnate, Inspector. If I did then I could employ illegal immigrant crews, and skim my taxes, and fly flags of convenience to avoid customs; and furthermore I could say, “*Something must be done about these dreadful pirates who flout our laws*”.’

‘Bravo, Mr Abdulle,’ Jouma said contemptuously. ‘Spoken like a true western capitalist.’

Jake looked up from his bowl and stared across the table at Julius with contempt in his eyes. ‘Well, something went wrong today, didn’t it, pal? Looks to me like you got your arses well and truly kicked. Who was it? The Royal Navy? The Americans?’

‘Jake—’ Jouma said, but Jake brushed away his hand.

‘No, I’ve heard enough of this crap. These pricks can call themselves what they want, they can pretend that this place is the fucking Ritz; but I’m the one who’s had his boat nicked, the shit kicked out of him, a gun pointed at his head and some poor bastard’s brains splattered all over his face. Right now I should be getting pleasantly pissed after a good lunch at Gunther’s bistro with my friend here.’

Omar’s bonhomie evaporated. ‘I am very sorry that

your lunch has been so rudely interrupted,' he snapped, knuckles white as he gripped the table. 'But what of *my* people? What of Somalia?'

'Oh, fuck off, Abdulle,' Jake said. 'You don't give a damn about Somalia. All you care about is your next buck.'

A leaden silence descended on the room, and behind the pirate's imperturbable façade something dangerous glinted.

'If you are finished your lunch, gentlemen, perhaps you would care to accompany me outside,' he said. 'There is something I would like you to see.'

Omar led them onto the aft deck. Here, amid the untidy tangle of mooring ropes and cables, was a canvas tarpaulin covering an object the size of a small car. When the pirate removed the covering, they saw it was four large plastic barrels, each as tall and broad as Omar himself. Each barrel was marked with a stencil that read $NH_4$ $NO_3$.

'Do you know what ammonium nitrate is, gentlemen?' he asked matter-of-factly, leaning against the stern rail. 'Probably not. Neither of you look like chemists or farmers. Let me tell you then: ammonium nitrate is mainly used as high-yield agricultural fertiliser.'

As he spoke, he slipped a reinforced rubber gauntlet onto one of his hands. He carefully unscrewed the cap at the base of one of the barrels, and a steady stream of what looked like seasalt crystals spilled out. Omar caught some in his palm, then quickly replaced the cap.

'Pretty, isn't it?' he said, letting the crystals slip through his fingers to be whipped away on the breeze. 'But in this concentration it is, of course, highly toxic and corrosive. For several years now – and if we are to judge them by their own laws, gentlemen, quite illegally – European countries have been routinely dumping barrels of ammonium nitrate, and other industrially-produced chemicals, off the coast of Somalia. And, of course, once these barrels have been dumped at sea, all it takes is a storm to bring them to shore. The ones that haven't already eroded and killed all the fish, that is.

'These barrels were found on the beach near to Rafael's mother's house. His little nephews were playing with it. One of the barrels split open – and one of the nephews thought the white crystals might be good to eat. He thought it was sugar. The boy was three years old,' he said, removing the glove and tossing it over the side. 'So don't talk to me of *laws*. Not unless you have seen a young boy writhing in agony, but unable to scream because his throat has been eaten away.'

Jouma stared at the barrels, then looked at Omar.

'What are you going to do with us?' he asked.

'I am going to use you, Inspector Jouma,' the pirate said, his voice steely. 'Just as my people have been used.'

# The Second Day

# 14

It had been a busy night, a late night, but after just five hours' sleep that seemed to pass in five seconds, WPC Lucie Mugo of Mombasa police was back on duty. Such were the vagaries of the shift pattern, the desk sergeant had explained, especially with so many uniformed officers off sick with this tummy bug doing the rounds. Mugo knew fine well that it had more to do with the fact that she was young, she was new, and she was female. She was also acutely aware that she had just returned from a two-week secondment to plainclothes division and certain people at central precinct thought she needed to be brought down a peg or two.

She was sanguine about it. Indeed Inspector Jouma had warned her to expect just such treatment when she returned to uniform. It was, he told her, something she would have to contend with all her career.

It was 9am and Mugo was exhausted. In fact, had she not been woken by the blaring air horn of an eighteen-wheel pantechnicon travelling in the opposite direction along the Mombasa to Malindi highway, her patrol car would have ploughed straight into it and they would have been picking bits of her from the roadside for weeks. Hands trembling, heart thudding, she parked in the dirt by the side of the road and stared meaningfully at an unopened packet of ten menthol-tipped cigarettes on the dashboard in front of her.

They belonged to Mrs Nderitu, who worked the switchboard at central precinct on Makadara Road. Her hair was white except for the front, which had been turned ochre by the cigarette that was permanently clamped in her mouth. If Kenya had an international smoking team, then she would be its captain and star player – and she was always looking for new recruits.

'Keep them close by, my dear,' Mrs Nderitu had told her, slipping the packet of ten into the breast pocket of Mugo's uniform shirt. 'This is a stressful job and you never know when you might need one.'

'But I don't smoke, Mrs Nderitu,' Mugo had protested.

'*Everybody* smokes,' the older woman said. 'Some people just don't know it yet.'

Lucie Mugo had never smoked in her life – and until a week ago, when Mrs Nderitu had given her the packet of ten, the idea had never even crossed her mind. Now, as her heart raced and her near-death experience burned in her mind, she wondered if the wheezing old telephonist was right.

'Smoking keeps the mind alert and the spirits buoyant,' Mrs Nderitu said with the enthusiasm of a TV evangelist. 'It calms the nerves, settles the internal organs, and improves mental performance and eyesight.'

Mugo could do with some sort of pick-me-up, and right now Mrs Nderitu's cigarettes looked pretty appealing. But no – she would not succumb. Sleep was what she needed, not cigarettes. Even so, as she started the engine of the patrol car and gingerly pulled onto the highway again, she was careful to replace the packet in the pocket of her shirt.

Just in case.

The headquarters of Coast Province CID is situated at the provincial police compound on Mama Ngina Drive, a sweeping thoroughfare of municipal and government buildings on the south side of Mombasa island. Behind a rosewood desk in a spacious office overlooking the ocean sat a well-built black woman wearing a floral blouse tied at the neck with an elaborate bow. Her name was Superintendent Elizabeth Simba, she was forty-five years old, and she was in charge of the day-to-day running of the department and the small team of detectives it employed.

Sitting opposite her, and in direct contrast to the superintendent's imposing bulk, was a slight, almost mouse-like African woman with short white curls framing a delicately-boned face. Her name was Winifred Jouma, and she was the wife of Simba's chief investigator.

'Are you sure you wouldn't like some tea, Mrs Jouma?' Simba said. It was the third time she had asked the question that morning, but she had long run out of polite conversation. Had Winifred Jouma been anyone else's wife, the superintendent would have farmed her out to one of her deputies long ago.

Winifred shook her head. 'I just need to be sure that my husband is all right,' she said.

'Boys will be boys, Mrs Jouma.' Simba smiled unconvincingly. 'Always disappearing off without telling anyone when they'll be back.'

'But that's the point, Superintendent Simba. Daniel *did* say when he would be back.'

Simba sighed. *Yes, of course he did.* Jouma was supposed to be back from his fishing trip in good time to pick his wife up from the airport last night, where she was returning on the 10.30pm shuttle from Lake Turkana after visiting her sister. And when he had not been there, waiting dutifully in the arrivals lounge, nor at their apartment in Makupa either, instead of doing what any other wife would have done and assumed her husband was unavoidably detained in a bar somewhere after a good day's sport, Winifred had called the police and reported him missing.

And now she was here.

In truth, Simba conceded, Winifred had a point. Jouma was not the type of man to go carousing, and certainly not when he was supposed to be meeting his wife at the airport. Simba found it hard to believe that he had gone on a fishing trip in the first place. As far as she was aware, the little detective hated the water.

'This Englishman, Jake Moore,' she said. 'Do you know him, Mrs Jouma?'

'I have met him on a couple of occasions,' Winifred sniffed.

'And how does he strike you?'

'Strike me?'

'Yes. Is he the reliable sort? Trustworthy?'

The older woman frowned. 'He attracts trouble like a moth to a flame, Superintendent Simba. I wish my husband had never met him.'

Harry Philliskirk was sitting on the toilet when the blue-and-white patrol car pulled up outside the workshop and office of Britannia Fishing Trips Ltd at Flamingo Creek.

He watched the female officer pensively though the slatted door of the wooden outhouse, which was situated a safe distance from the main cinderblock building. A visitation from the police was never a good thing, and certainly not at nine-thirty in the morning. Early morning visitations from the Plod usually meant one of two things: the death of a close relative, or you were under arrest for something you'd done the night before but could not remember. As he squatted, Harry considered the latter possibility and swiftly dismissed it. Last night he'd been at Suki Lo's bar along the creek road – and although he had been very drunk, and may even have got into a bout of fisticuffs with a particularly annoying grease monkey from one of the yards at Kilifi, there was nothing out of the ordinary about that. It was, in fact, an average night out at Suki's. In fact, now that he thought about it, he was pretty sure Suki had joined in at one stage, too.

That left the first option, and this made his flesh creep because Harry knew all about the death knock. He'd been there, bleary-eyed, still stinking of the previous night's booze, when two solemn-faced officers from Thames Valley constabulary had informed him that while he'd been out carousing until the early hours with his chums from the City, his wife and two boys had been killed in a head-on collision.

Harry finished up, belted his trousers, and went outside.

'You looking for me, officer?' he said.

'Mrs Jouma, I really do think that you would be better off at home,' Simba said, trying to disguise her exasperation. 'What if your husband is trying to call you?'

Winifred Jouma tapped her fingertips on the clasp of her handbag, and with some relief Simba saw uncertainty in the old woman's eyes.

'I assure you that as soon as we hear any news at all we will let you know.'

'Well—'

'As I say, I'm sure there is a perfectly rational explanation for all this. I myself was married for ten years. I know what men are like.'

Winifred's expression hardened. 'Daniel and I have been married for more than thirty, Superintendent Simba. I know my husband better than anyone.'

*Damn*, Simba thought.

'But,' Winifred continued, 'perhaps you are right. Maybe I should go home.'

Simba was already halfway to the door. 'It's for the best, Mrs Jouma. I will get one of my officers to give you a lift.'

'I am perfectly capable of walking. Besides, the cupboards are bare. I need to get some vegetables from the market. For Daniel's—'

She paused for a moment and suddenly she seemed incredibly small and helpless. Then she gathered herself up, nodded politely, and left the office.

'There is an old saying in England,' Harry said. '"You know you're getting older when the policemen start looking younger".'

Lucie Mugo thought about this, then wrinkled her nose at him across his desk, partly to avoid the smell of stale alcohol. 'But you could say that about any profession,' she pointed out.

'You'll go far, Constable. How old are you, out of interest?'

'I am eighteen. Now about your business partner and Inspector Jouma.'

Harry sat back in his chair. 'You know Jouma?'

'I worked briefly as his administrative assistant after Detective Sergeant Mwangi—'

Ah yes, Harry thought. He'd heard all about what had happened to the unfortunate Detective Sergeant Mwangi up in the swamps of the Sabaki river. It was not pleasant.

'What more can I tell you? They were going for lunch

at Gunther's restaurant at Lamu.'

'And after that?' Lucie asked, scribbling in a small black notebook.

'I assume they were coming back.'

'Last night?'

'Well, clearly not, because they're not here.'

'And that does not concern you?'

'Constable Mugo, you have clearly never been for lunch at Gunther's in Lamu. My own personal record is three days.'

'Inspector Jouma's wife is very concerned as to his whereabouts.'

Harry looked at her, then shook his head in resignation. 'OK, OK. If it makes Mrs Jouma feel better, I'll raise Jake on the ship-to-shore.'

'I would be very grateful, Mr Philliskirk.'

Harry levered himself out of his chair and went across to the radio, which rested on a half-sized metal filing cabinet on the other side of the office. He grabbed the handset from its cradle and, in a theatrically booming voice, hailed *Yellowfin*.

There was no reply other than a sustained burst of static. Harry frowned, and fiddled with the frequency dial. But when he tried again, and for a third and fourth time, there was still nothing.

'Odd,' he said.

'There is no signal?'

'There doesn't appear to be anything at all.'

He returned to his desk and picked up the phone.

'Gunther! Harry Philliskirk. *Wie sind Sie, mein Freund? Gut. Ausgezeichnet.* Now listen, old boy – I'm looking for Jake, and I understand he was at your place for lunch yesterday. No doubt he's under one of your tables, but—' Harry's face fell. 'I see. And he didn't leave a message?

OK. No, no – nothing to worry about. *Auf Wiedersehen*, Gunther.'

He hung up the phone and sat for a moment staring at the receiver.

'Well?' Lucie asked.

'Well, he booked a table for two,' Harry said. 'But he didn't show up. Listen, Constable Mugo, Jake's a big boy. He'll be fine, you'll see.'

'I hope so, Mr Philliskirk,' Lucie said. 'But Inspector Jouma was due back at work this morning. It is most unlike him that he is not.'

When Winifred Jouma had gone, Simba released a long sigh. She had heard through her sources that Jouma's wife was a formidable woman. Now she knew at first hand.

She wandered back to her desk, but kept on going to the window. Beyond the stand of palms the Indian Ocean was a vast and placid expanse of blue.

*Damn you, Daniel*, she thought. *Where the devil are you?*

# 15

'Are you pissed off, Nancy?'

'Me? No. Why should I be pissed off?'

Red Sheppard lowered the rubber eyepiece of the digital Betacam resting on his shoulder and gave Nancy Griswold a withering stare. 'Because you *look* pissed off, that's why,' he said. 'Your face is hurting my lens.'

Nancy shrugged. 'OK – maybe I am a little pissed off.'

'Why?'

'*Why?*' She gestured with theatrical frustration at the tumbledown wattle shacks, at the stupid goats wandering untethered through the filthy streets, at the even filthier stray dogs, and at the knot of blank-faced villagers silently watching their every move. 'Because we're still bloody well *here*, that's why.'

'Listen, these Somali pirates are slipperier than a box of snakes,' Sheppard counselled, scratching his thick white beard with a thumbnail. 'The fixer told us we would have to be patient if we wanted to talk to one of them.'

'We gave the bloody fixer three Gs of network money to make *sure* he got one to bloody talk,' Nancy pointed out. 'I'll be amazed if we see him or the cash again.'

Sheppard sighed. The cameraman was used to Nancy's

tantrums, but that did not stop them from being wearying. He was fifty-seven years old now and when he stopped to think about it he no longer needed this shit. 'Listen, Nance – let's just do the colour piece to camera. Then at least we've got it in the bag in case anything does come up.'

Nancy's lip protruded petulantly. 'OK – but it's my reputation on the line here, Red.'

'Sure it is, Nance,' Sheppard said, peering through the viewfinder and fiddling with the focus to ensure Nancy's mane of copper-coloured hair was in the frame. 'OK – when you're ready.'

She took a deep breath, composed herself, and began walking slowly towards the camera, violet eyes fixed on the lens. 'This primitive village, on the Kenya-Somalia border, is on the very cusp of civilisation,' she began. 'These people – the Boni people – are peace-loving hunter-gatherers who lead their lives as they have for thousands of years. Yet just a few miles north of here is a very different world. A world in which there is no law. It is the world of the pirates.'

*Oh, but she was bloody good*, Sheppard thought admiringly. He had worked with them all over the years – Kronkite, Rather, Amanpour – but none of them could bullshit to order like Nancy Griswold. Maybe, he thought, all of the great names in journalism could benefit from ten years in soap opera.

'Pirates who – *Jesus Christ!*'

Nancy broke off as two small boys in soccer shirts ran in front of her and began dancing for the camera.

'OK, Nance – we'll leave it there for now,' Sheppard said hurriedly. 'It's too bloody hot here anyway. Hard to think straight. Let's head back to the hotel, grab a shower and a beer.'

'Yeah. OK. That sounds good.'

*Thank Christ for that*, Sheppard thought, lifting the camera from his aching shoulder. She might have gravitated from light entertainment to heavy news documentaries, but Nancy could still throw a theatrical tantrum. Sometimes he felt less like her cameraman and more like her bloody agent.

Later, in the stone-flagged bathroom of her $300-a-night hotel suite, Nancy wrapped her freshly-washed hair in a towel and examined her thirty-eight-year-old face in the mirror. Without make-up it was a face that was blandly handsome without being overly pretty. There were flaws. One eye was slightly lower than the other. There was the faintest of scars on her chin. Once upon a time she had considered plastic surgery to iron out the kinks – but in retrospect her decision to live with her looks was the best she'd ever made, because it set her apart from every other wannabe TV star clamouring for attention from Australian casting directors.

The reward for her mediocrity had been a small part in *Midway Bay*, a cheap daytime soap screened to a few thousand benefit scroungers on Channel Seven. She'd played a hard-pressed single mother trying to bring up baby, the show's mandatory, patronising nod to the real world. She was contracted for six episodes, at the end of which her character swallowed a bottle of Nembutal washed down with a slab of tinnies. That should have been that – except to everyone's surprise, the public outcry at her squalid death was such that the producers had no choice but to bring her back to life. The dramatic scene in which frantic hammering was heard coming from her coffin as it rolled towards the crematorium flames would register the fourth highest ratings on

Australian TV that year, and convince the network to bump *Midway Bay* to a primetime slot. Overnight Nancy Griswold was a star, at least within the claustrophobic confines of domestic soap opera. Eight years down the line, however, she had mutated into a permanent fixture, indistinguishable from the character she played on TV. It was time to get out – and she instructed her agent to start tunnelling.

Escape came from the most unexpected quarter. A producer at Channel Seven was looking for a celebrity to narrate an otherwise unappetising documentary about single mothers in Australia. With her background, Nancy Griswold was the ideal choice – but Nancy was not content to provide the voice-over. No, she wanted to *present* the bloody thing. Browbeaten by Nancy and her equally pushy agent, the producer reluctantly gave in. He was rewarded with a factual documentary with the fifteenth highest ratings of any show in Australia that year.

Three months later the first edition of *Nancy Griswold Reports* aired on Channel Seven. She had progressed from single mums to dictators, warlords and drug barons. During its four-year run it had never been out of the top five most-watched programmes.

In the bathroom of her suite, Nancy applied a sheen of moisturiser to her face, but that was all. Viewers, she knew, liked eye candy on their screens – but they also demanded legitimacy when it came to serious reporting. Facelifts, pancake and hairpieces were for the anchors and the weather arseholes back in the warmth of the studio; out here in the field there was a fine line between glamour and realism, and Nancy had walked it successfully through war, natural disaster, civil uprising and brutal suppression. She was well on the way to becoming a legend in the industry, a name mentioned with breathless reverence.

And it felt bloody good.

But Nancy, for all her self-regard, had not achieved what she had by ignoring the fundamental tenet of her new career: that you were only as good as your last story. That was why it pissed her off that her latest assignment – securing an interview with one of the pirate warlords currently running amok with shipping off the east coast of Africa – appeared to have hit a brick wall. Was it *so* difficult to get one willing to talk? Surely the whole point about these people was that they were mercenaries who would ransom their own grandmothers for a few thousand dollars?

In the bathroom mirror Nancy Griswold's violet eyes burned with fury.

*Where the bloody hell was the fixer?*

She woke to the sound of someone hammering at the door. For a moment she stared up at the swagged mosquito net above her bed, piecing together where the hell she was.

The hammering continued. *Bloody housekeeping!* She was sure she'd left the Do Not Disturb sign hanging on the doorhandle.

'Come back later, will you?' she called irritably.

'Nance, it's me.'

She opened the door to find a grinning Red Sheppard in the corridor.

'What is it, Red?'

'He's back,' the cameraman exclaimed. 'The bastard came back.'

Nancy tied her hair back, dressed quickly in casual attire

of jeans, T-shirt and Timberlands, and hurried downstairs. Sheppard was sitting at a corner table of the hotel bar with Hafiz, the fixer. As usual the little Arab merchant looked like shit in a *dishdasha*, and if it hadn't been for the Australians' endorsement the management would have kicked his sorry arse out onto the street before he'd got past the reception desk.

'Miss Griswold!' he exclaimed, his narrow face split by an enormous smile. '*Salaam alaikum!*' He opened his arms and, to her horror, puckered his lips to kiss her on the cheek.

'I was beginning to think you weren't coming back, Hafiz,' Nancy growled, pushing past him to a vacant seat. A waiter materialised at her shoulder and she ordered a diet Coke.

'A thousand apologies,' the fixer whined, 'but I have travelled many difficult miles in order to—'

'I'm sure you have. So what's the deal? Did you get me a pirate?'

Hafiz puffed out his chest with pride. 'Indeed I did, Miss Griswold. It took much persuasion on my behalf, many long hours of negotiation, but I finally managed to—'

'Who?' Nancy snapped.

'Few know his real name … but they call him The Poacher. He is the most feared pirate in all of Somalia.'

The Australians glanced at each other. Sheppard shrugged.

'All right,' Nancy said presently. 'So where do we find him?'

'His location is a closely guarded secret. But I will take you to him.'

'When?'

'*Now*, Miss Griswold! The Poacher will speak with you *now*!'

'Good,' Nancy said, rising from her chair. 'Then I'll get my stuff.'

'There is one small consideration,' Hafiz said cagily.

Nancy grimaced and sat down again. 'Oh yeah? How much?'

'He wants ten thousand dollars.'

'Ten thousand? He's already getting three up front and another five after the interview. You *did* explain that to him, didn't you, Hafiz?'

'Indeed I did, Miss Griswold.'

She sighed. 'OK – we'll raise it to seven thou for the interview. That's a round ten.'

Nancy stood again, but Hafiz cleared his throat uncomfortably. 'What I meant was, he would like ten thousand dollars *up front*. And a further twenty on completion of the interview.'

'*Thirty thousand dollars*?' she squawked, and all eyes in the bar swivelled in her direction. She reached across and grabbed the front of the fixer's *dishdasha*. 'You've got to be bloody joking, Hafiz! When we interviewed Charles Taylor of Liberia he only wanted a Lincoln Convertible – and he was responsible for bloody *genocide*. That's slightly higher up the scale of human evil than jacking a few boats, wouldn't you say?'

The fixer nodded frantically. 'Believe me, Miss Griswold, The Poacher would be a big catch. There is none bigger! In Somalia his name is spoken of with awe.'

'So you say. But I don't trust you, Hafiz. He could be your fucking cousin for all we know.'

Sheppard sat forward. 'Listen, Nance – the network will stump up the thirty Gs. And if this Poacher guy is who he says he is, then it'll be a bargain.'

Nancy released Hafiz and sat back in her chair. 'All right,' she said. 'Thirty Gs it is.'

'You will not regret it, Miss Griswold,' Hafiz said, clapping his hands in delight.

'I hope not, Hafiz,' Nancy said. 'Because I'll make bloody sure that you do.'

# 16

After their lunch with Omar the previous day Jake and Jouma had been locked in a tiny, two-bunk cabin in the crew's quarters, adjacent to the stairs leading to the engine room. In terms of comfort it was an improvement on the brig – but it was a prison cell nevertheless, airless, hot, and with a pervading stink of diesel fuel. The noise and vibration from the ship's engines was constant and deafening, precluding any conversation, and it was only when the *Kanshish* stopped moving, shortly before midnight according to Jake's watch, that the two prisoners had been able to get to sleep.

Even then Jouma had slept fitfully, to the extent that he was not even sure if he had slept at all. Eventually, at around four in the morning, he had risen and dressed quietly in Karim's clothes so as not to wake Jake, snoring on the top bunk. How he wished he had a crisp white shirt, a pressed tie, and a suit that had been aired overnight to change into.

*How he wished he had his wife to kiss good morning.* Suddenly that routine peck on the cheek seemed like the most important thing in the world.

He had been trying not to think about Winifred, but now, as he lay on his bunk, he could not help himself.

She would be back from Lake Turkana now. He was supposed to have been at the airport to meet her. By now bewilderment would have turned into frantic worry. He wished he could somehow reach out to her, to let her know that he was all right. But all he could see was her sitting alone in their little apartment – and for a moment he had to pause and compose himself.

Jouma lay there for a while until, over the regular rasp of Jake's snores, he became aware of a sound at the door. Someone outside was wrestling with the chain and padlock that had been used to secure it. He sat up and slid back against the wall, instinctively bringing his knees to his chin. *What now? More beatings? Or had Omar finally decided to kill them?*

'Jake—'

On the bunk above, Jake grunted and rolled over.

The door opened.

'*Jake!*'

'Give me some good news, Inspector,' Jake muttered, opening one eye. 'Tell me the British Navy are surrounding the ship.'

'We have a visitor,' Jouma said.

Jake opened his other eye and sat bolt upright. Standing sheepishly in the doorway was a small African boy in a sun-faded football jersey. He was thin and fragile-looking, an appearance accentuated by the cumbersome leather and metal calliper on one leg.

'Who's this?'

The boy looked at the floor bashfully.

'Well?' Jouma asked. 'Speak up, boy.'

'My name is Jalil,' the boy said. 'Omar said I must take you to breakfast.'

The *Kanshish* was at anchor again. To the east a watery

sun was beginning to burn off the early morning mist, and to the west mounds of cumulonimbus suggested they were near the mainland. The majority of the crew were lounging topside, smoking, playing cards, listening to thumping rap music on suspiciously expensive-looking beatboxes, or just sheltering beneath tarpaulin shades. The sight of the two captives emerging from the superstructure stirred them from their torpor. They watched with surly curiosity, nudging each other and muttering in low, indistinct tones as Jalil led them towards a makeshift mess tent situated in the bows of the ship. Under the greasy canvas awning a large steel pot bubbled over a filthy range. In it was some sort of communal slop made of maize, and Jalil spooned some into two plastic bowls which he handed to Jake and Jouma. The two men sat down in the shade as the boy filled his own bowl.

Jouma considered his breakfast long and hard, but he found it difficult to concentrate. He could feel eyes boring into him. Men were lounging in untidy gaggles, smoking *bhang*, rolling dice, cleaning automatic weapons. Their unspoken hostility was almost tangible. But there was something else, and only after a while did he realise that the vicious stares were not only directed at him and Jake, but at the boy, too – and if anything their venom was even more toxic. *Why?* Because he was a cripple? Because he had served the captives breakfast?

Jalil seemed if not oblivious then resigned to it. He hungrily shovelled maize porridge into his mouth with his fingers, and when he saw neither man was eating he seemed surprised.

'You don't like it?'

'I'm still not certain what it is,' Jake said.

But the low grumbling in his stomach convinced him that he should at least try one mouthful. He scooped some in the crook of his finger. It tasted much as he expected – like wallpaper paste.

'So – are you a pirate, too, Jalil?' Jouma said, nodding at the men slumped nearby.

Jalil scraped the bowl. 'Pirate?'

'Do you go out hijacking ships?'

'Omar says I am too young, but that soon I will be ready.'

Jouma looked at the boy's cumbersome metal and leather calliper and suspected that the pirate leader was being diplomatic. 'Omar seems to think a lot of you.'

'He is a great man,' the boy said, his eyes shining. 'It is an honour to serve him.'

'How old are you?' Jake asked.

'Eight.'

'What about your mother? Is she down in the hold?'

'She is dead,' Jalil said with finality.

'Sorry to hear that.'

'Don't be.'

They continued to eat in silence. Then the boy said, 'Did you see the soldiers who killed Julius's men yesterday?'

'No,' Jake said.

The boy shrugged. 'No matter. Omar will have his vengeance.'

The boy clearly had confidence in the pirate leader, Jouma thought. Most probably because he had been brainwashed into it. But what sort of vengeance could Omar possibly hope to exact against the sort of heavily-armed naval force that had, in the blink of an eye, wiped out twelve of his best men? He could beat his chest as much as he liked – but at the end of the day he presided over the rag-tag crew of an ageing coaster that wouldn't last ten seconds against that sort of firepower. No, Omar was not interested in vengeance. If he was he wouldn't have spent the best part of the previous day running away.

'*Jaliiiil!*'

The shout was as piercing as the keening of an albatross, and shattered the subdued peace of the early morning. Up on the bridge gantry a small, dumpy little figure in white was waving urgently at the boy.

'*Ja-liiiiillll!*'

'What the hell is that?' Jake asked.

'Sheba,' Jalil said disconsolately.

Jake noticed that all around them, the crew were laughing quietly to themselves. One or two of them were making surreptitious squawking noises. Whatever this little domestic drama was about, it clearly amused them.

'Omar is her uncle,' said the boy, quickly scooping the last of his maize porridge from the bowl and levering himself to his feet. 'I have to go.'

Sheba shrieked Jalil's name again, and Jouma flinched as if he had just been strafed by a low-flying jet. Jalil was already hobbling towards his mistress's voice as if his very life depended on it.

'Omar's *niece*?' Jake said. 'I never took him for a benevolent uncle.'

'There is nothing benevolent about our host,' Jouma said sourly, thinking back to what the pirate had told them the previous day. 'He regards himself as a businessman, and a highly successful one at that.'

Jake nodded. 'Yeah. If he was British they'd probably give him a knighthood for services to industry.'

'Then we must assume Omar thinks like a businessman. That means everything he does is carefully calculated, and every risk is weighed against the potential benefits. Yesterday he said he planned to *use* us. What I don't understand is *how*. He knows our respective governments will not pay a ransom for our release, and therefore we should be worthless to him as a commodity. Yet he has clearly decided we are valuable to him.'

'I suppose I should be grateful to feel so wanted,' Jake said. 'But right now I'm starting to feel like a turkey being fattened up for Christmas.'

There was a sudden flurry of activity all around them as, like birds startled by a gunshot, the crew scattered to other parts of the deck. Approaching from the direction of the superstructure, smiling beneficently and looking for all the world like a Third World dictator on a choreographed walkabout, was Omar himself. He was shadowed, as ever, by Rafael – but he was also accompanied by a small retinue consisting of Jalil, a bearded man in the robes and skullcap of a Muslim cleric, an old woman, and the girl they had seen on the bridge gantry a few moments earlier. She was perhaps ten years old, although it was hard to be sure because she was extremely overweight beneath the straining fabric of her cotton robe. There was a self-satisfied expression on her face – but again that could have been because her Arabic features were distorted by the wads of subcutaneous fat in her cheeks and under her chin.

'Good morning, gentlemen!' the pirate leader called out cheerily. 'It is going to be a beautiful day, don't you think?'

'For some perhaps,' Jouma said.

The pirate leader placed one hand on Jalil's head, the other on the girl's. 'I take it you have already met young Jalil,' he said. 'This is my brother's daughter Sheba. I am looking after her while he is otherwise engaged on business. She is on her way to religious instruction with the Imam here – but ever since you arrived she has insisted on meeting you.'

Jouma had never been good around children, unless they were engaged in criminal activity, in which case he found it best to treat them like adults.

'Charmed, I'm sure,' he said.

'You are the policeman?' Sheba demanded. Jouma nodded. 'I hope you don't think you can put my uncle in jail. Nobody can put my uncle in jail.'

Jouma raised an eyebrow, thinking that the girl displayed all the same cocksure arrogance as the juvenile gangsters from the slums of Mombasa. 'Is that so?'

Omar chuckled and tugged her fat cheek. 'Now then, Sheba – you've met our guests. It's time to run along.'

'But—' the girl whined.

'Come, Sheba,' the Imam said, gripping her shoulder. 'Do as your uncle says.'

The cleric led the still-protesting girl back towards the superstructure, trailed like obedient dogs by Jalil and the old woman.

'You must be very proud,' Jake said, his voice laden with sarcasm.

Omar shrugged. 'She is a salutary lesson in what happens to children when you spoil them. I find her offensive to the eye and the ear – but she is my brother's daughter and it is my solemn duty to look after her welfare while she is aboard my ship. Fortunately my brother has brought her up as a strict Muslim, which means she spends at least three hours a day with the Imam. The rest of the time she has poor Jalil to torment.'

'And the old woman?' Jouma said.

'Maira? She has been with the girl since she was her wet nurse. I can only assume that, in a previous life, she committed a sin so dreadful that her punishment was to spend this one looking after Sheba. Do you have children, Inspector?'

'My wife and I were not so blessed.'

'Think yourself lucky. And you, Mr Moore?'

'I could never keep a girl long enough.'

Omar laughed again. 'It is a shame you will not be staying with us longer,' he said. 'I find you amusing.'

Jake blinked. 'You're letting us go?'

'In a manner of speaking,' the pirate leader said. 'Let's just say that after much contemplation I have reached a compromise that will keep everyone happy.'

# 17

In a spacious conference room with views across the office blocks of central Nairobi, three men sat at the top end of a rosewood table made to hold thirty people. Two of them wore short-sleeved white shirts and ties, and worked for the Internal Division of the Kenyan National Security Intelligence Service. The older of the two was the head of the division. The third man was a high-ranking general in the Kenyan army.

The subject of the meeting, which had been called thirty minutes earlier and designated with the highest possible level of secrecy, was a satphone message which had been received the previous evening by the warden of Nairobi prison and dutifully passed through the relevant government security channels until, shortly after 10pm, it reached the desk of the Minister of the Interior. The text of the message had been transcribed and now took the form of three hundred carefully typed words on a sheet of A4 paper in front of each man in the conference room.

The Internal Division chief was in his late fifties, white-haired and baggy-faced. His name was N'Kuma and he was a good thirty years older than the second man, an agent called John Nola, whose heavy horn-rimmed spectacles nevertheless gave him a solemn maturity that belied his youth.

'What do we know of this man Omar Abdulle?' the senior man said, tapping the sheet of paper.

Nola leaned forward. 'Very little, sir,' he said. 'Our initial research has come up with a couple of namechecks dating back to the mid-90s, which – if it is indeed the same person – suggests that he was a minor gangster allied to General Aidid in Mogadishu. As you know, a number of those gangsters who survived subsequently turned their hands to piracy.'

'No intelligence from our people on the Somali mainland?'

'Obviously we are continuing to check. But Abdulle's name does not come up in connection with the primary pirate gangs known to be in existence.'

'Then he is new?'

'Possibly. Or possibly he has chosen to remain under the radar.'

'Until now.'

'Yes,' Nola said. 'Until now.'

The army general shifted impatiently in his chair. 'What about the prisoner—' he checked the sheet in front of him '—Qasim Fadir? Surely he will tell you what you need to know, given encouragement.'

Nola smiled to himself. 'Trust me, General, since his arrest Fadir has been given *plenty* of encouragement to tell us what he knows about ongoing pirate activity. In fact you could say he has been encouraged to within an inch of his life.'

'He didn't tell you that his boss was Omar Abdulle, or where Abdulle's base is, though,' the general grunted, his contempt for the methods and indeed the very existence of the security services plain to see.

'In certain respects he has proved stubborn,' Nola admitted.

The general grunted again. He was a military man and in his experience there was no such thing as a stubborn prisoner, just one who had yet to be broken.

'What Fadir knows or does not know is irrelevant now,' N'Kuma said. 'The point is, we have received this message and the Minister has instructed us to deal with it. Furthermore, we are working to an extremely tight deadline. General, you have already indicated to me that your men are ready to carry out their orders should they be required to do so.'

'Yessir.'

N'Kuma scratched his head wearily. 'John – I need to know the veracity of Abdulle's claims. Especially the hostages. Check the names, make sure they are actually missing. It would be highly embarrassing if these two men were to simply turn up having spent the night getting drunk in Malindi.'

Shortly after 11am, dozing in her bed at the police hostel in downtown Mombasa, Lucie Mugo jerked awake. After flinging on her uniform, she ran the short distance to Mombasa central police station on Makadara Road.

The desk duty officer was a time-served sergeant with a vast pot-belly. When Mugo came sprinting into the lobby he regarded her with amusement.

'Constable Mugo! I thought you were on nightshift this week.'

'I am, Sergeant,' Mugo said. 'As you can see, I am also on dayshift.'

'You really *are* keen, aren't you? Your little secondment with CID has clearly whetted your appetite. I heard you were assigned to the great Inspector Jouma himself!

Standing on the shoulders of giants, eh?'

'I am sure he does not even remember my name.'

The sergeant leaned forward across his high desk, the only way he could see her properly. 'So how can I help you?'

'A man was brought in last night. Foreign national. Very drunk. He was arrested following an altercation in the Old Town.'

'What sort of altercation?'

'He was in a fight with some sailors from the dhow harbour.'

'Did he win?'

'It was an honourable draw.'

'I see. What about him?'

'I arrested him, sir. And now I would very much like to speak to him.'

'*You* arrested him?' He regarded the diminutive officer doubtfully. 'Have you taken up karate since I last saw you? Or have you got a big stick?'

Mugo flushed. 'When I reached the scene he was ... incapable of standing, sir. I merely helped him into the back of the wagon.'

'Back to the real world, eh? Drunks in wagons.' The sergeant smiled. 'Well, if this fellow was thrown into the tank he may well have been processed by now. What is his name?' He slid a pair of spectacles onto his nose and peered at the overnight admissions register on the desk in front of him.

Mugo had brought her notebook with her. '*Aristo-Aristophe—*'

'*Aristophenedes*,' the sergeant read. 'Is that the one?'

'Yes, sir.'

'You are too late, Mugo. *Captain* Aristophenedes clearly has friends in high places.' He shrugged. 'A gentleman from the Greek Consulate collected him from the cells shortly after six o'clock this morning.'

Seventy miles inside the sanctuary of Tanzanian waters, the crew of the *Arturet* were making repairs to those areas of the ship's superstructure damaged in the firefight the previous day. Until now plastic sheeting and white emulsion paint had sufficed; it was not ideal but it had covered up the bullet holes and meant there were fewer questions to answer in Mombasa. More substantial repairs would be undertaken once the ship docked in Cape Town.

Stewart and Chief Wojcek were watching the work from the shade of an awning strung between two containers.

'Situation Normal, All Fucked Up.' The Chief smiled grimly.

Stewart chuckled. It was an old Marine maxim, but one that was rarely inappropriate and certainly not when applied to this particular mission. So far everything they had touched had turned to shit – and the main reason for that was now swilling ouzo on the bridge. There were certain members of the unit who would have quite happily throttled Aristophenedes after discovering that he had escaped from the ship the previous day; but now that they were out at sea it seemed churlish to keep the Greek skipper under lock and key. And while he was undoubtedly a loose cannon, he was also the only person on board the *Arturet* who was qualified to sail the damn ship.

It had taken a while to track him down to a police cell in Mombasa. Shortly after dawn that morning, however, Wojcek – whose ancestry was in fact Albanian – had put on a shirt and tie, strolled up to the front counter, and announced he was from the Greek Consulate with instructions to collect one of his countrymen. He had neither identification nor warrant, and had it been the US he would have most probably ended up in a cell as well. But as with all things official in Kenya, the only paper-work that mattered was the stack of dollar bills that Wojcek had pressed, smiling, into the desk sergeant's eager palm. Ten minutes later the Chief and an exceedingly jaded Aristophenes were in the back of a cab heading for Kilindini. Two hours later, the Greek was guiding the big freighter out of the harbour mouth.

'I guess you have to admire him,' Wojcek said. 'A guy needs a drink that bad, he's got to be inventive.'

Stewart nodded. 'It could have been worse, I suppose. At least we got to the drunken sonofabitch before he had a chance to shoot his mouth off to the cops.'

'Did you tell the Limey that he escaped?'

'Who, Pottinger? What do you think, Chief? The captain's walkabout is something that we'll just keep to ourselves, I think.'

'*Semper Fi*,' Wojcek grinned.

'You look tired, Mugo,' said Superintendent Simba. 'Would you care for some coffee?'

'No, thank you, ma'am,' Mugo said. Her voice was trembling because even though Elizabeth Simba was the woman every female officer in Kenya Police wished to emulate, the only one who had risen through the male-dominated ranks to become head of a provincial CID division, the young constable found it more nerve-racking speaking to her than to any man.

Simba was looking at a copy of an arrest sheet Mugo had brought with her from the central precinct. Although she would never say, the superintendent was impressed with its economy and precision. The forms her own detectives filled out invariably resembled the scrawls of unruly children.

'*Aris – Aristoph—*'

'Aristophenedes, ma'am. He is Greek.'

'Skipper of a vessel at Kilindini?'

'The *MV Arturet*. It berthed yesterday afternoon.'

'Well, I am sure that it will come as no surprise to you that all sailors like a drink,' Simba said. 'And when they have had a drink, they usually want to fight. I see from Captain Aristophenedes's file that this is not the first time he has spent the evening in one of our cells.'

'Yes, ma'am. But last night, after he had been put in the wagon, I interviewed the barman at the Bosun's Chair – the establishment where Captain Aristophenedes had spent the evening. He mentioned something that I think now, in retrospect, might be pertinent to the current situation regarding Inspector Jouma.'

Simba's eyes narrowed behind her designer spectacles. 'Go on.'

In that instant Mugo realised the utter folly of what she was doing. She pressed on nevertheless.

'He said . . . He said that . . . '

'Out with it, Mugo – I don't have all day.'

'He said Captain Aristophenedes was . . . *celebrating*.'

'Celebrating?'

'Apparently the captain's vessel was attacked by pirate boats yesterday morning. The captain said that he had driven them off single-handedly.'

For several seconds Simba stared at her blankly, as if she'd just recited a poem in Martian. 'And that's it?'

Had a big hole opened up in Simba's office at that moment, Mugo would have happily jumped into it. 'Yes, ma'am.'

'And how is that pertinent to Inspector Jouma's disappearance?'

'Is it not possible that the Inspector and Mr Moore were captured by the fleeing pirates, ma'am?'

Simba sighed. 'Mugo, you are a very promising police officer, and one day I have no doubt you will achieve great things as a detective. Before that day, however, you must learn that you do not waste your superintendent's time with the drunken utterances of a Greek sea captain. The fishing boat was found in Kenyan waters. Even Somali pirates have more sense than to operate in that area.'

'Yes, ma'am,' Mugo said, deciding that it was better now to be hung as a lion than a lamb. 'But according to the barman, Captain Aristophenedes was quite adamant: *his vessel was attacked in Kenyan waters.*'

Simba looked up at her from beneath the rims of her spectacles. 'The barman told you this?'

'Yes, ma'am.'

The superintendent levered herself from her chair and went across to a framed map of the Coast Province on the wall. She studied it closely.

'I do not make a habit of acting on drunken boasts,' she said. 'But under the circumstances I think it would be wise to pursue every possible lead, however flimsy.' She turned. 'Go to central precinct. Find out what this Greek has to say now that he is sober,'

'I already did, ma'am.'

'And?'

'He is no longer in custody.'

'Then where *is* he, Mugo?'

'He was collected from the cells by a member of the Greek Consulate this morning.'

Simba's face froze. 'The Greek Consulate? Who told you this?'

'The desk sergeant, ma'am.'

'There *is* no Greek Consulate in Mombasa, Mugo!' the

superintendent erupted. She strode across to her desk and grabbed the phone. 'Helen – put me through to the duty officer at Kilindini Port Authority.'

Mugo listened, trembling, as Simba was connected. A series of short, barked questions were fired down the line, and then the superintendent slammed down the receiver.

'The *Arturet* left port at seven o'clock this morning, bound for Cape Town,' she said, trying hard to keep her voice even. 'By now they will be in Tanzanian waters.'

Mugo's face fell. If only she had remembered about the Greek captain sooner. If only she had gone straight to central precinct that morning instead of going to bed. If only—

Simba's phone rang. She put it on speakerphone.

'Sorry to disturb you, ma'am,' her secretary said. 'But I have a gentleman on the line who wishes to speak with you urgently.'

'Who is it?'

'He did not give his name. But he says he is from the security service in Nairobi.'

Simba rolled her eyes. 'That will be all, Mugo,' she said. Then, 'Very well, Helen – put him through.'

Mugo was on her way out of the building when Simba's secretary caught up with her. Helen was a big lady, and she was clearly not accustomed to running.

'Superintendent Simba wishes to see you in her office, Officer Mugo,' she gasped.

When she returned, she found Simba staring at the map on the wall.

'You wanted to see me, ma'am.'

'Yes, Mugo,' the superintendent said without turning. 'It would appear that your theory may have been correct after all.'

'Ma'am?'

'Jouma and the Englishman were indeed kidnapped by pirates.'

Mugo's eyes bulged. 'How do you know?'

'Because the pirates who kidnapped them have just made a phone call to the security service to tell them that very fact,' Simba said, staring at the map of Somalia as if it was a bewildering piece of modern art.

'Well?' N'Kuma said.

'The story checks out, sir,' John Nola said. 'I contacted Mombasa Port Authority and they confirmed that a Korean-registered freighter docked at Kilindini yesterday morning. However, the skipper of the vessel made no report of being attacked by pirates.'

'That is not unusual. They were probably transporting contraband. What about these two men from the fishing boat? Abdulle claims one is a Coast Province detective?'

The younger man nodded. 'I have just got off the phone with the CID superintendent in Mombasa. She confirmed that the wife of one of her detectives has reported him missing.'

'Missing?'

'Yes, sir. It seems he went out on a fishing boat yesterday morning and never returned.'

'His name?'

'Jouma. Detective Inspector.'

N'Kuma's brow furrowed. '*Jouma.* Why do I know that name?'

'He was involved in the corruption investigations in Mombasa a couple of years ago,' Nola said.

'Ah, yes. I remember. Half of the city's politicians and police ended up behind bars thanks to him, didn't they?'

'The actual number jailed was comparatively small, sir. Those that didn't flee the country employed highly-paid lawyers to throw spanners into the machinery of the judicial system.'

'Shakespeare was right, John.'

'Sir?'

'"*Let's kill all the lawyers.*" Henry VI Part Two. What was Jouma doing on board a fishing boat in the first place?'

'I understand it was a pleasure trip.'

'Then I take it he was not alone.'

'No. The boat is registered to a British national, who is also reported missing. Name of Moore.'

'You told this superintendent that the two men have been taken captive?'

'Yessir. But I mentioned nothing about Abdulle's offer.'

'Good. This is a very sensitive issue. I don't want it out in the public domain until it is over. If anybody asks, tell them we are making ongoing inquiries.'

'There is one other thing, sir.'

'Yes?'

'The boat, sir.'

'What about it?'

'It was found this morning. A coastguard aerial crew spotted it drifting around forty miles north-east of the Lamu archipelago, close to Somali waters. A gunboat was scrambled from the navy base at Manda Island, but there was no sign of the two men supposed to be on board.'

'Where is the boat now?'

'It was towed to Manda.'

'Good,' N'Kuma said. 'Make sure it stays there. And make sure nobody knows about it, understand?'

'Yessir.'

Nola turned to leave.

'John.'

'Yessir.'

'I know you have worked hard on Qasim Fadir, and I know you must be disappointed with the decision of the Minister. But I want you to supervise this handover, and I want you to ensure that it goes smoothly.'

'Of course, sir. Thank you, sir.'

'Politicians are spineless idiots, John,' N'Kuma said. 'But don't forget they pay our wages, and they do not last for ever.'

# 18

'Hey, Red,' Nancy Griswold called out over the roar of the Hummer H2's powerful engine. 'Is it just me, or has Hafiz got a couple extra gold teeth since we last saw him?'

Sheppard was behind the wheel of the monstrous vehicle, which had been modelled on the US military-issue all-terrain Humvee and guzzled an eye-watering twelve miles to the gallon. He looked in his rear-view mirror at the fixer sitting in the back seat. 'Maybe so, Nance,' he grinned.

'My friends, please,' Hafiz said, proffering his hands in a gesture of goodwill but keeping his mouth puckered. 'I assure you that any expenditure incurred is legitimate.'

'It had better be,' Nancy snarled, turning in her seat. 'Or I'll pull every damn one of them out of your head with my own bloody hands.'

They had been driving for two hours, most of it along unmarked and unmetalled roads designed to get them into Somalia without attracting the attention of border patrols. The occasional half-arsed police official was easily bribed, but the Australian documentary team was keen to avoid military roadblocks. These had been erected to prevent Islamic fundamentalists flooding into Kenya, and the soldiers manning the primary guardposts were all US army trained.

Now, according to the GPS monitor on the dashboard, they had at last crossed the frontier. Nancy peered through the Hummer's tinted windshield at a long, straight road cutting through seemingly endless and arid scrub. She nodded to herself. After all the bullshit, it was time to focus on the job in hand. They had entered the snakepit.

Her mind flipped through the relevant facts about Somali pirates she and her team of researchers had gleaned from the cuttings files and the internet prior to her departure for Africa.

It was not much. In fact, she reflected, it amounted to bugger all. From what she could gather, up until a few years ago piracy had been small-scale to the point of being non-existent. Those who practised it were generally disaffected fishermen and their targets tended to be nothing more significant than the occasional unfortunate cargo dhow. The real money in Somalia was to be made on the mainland, in the cities, by the clan warlords who ran the country in the absence of any recognisable law. But that was before an already dysfunctional country spiralled into total meltdown and was overrun by al-Shabaab Islamists in the mid-2000s. Suddenly there were a hell of a lot of out-of-work gangsters desperate to reinvent themselves – and organised piracy soon proved an extremely lucrative form of alternative employment.

There were, as far as Nancy could make out, four major players in Somalia: the self-styled National Volunteer Coast Guard operating out of the south; the Marka Collective, from Mogadishu; the Puntland Group, who preyed on shipping off the Horn; and the Somali Marines, an organisation so regimented that its leader had given himself the title Fleet Admiral.

The one thing they had in common was that they had cashed in unreservedly on the attitude of the shipping companies, whose seemingly boundless generosity in paying out multi-million-dollar ransoms was matched only by the mindblowing ineffectiveness of the international community to do anything about the problem.

Oh, it looked just dandy on paper. The international naval convoy assembled to protect commercial shipping from attacks by Somali pirates was known as Combined Task Force-151, a fleet made up of over a hundred ships from more than twenty countries as diverse as Canada, Denmark, the USA, Singapore and Pakistan. But at any one time most of the CTF-151 fleet was concentrated on what was called the Recommended Transit Corridor, a narrow, heavily-patrolled sea lane through the Gulf of Aden. It did not take a rocket scientist, let alone a Somali pirate, to work out that the safest place to attack ships was therefore the several hundred thousand square miles of ocean outside the RTC.

In truth, though, Nancy didn't give a damn for the whys and wherefores. She was interested only in the human story, which was why she was so keen to sit down with one of the pirate leaders – and why, now, there was a buzz of excitement in the pit of her stomach as the Humvee headed over the border.

*Just who would she be meeting?*

The fixer had been almost theatrically vague about his identity which, while it irritated her, also added a frisson of excitement to the whole adventure. Pirates by their very nature tended to shun the limelight. Only on very rare occasions did they allow journalists into their encampments, and then for the sole purpose of interviewing foreign hostages. She'd seen plenty of footage of bedraggled captives begging their governments to stump up the ransom money, but on these occasions the pirates themselves remained stubbornly behind the camera.

All of which made Nancy wonder why this particular pirate had chosen to raise his head above the parapet. Was it the money? Hardly – thirty grand was peanuts compared to the lucre they were used to raking in from the shipping companies. Or was it because he had realised that, in the land of the illiterate cutthroat, the man with public relations savvy is king? If so, this exclusive interview would be a testament to Nancy Griswold's finely-honed instincts for a good story. She knew that Somali pirates had been getting some bad press of late. No one was buying their poor, exploited Third World fishermen schtick anymore; not when they were bagging upwards of two or three million bucks for every ship they hijacked. Most of the bastards were driving round in SUVs and living in palaces on the mainland. Nancy had come to Africa precisely because her instincts told her one of them would eventually realise the importance of having the public on his side.

'You must pull over now,' Hafiz said anxiously.

Up ahead was a burnt-out Texaco filling station, its sign riddled with bullets.

'Here? Are you sure?'

'That is the arrangement.'

Nancy glanced at Sheppard, who shrugged as he swung the vehicle into what had once been a forecourt but was now a collection of twisted metal heaped outside a windowless cinderblock building.

'Now what?' she said to Hafiz.

The fixer's eyes widened. 'Now we wait.'

Thirty minutes later a dust cloud on the road ahead

coalesced into the shape of a ten-year-old Ford saloon that clattered into the ruined filling station and screeched to a halt next to the Hummer. Two scrawny Somalis got out, their faces mostly hidden by *keffiyeh* headscarves. Inevitably they were toting AK-47 assault rifles, which round here was the same as carrying a leather attaché case on Market Street in Sydney. They gave Nancy and Sheppard a cursory once-over, but it was clear they were more interested in the $70,000 vehicle the Australians had arrived in.

'Good morning, gentlemen,' Nancy said in a firm voice. 'My name is Nancy Griswold, Channel Seven in Australia, and—'

One of the men said something to Hafiz.

'He says he knows who you are, madam,' the fixer said anxiously. 'He wants you and Mr Sheppard to get into the car.'

'Fine.'

Nancy stepped towards the Hummer, but the man who had spoken moved towards her aggressively.

'No, madam,' Hafiz said. 'You are to get into *his* car.'

'*His* car?' Nancy looked disdainfully at the saloon. 'But what about *my* car? That's Seven News property. I'll be damned if I'm leaving it here.'

'He says *he* will drive it,' the fixer explained. 'You can pick it up later.'

The eyes behind the *keffiyeh* shone, and Nancy could tell the bastard was laughing at her.

An hour later the ill-matched convoy came to a halt at a tiny fishing village on the banks of a wide river. The Australians, who had both been blindfolded, were dragged unceremoniously out of the Ford and into a wooden skiff powered by a large outboard motor. Hafiz, who had travelled in the Hummer, joined them in the boat as it cast off.

Words were exchanged between the armed men.

'What are they saying?' Nancy asked Hafiz.

'They are saying that they are very thrilled to be bringing a world-famous Australian television celebrity to meet the great Omar Abdulle,' the Arab beamed.

'Omar Abdulle, eh? So now at least we know this mystery man of yours has a name.'

Red Sheppard, who understood a smattering of Somali, said nothing, because he was pretty sure one of the phrases that had been used had been a vivid description of how they would like to sexually violate Nancy given the opportunity. The veteran cameraman, a man who was not usually given to second thoughts, was beginning to wonder if this was such a good idea after all.

# 19

They were going home. And even though the news had come from the man who was keeping them against their will, whose men had beaten them, and who had made them sink to their knees while he waved a gun in their face, it was so unexpected, so *welcome*, that Jake found himself feeling *grateful* to him.

Only later, in the stuffy confines of their cabin, was the gratitude replaced by waves of resentment when he considered the sheer scandalous affront to his own liberty that the kidnapping represented. He felt *violated*.

Yet they were being released. Omar had told them so, his hard face split by a smile of genuine pleasure, as if he was announcing they had just won the Lottery. And despite it all, the thought that their hellish ordeal would soon be over was what Jake clung to amid the anger and recrimination.

Jouma was not so sure. He had long since annexed all thoughts of his wife to a part of his mind where they could not be accessed. To do so would be unbearable, and he knew that he had to remain strong and focused on their present predicament. What Omar had told them was indeed welcome news – but what concerned him were the terms of their release. When it came to the specifics, the pirate leader had been evasive.

'You will be taken to the mainland at dawn tomorrow, and there you will be reunited with your people,' was all he had told them.

But Jouma knew there was more to it than this. Omar was, as he kept insisting, a businessman – and by their very nature businessmen were not inclined to be philanthropists. No, if he and Jake were being released then it was only because Omar stood to benefit. They were pawns, and their fate remained in the pirate's hands until such time as they were back in Kenya.

And that made Jouma uneasy.

'This time tomorrow I will be drinking the biggest, coldest beer Suki Lo has on offer,' Jake said.

'It is only eleven o'clock in the morning,' Jouma pointed out.

'I don't care.'

'Then I am happy for you, my friend.'

'What about you?'

The Inspector shrugged. 'Life goes on. I expect I will be back at my desk.'

'You are truly an amazing man, Inspector.' Jake smiled.

'Amazing? No. I am simply an employee of the state – one who is already absent without leave.'

'I'm sure Superintendent Simba will understand when she hears the circumstances.'

'You don't know Simba,' Jouma said gravely. 'The only legitimate excuse she will accept for taking time off outside of a holiday entitlement is death.'

There was a light tap at the door. The two men looked at each other warily.

'Come in,' Jouma said, and even as he said the words it struck him how out of place they were on this ship.

There was hesitation and then the door – which was not locked – opened slightly and Jalil squeezed in awkwardly on his calliper. The boy nodded, but as he quietly closed the door behind him it was clear he was wary of being caught. Unlike his visit at breakfast time, this was obviously not sanctioned by Omar.

'I have heard you are leaving,' he said timidly.

'So have we,' said Jake.

'Why don't you sit down, boy,' Jouma said, patting the thin mattress on his bunk. But Jalil shook his head.

'Will you come back for Omar?' he said.

Jouma took a moment to reply. 'Omar is a criminal, Jalil. Those who break the law must pay for their actions.'

'*Will you come back for him?*' The boy's voice was tense with anxiety.

'No,' Jouma said. 'I don't think so. But somebody will. One day.'

Jake peered down from his bunk. 'Do you *want* somebody to come back for him, Jalil?'

Jalil gasped and shook his head, as if the question was breaking some sort of unspoken taboo. 'Omar is a great man. He is my father.'

'No—' Jake began, but Jouma cut him off.

'Where are you from, Jalil?'

'Kismaayo.'

'You were born there?'

'Yes.'

'And you say your mother is dead.'

'Yes.'

'You do not miss her?'

'No.'

'Why? Did she not love you?'

'She was a whore.'

The word coming from such a young mouth was shocking, but Jalil said it with the matter-of-factness of one who had said it many times.

'That is no reason for her not to love you,' Jouma said.

'She did not love me. Only Omar loves me. That is why he killed her.'

Again there was a beat as the boy's words sank in.

'What did she do to you, Jalil?' Jake asked.

Jalil looked at his feet, and mumbled something indistinct.

'*What did she do?*'

Slowly he turned and raised his football shirt to expose his thin, bony torso. Plain to see against the dark skin was a series of discoloured ridges and furrows, permanent evidence of years of savage abuse.

'My God,' Jouma said.

The boy turned. 'Don't come back for Omar,' he said, his voice rising. 'Please.'

# 20

Captain Milton Mabuto of the Kenyan army did not regard himself as a monster, even if his reputation suggested otherwise. Thirty-two years old and from a family of professional soldiers, he regarded himself as a devout Christian and a loyal patriot who believed in the sanctity and the security of his beloved country – and this, when he analysed it, was most probably where the misunderstanding arose.

Mabuto believed firmly that the root of all evil in Kenya lay not in the ancient tribal rivalries that occasionally spilled over into internecine unrest, but in the unchecked influence of godless foreigners. By that he did not mean Europeans – Mabuto was a great admirer of the white man in general and the British in particular. He knew it was not a popular view, but he was convinced that without the guiding hand of her colonial overlords, Kenya would today have none of the technological and infrastructural advances that set it apart from the rest of Africa.

No, it was the rest of Africa that concerned Captain Milton Mabuto. Specifically Somalia, which as far as he was concerned was a pustulent sore leaking its poison across the border in the form of criminals, illegal immigrants, and filthy Muslim zealots.

And as commander of the border garrison at Kiunga, he prided himself on being his country's first line of defence against the steady toxic drip from its benighted neighbour. The words of his favourite hymn were *Onward Christian soldiers, marching as to war.* And as far as he was concerned, it *was* a war.

Moreover, it was a war he was determined to prosecute at all costs.

Kiunga was a small coastal town a few miles south of the Somali frontier, and the garrison and its various checkpoints guarded the main road connecting the two countries. The garrison was situated in a fort dating back to the seventeenth century, which had once been used by the Portuguese to control the passage of contraband across the border. Over the centuries it had fallen into disrepair, but ever since the Muslim menace had reared its ugly head – and especially since anarchic Somalia had become a breeding ground for Islamic fundamentalists – its strategic importance had returned. Funded largely by the Americans, the Kenyan military had rebuilt and reoccupied it, and for the last two years Mabuto had been in charge of a company of twenty men loyal to their commanding officer and to his beliefs.

And it was, Mabuto reflected, a rewarding job. Just that morning a southbound grain truck, stopped and searched at one of the checkpoints, had been found to contain a Somali stowaway hiding in a false fuel tank. It was one of the oldest tricks in the book, and it never ceased to amaze Mabuto that the idiots continued to think they could get away with it.

The stowaway was now manacled, naked, to a metal chair in one of the garrison's subterranean interrogation chambers. He was a young man of about twenty-five years, and he claimed he was fleeing Somalia because one of the local warlords had put a price on his head.

Mabuto had heard it all before, of course.

'Why would anybody put a price on *your* head, Ahmed?' he demanded, using the name the man had all-too willingly given him.

The beads of sweat on the young man's forehead were almost as large as his bulging eyeballs. 'They . . . they said I was providing information to the American CIA,' he said.

'What sort of information?'

'I don't know – I wasn't talking to the CIA.'

'Do you believe in God, Ahmed?'

The sudden change of subject left Ahmed momentarily dumbstruck.

'I said, do you believe in God?' Mabuto repeated, only this time he fractionally twisted the handle in front of him. The handle increased the tension in a strip of rolled wire that was looped around Ahmed's exposed testicles. The Somali stowaway shrieked.

'Do you believe in God?'

'Yes! *Yes!*'

'The Christian God, father of our Lord Jesus Christ?'

'*Yes!*'

Another small twist. Another prolonged squeal of agony.

'But your name is Ahmed. That is a Muslim name. Do you wish to kill the followers of the Christian God? Do you wish to cleanse the earth of the Infidel? Is that why you have come to my country, Ahmed? Do you want to kill me? My wife? My children?'

Ahmed's screams obscured the sound of the wooden cell door opening. One of Mabuto's junior NCOs entered the chamber and whispered something in the captain's ear.

'We will talk later, Ahmed,' Mabuto said, giving the handle one last tweak before leaving the room and heading upstairs.

Mabuto's office was in a whitewashed blockhouse built in one corner of the old fort. As he crossed the dusty parade ground, the captain noticed an olive-green military van parked outside. The rear windows of the vehicle had been reinforced with steel mesh, and cut into the armoured side panels were weapon ducts. Three burly soldiers carrying automatic rifles were guarding the van. They saluted smartly as he strode into the cool of the blockhouse.

A man was waiting in his office. He was wearing a suit and a pair of horn-rimmed spectacles. John Nola introduced himself, showed Mabuto a laminated identity card, but did not shake hands.

Mabuto, who was not used to government officials and had therefore developed a finely-honed distrust of them, sat down at his desk and regarded his visitor with a studied indifference that belied his own apprehension.

'You are from Nairobi, Mr Nola?'

'That is correct.'

'Then you are long way from home.'

'Less than an hour by plane is no hardship,' Nola said.

'I take it that is your truck that is parked outside?'

'Indeed. It is carrying my prisoner.'

This time Mabuto could not hide his surprise. 'Prisoner?'

'Somali national. He accompanied me from Nairobi, where he has been residing in a high-security jail cell. Here are his papers.'

Mabuto scrutinised the typed sheet. 'Qasim Fadir?' He twitched slightly at the Arab-sounding name. 'He is a terrorist?'

'Pirate,' Nola said. 'He was picked up three weeks ago

in Zanzibar, attempting to launder money on behalf of one of the Somali cartels. We have been holding him in Nairobi for interrogation.'

'Why have you brought him here?'

'Because he is to be exchanged.'

'*Exchanged?*'

'Tomorrow morning. You are to facilitate the operation.'

'By whose authority?'

'The Justice Minister and Chief of the General Staff.'

Mabuto's mouth dropped open. He had no idea who the Justice Minister was, but the Chief of the General Staff was the highest-ranking officer in the Kenyan army. 'I have heard nothing about this.'

'These are your written orders,' Nola said, dropping a second sheet of paper on the desk.

Mabuto scanned it greedily until his eyes fixed on the joint signatures at the bottom of the page.

'There is no mention of who is to be exchanged for this prisoner,' he pointed out.

'No,' Nola said. 'It is not necessary that you know that information. Your orders are to arrange the necessary security at the rendezvous point and ensure the cargo is returned across the border.'

'And you?'

'I will be present in a supervisory capacity.'

'I see.'

'Now, despite his circumstances the prisoner is of high value. I suggest you find him a nice cool cell and ensure that he is fed and watered. He has a big day tomorrow.'

'As you wish. And you?'

'I am staying in Lamu overnight,' Nola said. 'I will be back here at 0530 hours tomorrow, and I will expect you and your men to be ready.'

*Yes*, Mabuto thought, when the NSIS man had gone. *He would be ready all right.* He checked his watch. Arrangements would have to be made if the exchange was to go smoothly.

He had a little over eighteen hours. That was not much time at all.

# 21

On the secluded quarterdeck behind the *Kanshish*'s superstructure, hidden from the moronic stares of the crew and out of earshot of Omar's constant bidding, Moses Bani completed his third *rak'a* – the formal cycle of Muslim prayer – recited the required lines from the *Tashahhud* and, with his ritual completed, stood and gathered up his prayer mat. His religious beliefs had always given him solace, and the contemplative nature of prayer helped to revive his tired mind.

Now, though, it was back to work, a prospect that did not fill him with joy because it involved filling out requisition forms for supplies. Hardly glamorous, but without it Hafiz would not come and the men would starve. Preventing mutiny was just one of the many thankless administrative tasks Moses performed in the service of the great Omar Abdulle.

He did not mind. He had never lusted after glory like Omar, nor had he ever relished hand-to-hand action like his younger brother. Julius was never happier than when he was leading a boarding party, just as Moses preferred the peace and quiet of his work. He knew they mocked his bookishness. But Moses contented himself with the knowledge that without him Omar's business would cease to function.

He stepped into the corridor that led to his cabin – and was nearly knocked off his feet by Jalil coming up the stairs from deck level.

'Watch where you're going, damn you!' he exclaimed.

The boy looked at him as if he wasn't there, eyes wide, mouth open.

Omar frowned. 'What is the matter, boy? Where have you been?'

'Nowhere, sir,' Jalil said. 'I have to see Sheba.'

'Then go and see Sheba. And watch where you're going next time.'

Jalil pushed past him and Moses watched him disappear round the corner in the direction of Sheba's cabin. He shook his head. Damn cripple. Why on earth Omar had seen fit to bring him aboard the ship was beyond him. Just because Jalil's whore mother had beaten him didn't detract from the fact he was nothing more than a filthy street urchin. Omar, of course, would argue that the boy was company for the insufferably vile Sheba – whose presence was an even greater mystery to Moses. So what if she was the daughter of Omar's feckless brother? Weren't there enough mouths to feed on board this ship already? One of the reasons he was having to amend the stores was because that fat little bitch consumed as much as ten crewmen.

With no little relief Moses went into his cabin and retrieved the relevant paperwork from a filing cabinet beside his bunk. Then he sat down at the dressing table and quietly got on with the business of running his master's empire.

'Where have you been, cripple boy?' Sheba crowed into the silvered mirror of her cabin dressing table as Maira fixed a bone chopstick into her freshly washed and brushed hair. 'You were supposed to be here five minutes ago.'

'Nowhere,' Jalil said, head bowed as he stood in the doorway of her cabin.

'Don't lie to me. You were with the prisoners, weren't you?'

'No, I—'

'Maira saw you,' Sheba said triumphantly. 'And Maira tells me everything, don't you, old woman?'

'No—'

'*Yes!* You think you can do *anything* on this ship without me knowing? You really think you are cleverer than me, you filthy cripple son-of-a-whore?'

By the door, Jalil clenched his fists so hard he felt the nails digging into his palms. '*Shut up!*' he exclaimed.

Sheba turned her head so quickly, the chopstick was yanked from the old woman's frail grasp and fell to the floor.

'Pick it up, you old bitch!' the girl shrieked. 'Then get out! I am tired of you pawing at me.'

When Maira had bowed and scraped her way out of the cabin, Sheba glared at Jalil with a look of pure hatred. 'As for you, little metal leg, I can say what I want and when I want – and don't you forget it.'

'Why?' Jalil demanded. 'What gives you the right?'

For a moment Sheba looked stunned. Then her pudgy features hardened again. 'I'll tell you who gives me the right,' she hissed. 'The same person who will slit your throat and throw you to the sharks if I ask him to.'

'Omar would never do that,' the boy retorted defiantly. 'He would never harm me.' It was the one thing in his miserable life that he could be sure of.

'Oh no? What if I told him that you *touched* me?'

Jalil's eyes bulged. '*What*?'

'Yes,' Sheba said, sliding from her chair and sashaying towards him. She was wearing a thin cotton robe that hung open as far as the budding swell of her breasts. 'What if I told my father that you grabbed me here,' she said, pulling the flimsy material aside to expose one dark nipple.

Jalil could not help but stare, even though the sight repulsed him.

'And *here*,' Sheba continued, placing one hand between her legs and rubbing it lasciviously. 'Don't deny you haven't thought about it, cripple boy.'

'I – I have done no such thing.'

'No?' she said, her face so close now that he could smell the rich food trapped between her teeth. 'You've never wanted to put *this*—' she snatched his left hand '—*here*?'

She yanked his hand downwards and Jalil's fingertips brushed against something soft and wet. Then she laughed and pushed him away.

'You think I would let a disgusting cripple come anywhere near me?' she brayed, walking back to the dressing table.

And as she did so, Jalil could feel the blood in his head thumping so hard he felt it was about to explode. His vision seemed to fade in and out in great dizzying waves, and as he stared at the violated fingers of his left hand, those of his right closed around the handle of the gutting knife that he kept against the leather of his calliper, and as he withdrew it he felt the cold, sharp steel brush against his own boiling skin.

# 22

The bell on the roof of the wheelhouse was ringing, a nerve-jangling racket that had the immediate effect of stirring the crew of the *Kanshish* to life. Grabbing their weapons they hurried to the superstructure and gathered on deck beneath the bridge gantry like a crowd in St Peter's Square awaiting an appearance by the Pope.

Down in Jake and Jouma's cabin the door opened and Rafael leaned in through the frame. With one twitch of his enormous head, he indicated that the two prisoners were to go with him.

Jake and Jouma followed Omar's henchman up two flights of narrow stairs to the bridge, where the pirate leader was already waiting, resplendent in a freshly-pressed uniform. Lurking by the wardroom door were the Bani brothers, their suspicious scowl clearly a genetic trait.

'Gentlemen!' Omar beamed. 'The hour is at hand!'

And with that he escorted them onto the bridge balcony where, forty feet below, the crew of the *Kanshish* gazed up expectantly.

'Yesterday,' Omar began in a firm, clear voice, 'twelve of our brothers were slaughtered in cold blood. They died doing their duty. Duty to their families. Duty to *your* families. They were loyal to their country, and they were loyal to me. I grieve for them still. I will *always* grieve for them.'

*Oh, he's good,* Jouma thought. The pirate leader had the oratory and the charisma of the truly great dictator.

'I know that life on board this ship is hard,' Omar continued. 'And I know that you look to me, Omar Abdulle, to guide you, to *provide* for you. To be your father! That is the burden I must carry. But I carry it gladly because you are my children.'

Jake peered surreptitiously down at the mob. What he saw were rapt, adoring faces staring up at the gantry. *Jesus* – they were actually buying this shit? Omar's children were obviously too busy grubbing around in the dirt to have seen their father's collection of fine wines, his silver cutlery, his Cuban cigars.

'But I too have lost a brother,' Omar said. '*Qasim Fadir!*'

The name meant nothing to Jake and Jouma, but it provoked a sudden outburst of shouting and wailing from the deck.

Omar nodded solemnly. 'Taken by the Kenyan dogs and left to rot in a stinking jail cell. My heart breaks when I think of what inhuman torture they must have inflicted on him to make him betray us. But where are the gunboats, my children? Where are the warships sent to hunt us down? They are nowhere – and why? Because my brother Qasim Fadir would *never* betray us. He would rather die!'

This time the mob erupted, punching the air, firing their weapons and chanting Qasim's name.

Again Omar waved for quiet. And then his head swivelled and his eyes fixed on Jake and Jouma with a murderous intensity. 'These are the two men brought to this ship by our valiant brother Julius Bani.'

They felt dozens of hot, angry stares drilling into them.

'I know many of you questioned why I chose not to kill them yesterday. I know that many of you thought they *deserved* to die, as vengeance for your dear brothers. But I have news for you, my children. Tomorrow they will be leaving the *Kanshish*. They will be taken to the mainland, where, in gratitude for sparing their lives – for my *wisdom* in letting them live – the Kenyan dogs will come on their knees. But they will not be empty-handed. No. This time tomorrow, my children, Omar Abdulle will stand here shoulder to shoulder with Qasim Fadir once again!'

Such was the noise and the jubilation that at first nobody noticed the small figure hobbling on deck through the superstructure door. Then, as if a wave had passed over them, the mob slowly fell silent – and Omar, who had been basking in the adulation from high up on the bridge balcony, frowned in puzzlement and looked to his henchmen. But, like the crewmen, and like Jake and Jouma, Rafael and the Bani brothers were staring down at the deck where Jalil now stood, his eyes wide and his shirt covered in blood.

'Jalil!' Omar roared. 'What is the meaning of this?'

The boy blinked then, as if snapping from some catatonic trauma, and as he looked up at the pirate leader his dry lips worked slowly and silently until, eventually, a tiny, bewildered voice emerged from his mouth, so quiet it was barely audible.

'She is dead,' he whispered, and when his fingers opened a bloodstained knife fell onto the deck at his feet. '*I killed her.*'

# 23

Harry Philliskirk gazed thoughtfully into the misted beer glass on the bar in front of him.

'You OK, honey boy?' asked Suki Lo, the Malaysian-born owner of the bar. Her thin face, furrowed by years of chain-smoking but also by a smile almost broad enough to split her head in two, was twisted with concern.

Harry looked up. 'I'm fine, Suki, my pet,' he said. 'It's Jake I'm worried about.'

Suki picked up a glass and began polishing it furiously with a cloth. Outside a sea squall had strayed into Flamingo Creek and rain was drilling on the tin roof of the bar.

'Jake is a good boy,' she said. 'I sure he OK.'

Harry smiled. 'I sure he OK too.'

But Harry wasn't. He wasn't at all. And Suki Lo, who knew her clientele better than they knew themselves, could see straight through him.

'You want another drink?' Suki asked as he drained his glass.

'No thank you, my pet,' Harry said. 'I'm not in the mood.'

Back at the workshop, he sat at his desk and unfolded

a large-scale map of the Kenyan seaboard. Even to scale the expanse of blue representing the Indian Ocean was vast. With his finger he traced Jake's route north from the creek towards the Lamu archipelago. All day, fishing boat skippers and coastguard helicopters had been criss-crossing the area, and the only crumb of comfort he could derive from the situation was that so far they had yet to spot any bodies floating on the surface. But it was cold comfort.

The office door opened and a young African boy came in. Sammy was *Yellowfin*'s fifteen-year-old bait boy from Jalawi village a couple of miles downriver. A gleaming, white-toothed smile was his default expression – but like everyone today the kid looked grim.

'No news, Mr Harry?' he said.

Harry raised himself from his trough of despair once again. 'No. Not yet. But there's nothing to worry about, Sammy boy,' he said brightly. 'You know what Jake's like: a bloody liability. My bet is he got a spot of engine trouble and hitched a lift to the mainland.'

'Then why has he not been in contact?'

'Dah, you know what Jake's like.'

It was a lousy answer and did nothing to reassure Sammy – because if anyone knew Jake as well as Harry it was the kid who spent most of the day with him out on the ocean. If anything had happened – if Jake was still alive – he would have been in touch somehow.

Just then the ship-to-shore radio on the other side of the office crackled to life and a gruff voice broadcast a call sign. Sammy's eyes lit up, but Harry recognised it as belonging to Kurt Anderssen, a particularly misanthropic Danish skipper based out of Watamu, a few miles south of Lamu.

'Good afternoon, Kurt,' Harry said into the radio handset. 'And how are you today?'

'Fucking pissed off,' Anderssen reported. 'I've got a party of six Frenchies, and not one of them would know a fishing rod if I shoved it up their arse.'

'Sorry to hear that, old man.'

'No you're not.'

'No – I suppose I'm not,' Harry admitted. 'What can I do for you?'

'Word is, your boy has gone AWOL.'

'Word is, you and the rest of the boys out there are helping to look for him.'

'Yeah, well,' Anderssen muttered.

'Anything to report, Kurt?'

'Nah. I was just wondering if you'd heard anything.'

'Nothing.' Harry smiled. 'Don't tell me you're *concerned*, old man? I'm touched.'

'Concerned? Me? Nah. But you've got to watch your own back, haven't you, Harry?'

'What do you mean?'

'I mean, if it was me who was missing out here I would like to think that you and Jake would be looking for me.'

'As opposed to thinking you're a miserable old Viking who can go screw himself?'

There was a burst of dry laughter that segued into the rumbling cough of a man who smoked eighty cigarettes a day. 'Something like that, Harry.'

'Don't you worry, Kurt, my friend. I'd search the ends of the earth for you.'

'Thanks.'

'You still owe me a hundred dollars from that race at Fairview last month.'

'Fuck you, Harry!'

'And you, Kurt!'

Harry was still grinning as he went outside. But his good humour dissolved instantly when he saw Sammy talking to Constable Mugo. At that moment he remembered his maxim about unexpected house calls from the police and his blood turned to ice.

'Hello, hello,' he said. He looked at Mugo's jeans and T-shirt. 'Off duty, are we?'

'Good afternoon, Mr Philliskirk,' Mugo said. 'Yes. My shift starts this evening.'

'How did you get here?'

She pointed to a moped leaning against a tree.

'I see. So to what do I owe the pleasure?' he asked.

'Perhaps we can talk inside? In private?' She glanced surreptitiously at the bait boy.

'Is it about Jake?'

Mugo nodded.

'Then Sammy comes too,' Harry said firmly.

# 24

Sheba's body was lying in a foetal position on the floor of her cabin. She was wearing a white linen robe, the front of which was soaked in fresh blood. There was blood on her hands and smears on the walls, the doorframe and on the carpet near where she lay. The dressing table in the corner of the room had been disturbed, and various pots, jars and utensils were scattered on the floor. The chair was upended and lying on its side close to the body.

Omar Abdulle stood at the doorway and looked at the murder scene with an expression of disbelief. In the corridor behind him was a small crowd consisting of his henchmen and his prisoners, all of them waiting to see what would happen next. Jalil was standing beside Rafael, and for once even the big enforcer seemed uncertain how to proceed.

Presently Omar turned. He looked, Jake thought, utterly shell-shocked – which seemed a strange reaction for a man who a little over twenty-four hours earlier had calmly blown one of his crewmen's brains out over the deck of the ship. But then wasn't Sheba his niece? Wasn't he supposed to be looking after her? Now she was dead. Murdered. How did you explain this to her father – especially when he was your own brother?

Omar knelt in front of the boy. 'Jalil – what happened?' he demanded. Then he shook him. '*What happened?*'

The boy raised his tear-stained face. He looked terrified. 'I killed her, Mr Omar, sir,' he said. 'I stabbed her with my knife.'

'But *why*?'

'I don't know.'

Omar slapped him across the face with the back of his hand.'You must know, Jalil.'

'She was—'

'She was what?'

Jalil swallowed hard. 'She was teasing me.'

There was a pause, then Omar nodded. 'She was teasing you.' Jalil nodded, and Omar stood. Then the pirate leader's hand swept round and connected with the boy's cheek again. He fell to the floor for a moment before Rafael grabbed him and pulled him to his feet like a rag doll.

'You killed her because she was *teasing* you?' Omar shouted, his voice deafening in the confines of the corridor, the veins in his forehead standing out like cables. Then: 'Get him out of my sight.'

Rafael looped his arm around Jalil's midriff and carried him away towards the stairs.

Jake moved forward, but suddenly Julius Bani was in his path.

'What are you going to do with him, Abdulle?' he demanded.

Omar glared at Jake and for a moment it was as if he was looking straight through him. 'I brought him on board this ship. I spared him from his whore of a mother because I believed in my heart that he would be grateful.' There was something in his hand now: Jalil's gutting knife. The two-inch blade was set in a wooden handle twice that length. The wood had been polished and inlaid with intricate twists of copper. 'I gave him this knife when he came aboard my ship. It was a gift. To show that he was a man.'

'For Christ's sake, he's eight years old,' Jake said. 'He's just a kid.'

Omar's eyes narrowed and his gaze turned cold. 'He is a murderer, and he has betrayed me,' the pirate leader growled. 'And that is why I will kill him.'

Jouma, whose attention had been fixed not on the confrontation between Omar and Jake but on the body lying on the floor beyond the cabin door, suddenly raised his finger. 'Mr Abdulle—'

'What?'

'I wonder if I might be permitted to examine the body.'

'What for?'

Jouma sighed. 'I may be your hostage, but I am also a detective inspector with the homicide division of Mombasa CID.'

The pirate shook his head irritably. 'The girl is dead and Jalil has admitted killing her. There is nothing to see.'

'In my experience, Mr Abdulle, there is *always* something to see,' Jouma said.

'You are a fool, Inspector.'

'Perhaps. But before you pass sentence on the boy, I would like the opportunity to see the crime scene. If only to satisfy my own curiosity.'

'And then? You will tell me that Jalil was not the killer after all? That I should spare his worthless life?'

Jouma shrugged. 'Why execute one who is innocent at the expense of a murderer?' he said.

For a moment Omar appeared to waver.

'You cannot afford to delay,' Moses Bani interceded angrily. 'You must kill the boy now and have done with it. If the crew think you consider them murder suspects, when the boy has admitted the crime in full sight, there will be chaos.'

'What difference do a few hours make?' Jake said. 'Like you said, Abdulle – you are the law on board this ship, not them.'

Omar glanced from one man to the next until his gaze settled on Jouma. 'You do not think Jalil is the killer, Inspector?' he said.

Again Jouma shrugged indifferently. 'Anyone is capable of murder, Mr Abdulle. But I have always believed that a man – or in this case a boy – is innocent until proven guilty.'

There was a long, heavy pause as Omar weighed the arguments in his mind. Then he said, 'I admire the sentiment, Inspector – but I have always believed it is the other way round. You have until dawn tomorrow to prove the boy is innocent.'

'I appreciate the opportunity, Mr Abdulle,' Jouma said. 'And if I don't?'

Omar smiled. 'Then your last act before you leave this ship will be to fire the bullet that kills him.'

# 25

It had taken a little under thirty minutes to drive the fifty or so miles north from Flamingo Creek to the beach resort of Watamu, which would have been impressive in a modern SUV. In Harry Philliskirk's twenty-year-old Land Rover it was little short of miraculous – but not as miraculous as the fact that its passengers had not been killed on the highway. Clinging to the roof strap for dear life, Mugo had spent most of the helter-skelter journey with her eyes tightly shut, listening to Harry's continuous and excited chatter only because it took her mind off the prospect of imminent death.

*This road wants to kill me today*, she thought. And she also thought about Mrs Nderitu's cigarettes which she had foolishly left in her room. And then she wondered what on earth had possessed her to allow the crazy Englishman in the seat beside her to drive her all the way to Watamu. She was, after all, officially off duty. There was no obligation to go to Flamingo Creek for a second time that day – except, of course, the personal promise she had made to Harry Philliskirk to keep him informed of any development, no matter how obscure.

Oh, she'd tried ringing. But she should have guessed he'd be drowning his sorrows. During her secondment to

CID she had heard Jouma describing the drinking habits of his English fishermen friends on many occasions, and never without a sense of wonderment.

So instead she'd driven there to tell Harry about the phone call Simba had received from the security service in Nairobi, and how his friend Jake Moore was somewhere in Somalia, being held captive by a gang of pirates.

And now, half an hour later, she was in a Land Rover that was rapidly approaching the beachside hotels of Watamu with Harry driving and Sammy the bait boy bouncing around in the back.

'Would you please tell me where we are going, Mr Philliskirk?' she said for the umpteenth time.

'Jake's in Somalia and we need to do something about it,' Harry said.

'But the authorities—'

'Bugger the authorities. They couldn't arrange a piss-up in a brewery. Have you got your badge with you?'

Mugo reached in her jeans pocket and removed the smooth wallet. 'Yes. Why?'

'That,' he said, grabbing it from her and waving it in the air, 'could come in very handy.'

'I am not a charity, Harry,' Kurt Anderssen said. 'And neither do I have a death wish.'

'You owe me a hundred bucks, Kurt,' Harry reminded him.

'A hundred bucks would not get you as far as Lamu. And that's if you wanted to catch some fish. As for what you are proposing . . .'

'How much?'

The Danish skipper made a swift calculation based on danger and greed. 'Six thousand.'

'You know I don't have six thousand dollars, Kurt,' Harry said.

'Then that's tough. Get someone else.'

They were standing in the bar of the Ocean Sports hotel, a renowned hang-out for fishing boat skippers operating out of Watamu. Next to the bar was a wooden rowing boat that had belonged to the intrepid, and probably crazy, Englishman who had first landed in the bay and started selling cold beer to the locals back in the fifties when there wasn't a hotel in sight. Now there were a dozen, and their clientele provided the likes of Kurt Anderssen with most of their business.

'What about all that crap about wanting Jake and me to help you in your hour of need, you skinflint Viking?' Harry said. 'It takes two to tango.'

'That was before you said you wanted to go to Somalia.'

'It's not a day trip, Kurt. You heard what Constable Mugo told me. This is a legitimate police investigation.'

Mugo was about to say she'd said nothing of the sort, but Harry fixed her with an imploring stare.

Anderssen peered down at her from beneath the floppy brim of his jungle hat. He was a tall man of around fifty, with a face so cracked and weatherbeaten it was often impossible to see his pale-blue eyes through the sharp folds of skin.

'I've got bait boys older than you, missy,' he pointed out.

Again Mugo was about to reply, but again Harry was not about to let that happen.

'I'd go myself, Kurt – you know I would. But I don't have a boat. I need someone I can rely on. Someone who knows these waters like the back of his hand.'

'Don't soft soap me, Harry,' Anderssen said. 'And don't

think you can use your pet dwarf here to convince me it's a matter of national security. I know Kenya cops and I know for a fact that they wouldn't go anywhere near Somalia.'

Harry stared at him, then shook his head sadly. 'All right, Kurt. Sod you. I thought I could rely on you, but it seems I was wrong.'

He tapped Mugo on the shoulder and the two of them headed for the door. Anderssen drained his pint of Tusker, swore, and called them back.

'Four thousand,' he said.

'Fuck you.'

'Three.'

'One hundred dollars, Kurt. And then we're quits.'

Anderssen shook his head. 'I must be mad.'

'It goes with the territory, Kurt,' Harry grinned.

Anderssen's boat, *Osprey*, was a forty-four foot Altair with a thousand horsepower in her engines and more expensive instrumentation than Harry had ever seen in his life. She was a beauty, in total contrast to her miserable skipper, who continued to grumble all the way across in the launch.

'I'm not happy about this, Harry,' he said, jabbing a finger at Sammy, who was steering the flimsy transport to where *Osprey* was moored a hundred yards out in the deeper waters of the bay. 'I've got my own boys, you know. This is costing them a day's pay.'

'We're not going fishing,' Harry reminded him. 'Sammy's here because he's got eyes like a hawk, and because Jake is his boss.'

'And what about you, missy?' Anderssen said, turning his attention to Mugo. 'You ever been on a boat before?'

Mugo looked at him indignantly. 'Many times. My

brother and I used to work for a skipper in Kilifi during our school holidays.'

'Oh yeah? And who was that?'

'Terry Baptiste.'

Terry Baptiste ran one of the biggest game fishing concerns in Kenya. He was also known to stamp hard on anyone he felt might be direct competition. At the mention of his name, Kurt Anderssen decided it might be diplomatic to shut up about Mugo's right to be here.

'Well, I'm still not happy,' he muttered. 'And you should know better than to get roped into this madcap fucking scheme. Harry's insane. Didn't you know?'

'I'm beginning to think you are right, Mr Anderssen,' Mugo said.

She felt a nudge on her arm and Harry, sitting beside her at the back of the launch, gave her a stern look. 'Kurt's right. I'm a bloody liability. You should go back,' he said in a low voice. 'This is no business of yours. It's not safe.'

'Forgive me, Mr Philliskirk, but this *is* my business. I should have kept my mouth shut. I should never have agreed to come here. In fact, I should stop you from embarking on this ridiculous journey.'

'Oh, yeah? And how do you plan to do that?'

Mugo opened her mouth, then shut it again. Harry was right. The only possible way she could stop him going in search of his friend was to arrest him. But on what charge? And what difference would it make anyway? Harry Philliskirk did not strike her as the type of man who would allow himself to be arrested by an eighteen-year-old rookie.

'You are fortunate that Inspector Jouma is also being held captive,' she said. 'This makes it an official police investigation.'

Harry grinned. 'That's the spirit, girl!'

'But I warn you, Mr Philliskirk – at the first sign of danger I will insist that we turn round. Do you understand me? Am I clear?'

'Crystal, Officer Mugo. And don't worry – I only plan to take a quick shufty. Ask a few questions, that's all. I won't be karate kicking my way through Somalia.'

'I sincerely hope not.'

'The truth is, if there's a chance, no matter how crazy, of getting them back safe and sound then we're going to take it. Am I right?'

Mugo nodded.

'Right. Well, if you're coming welcome aboard. But I suggest the first thing you do when you get on Kurt's boat is hide that badge. Where we're going, they don't like policemen.'

# 26

'So now what?' Jake said, exasperation in his voice.

Jouma, on his knees and peering beneath Sheba's bunk, said, 'You surprise me, my friend. You told me once that detectives never lose their instinct for clues.'

'I think I also told you that I was a detective in the Flying Squad,' Jake pointed out. 'My job was catching armed robbers, not sifting murder scenes.'

The inspector extracted himself from the bunk and sat up, groaning slightly as the bones crackled in his spine. 'A crime scene is a crime scene whatever department you work for,' he said. He used the edge of the bunk to pull himself upright then, stepping carefully around Sheba's body, went across to the dressing table.

'You're enjoying this, aren't you?' Jake said. He was leaning against a narrow fitted wardrobe beside the door, his arms folded in an attempt not to contaminate any evidence with his big, brutish, Flying Squad hands.

'Enjoying is not the word.'

'No – but you're back in your element. Happy at last.'

'It is a relief to be able to focus one's mind on something other than the probability of one's own violent death,' Jouma said, peering at the utensils on the floor by the dresser.

'Even though you're going to have to kill the boy tomorrow morning.'

'Yes,' Jouma said. 'That is a worrying consideration. But only if I cannot prove his innocence.'

'And you think you can?'

'We shall see.'

Jake unravelled his arms and slapped his own forehead in exasperation. 'This is a bloody pirate ship, Inspector! You don't have any witnesses, any forensics, any ... *anything*.'

Jouma straightened and looked at him. 'My friend, I work for Mombasa CID. I am used to such privations. Now unless you have anything constructive to add here, might I suggest you make yourself useful elsewhere?'

Jake looked at him blankly.

'*The boy!*' Jouma said. 'Surely you have not forgotten how to interrogate a suspect?'

Jalil was being held in the same foetid storeroom where they had been imprisoned the previous day. Rafael had placed a guard at the door, but Jouma had made strict stipulations about the terms of his investigation, and the bruiser was under grudging instructions to allow them access to the boy.

He was sitting on the floor, and when Jake entered he scuttled back against the wall, the struts of his calliper clanging against the harsh metal floor. It was only when he saw who it was that Jalil calmed slightly. Jake sat down beside him, and for a while the pair stared at the wall.

'Are you all right, son?' Jake asked him presently.

'Yes,' Jalil said, although his face was puffy with crying and with the slap Omar had given him across his cheek.

'You sure?'

'Yes.'

'So why don't you tell me what's going on?'
'I killed Sheba.'
'So you say. What I don't understand is why.'
'I . . . don't know.'
'You don't know?'
'I mean – I must have. It was my knife.'
'That's not the point, Jalil. I asked you why.'
'I don't know,' the boy repeated.
Jake sighed. He was chasing his tail here. Or, more likely, it was so long since he had conducted any sort of police interview that he had forgotten how to do it. He knew the key was patience, especially when dealing with a kid – but he was finding it hard to keep his rising exasperation in check.
'OK – let's start from the beginning. You were with Jouma and me this morning, right? Then you left. Where did you go?'
'I went to Sheba's cabin.'
'And what were the two of you doing?'
'I can't remember. Nothing.'
'Well, why were you there?'
'Sheba likes to have me around.'
*Yeah, so she can bully the shit out of you*, Jake thought sourly.
'Were you talking?'
Jalil thought for a moment. 'Maira was fixing her hair.'
'And where were you?'
'I was by the door.'
'Was Maira there all the time?'
'No. Sheba told her to leave. She was angry.'
'With Maira?'
'No. With me.'
'Why?'
'Because I had been to see you.'

'Why would that make her angry?'

'Because I was late. And because I was not supposed to be there.'

'What did she say?'

'She said she would tell Omar.'

Now they were getting somewhere, Jake thought. He could picture the vituperative little bitch threatening to tell tales out of school. And he knew that, for whatever reason, Jalil was in awe of Omar Abdulle. But was that motive enough for murder?

'Jalil – was Sheba teasing you?' Jalil looked down. 'I know she does, son. And I know it can be hard to take sometimes. Sometimes you just want to fight back. When I was a kid your age I was always getting picked on at school. There was this big lad called—'

'I don't remember,' the boy said flatly. 'I was in Sheba's cabin and we were talking and then the next thing I knew I had killed her.'

'You don't remember stabbing her with the knife?' Jake asked.

'No.' Jalil looked at him with an expression of profound sadness and confusion. 'But I must have done – otherwise she would not be dead.'

*He's just a kid*, Jake thought. Since when did that make a difference, though? What about those callous little bastards from Liverpool who tortured Jamie Bulger before leaving his mutilated body on a railway track? How old were they? Ten? Eleven? What about Mary Bell thirty years earlier? The schoolgirl from his own home town who strangled two toddlers before carving her initials into their flesh with a razor?

Just kids.

But murderers all the same.

Yet when he looked at Jalil he didn't see a cold-blooded killer. He saw a boy who had stabbed his tormentor simply because he had reached the point at which he could stand it no more. In any civilised country the charge would be manslaughter.

On the *Kanshish* there were no such legal niceties.

'What is the biggest fish you have ever caught?' Jalil asked suddenly.

Jake smiled. 'The biggest? Well, not so long ago I was with a guy who hooked a 500-pound bull shark. That's pretty big. I saw its teeth. Big sharp teeth. Teeth like you would never believe.'

Jalil shuddered. 'I don't like sharks.'

'Me neither.'

'My uncle in Kismaayo, he used to work on fishing boats like yours. His job was to cut open the little fish and put them on the hooks.'

'It's a vital job, I'll have you know. Much more important than driving the boat. I've got a lad just like your uncle who works on *Yellowfin*. His name's Sammy.'

'Does he have a knife like mine?'

'Yes. In fact he's got a few.'

'Did he cut open the shark?'

Jake smiled. 'No – it used those big teeth of his to bite through the line. Anyway, you'd need a much bigger knife to cut open a shark. Sammy's little blade would hardly make a scratch.'

Jalil considered this. Then he said, 'I would like to work on *Yellowfin* one day.'

'You're a bit young,' Jake smiled. 'But one day I'll take you on.'

'Promise?'

Jake paused. He looked at the boy's expectant face and felt his heart breaking. 'Sure.'

★

Every crime scene told a story. And the narrative of this particular scene, Jouma reflected as he stood in Sheba's cabin, was as straightforward as they came.

*Jalil and the girl have an argument. Somewhere around the middle of the room Jalil stabs her in the abdomen with the gutting knife. There is perhaps a moment or two of shock – the two children standing like statues as the blow registers. She puts her hands to the wound and feels her own warm blood. Then her instinct kicks in and she reels away from her attacker, gripped by fear and panic. Her bloodied hands claw at the wall. She crashes against the dresser, upending the chair. Perhaps she screams for help; but nobody hears her over the cacophony of cheers and gunfire coming from the mob on deck. By now Jalil has fled. She staggers to the door, leaving more blood smears on the jamb. Is she trying to reach Omar, her uncle, her protector? But the shock is beginning to kick in now. She feels weak. Her knees give way and she falls to the floor, curling into the instinctive position of the child in the womb.*

And it is there that she dies.

Jouma looked down at the girl's body again. In death she seemed diminished, as did all bodies when the essence of life had left them. She looked, he thought, precisely what she was: a vulnerable child.

He sighed. It was not in his professional nature to be affected by the circumstances or the protagonists of murder. And yet he could not help but feel an overwhelming sadness here in this rudimentary cabin on board this hellish ship. This was no place for children. A child's place was with its parents and its friends, not surrounded by rapacious thugs and murderers. There was, he thought, a tragic inevitability about what had happened here. The lives of Jalil and Sheba had been irreversibly tainted the very moment they had stepped aboard the *Kanshish*.

'Have you finished?'

Moses Bani was standing in the doorway. The wiry Somali was twisting his fingers with a mixture of anxiousness and impatience.

'Why do you ask, Mr Bani?'

'Because Omar wishes his niece's body to be prepared for burial. The Imam is waiting.'

'Where do you propose to take her?'

'A place has been made ready in the galley downstairs.'

Jouma nodded. There was little point in leaving Sheba's corpse here in the cabin. And while he had little knowledge of the Muslim code of burial, he could appreciate the need to act quickly; Sheba had been dead less than an hour, but in this heat it would not be long before her body began to decompose.

'I would like to examine the body before the Imam prepares it,' he said.

Moses's eyes flashed angrily. 'You haven't seen enough?'

'Not yet,' Jouma said – although it was with a sinking feeling that, deep down, he knew that he probably had.

# 27

'Could you just say something into the microphone, Mr Abdulle?' Nancy Griswold said. 'Anything. It's just to check the sound levels.'

The man in the green and black jungle camouflage uniform leaned forward and said: 'Hello. My name is Omar Raghib Abdulle.'

Nancy looked across at Red Sheppard, who was sitting on an upturned aluminium camera case, a pair of headphones connected by a curling wire to the Betacam on his shoulder. The veteran cameraman nodded. 'All good, Nance,' he said.

'That is a very nice camera,' Omar Raghib Abdulle said. 'How much did it cost?'

'Plenty,' Sheppard said tersely.

He put his eye to the viewfinder and adjusted the focus so Abdulle's narrow, pockmarked face bounced in and out of the frame. Then he zoomed out so the subject was captured in its entirety, seated somewhat grandiosely on a collapsible garden chair in the shade of a palm tree, the ocean forming a pleasing line of balance in the background. Zooming out even further he saw Nancy in the foreground, leaning forward in her chair, making final adjustments to the angle of the microphone stand between her and the interviewee. Further back still, and Sheppard could pan across to his left to where a canvas bell tent had been pitched by the sluggish brown waters of the creek. The skiff that had transported the Australians downriver had been pulled up onto a shale embankment, where Hafiz the fixer sat with the two gunmen, counting out the dollar bills he'd been paid for arranging this interview.

'You ready to roll?' Nancy said into his headphones.

Sheppard quickly snapped back to a medium shot of Omar Abdulle, who had now lit a cigarette and was blowing the smoke coolly through a large gap between his yellow front teeth.

'Ready.'

Nancy cleared her throat. 'I wonder if we could start with you explaining as clearly and concisely as you can who you are and who you represent.'

'My name is Omar Raghib Abdulle,' he began, drawing more smoke deep into his lungs, this time exhaling it through his nostrils. 'They call me The Poacher. I am the most feared pirate in Somalia.'

'I see,' Nancy said. 'And you don't mind being known as a pirate, with all the negative connotations that might entail?'

Abdulle grinned. 'Why should I care what the western imperialists think of me? They have raped my country and exploited my people, and now they tremble when they hear my name.'

He certainly talked the talk, Sheppard mused. And, with his ersatz military attire, Omar Raghib Abdulle was just as one might imagine a Somali pirate leader to look. And maybe that was what bugged him about this whole set-up. It was all too ... *as you might expect.* Furthermore he could tell from Nancy's body language – stiff, defensive – and the tone of her voice as she conducted the interview – wary, disengaged – that she was thinking the same thing.

'When I capture a ship it gives me great joy,' Abdulle was saying, 'because I see fear in the faces of the crew. They bow before me because they know that I hold their lives in the palm of my hand – and that I can crush them from existence in the blink of an eye.'

Nancy nodded. 'OK, Mr Abdulle, that's great. We'll just take a little break there.'

'But we have just started,' Abdulle said, clearly irritated to have been cut off in his prime.

'I just need to have a word with my cameraman about maybe doing a couple of different angles.'

'As you wish.'

As Sheppard unhitched his camera, Nancy stood up and he followed her to a spot a few yards away where they could not be overheard.

'Well?' he said. 'What do you think?'

She screwed up her face. 'This is bloody bullshit, Red.'

'Yeah, I know. It's like he's been boning up on the pirate's handbook.'

Hafiz came scurrying across, a look of consternation on his face. 'Is everything all right?' he asked.

Nancy glared at him. 'How many men did you say this bloke commands?'

'Five, six hundred at least. He is the most feared—'

'—pirate in Somalia. I know. He told me. It just strikes me as odd that a fellow as feared as Omar should turn up to an interview without any of his men to look after him. I mean, where's his base? We were kind of expecting to meet him there, not out in the middle of fucking nowhere.'

'The location of Omar's base is a closely guarded

secret, Miss Griswold,' Hafiz said earnestly. 'There is no amount of money that would persuade him to allow you to go there.'

Nancy's violet eyes bored into the little Arab. Then she looked at Sheppard. 'We'll carry on a little bit longer. See if he's got anything more interesting to say.'

'You're the boss, Nance,' Sheppard shrugged.

They went back across to the palm tree, and while Nancy readjusted the microphone and made soothing noises to the interviewee, Sheppard hooked his camera over his shoulder and began his own routine again.

But this time when he zoomed out, something seemed different. The balance was all wrong – and as he peered into the viewfinder he quickly saw what it was.

'Nancy – I think we've got company.'

He was pointing inland, almost directly over Omar Abdulle's head, at a puff of dust that was growing in size and intensity as its source approached at high speed.

'Friends of yours, Mr Abdulle?' Nancy asked, shielding her eyes as she stared out at the dust cloud.

Abdulle got to his feet, suddenly agitated, and shouted something to Hafiz and the gunmen. The fixer took one look and his mouth dropped open.

'We have to go now, Miss Griswold,' he said urgently, grabbing the reporter by the arm and attempting to lead her towards the creek where the two gunmen were already pushing the boat into the water.

'What the fuck is going on, Hafiz?' Nancy demanded, shaking her arm free.

'It is not safe here. We have to go.'

'I think the great pirate leader has already made up his mind,' Sheppard said sardonically. Abdulle had already folded up his chair and was sprinting towards the skiff with it under his arm. 'Come on, Nance. Let's get out of here.'

But it was far too late for that. Suddenly a muscular-looking open-tailed pick-up truck smashed out of a fringe of low scrub a hundred yards away. The vehicle had been pimped with steel bull-bars and roof spot lamps, and in the back, mounted on a welded stand, was a .50 Cal general-purpose machine gun.

*Jesus Christ,* Sheppard thought, because he had seen vehicles just like this one in the urban hotspots of Afghanistan, Sudan and Iraq. They were known as *technicals* and they were the preferred mode of transport of local militias in those lawless territories. This particular vehicle contained a driver and passenger in the cab, and five men in the rear, one of whom was manning the gun. They were all black, all mean-looking, and, had Sheppard been asked to describe what Somali pirates really looked like, this is precisely how he would have seen them.

As the technical drew near, the driver made a point of crushing the bell tent beneath its oversized tyres before slewing the vehicle to a halt near to the skiff. Armed with AK-47s the men in the back jumped out and marched across to where the two gunmen and Omar Abdulle were now standing on the shore, hands raised in abject surrender.

'The most feared pirate in Somalia,' Nancy said acidly, as now the men in the technical's cab disembarked and came swaggering across. In their baggy vests, low-slung Levis and Reeboks they looked like a couple of LA homeboys – or at least a Somali version. One of them was even pointing his big silver Glock so that the back of his hand was uppermost.

'Who the fuck are you?' he demanded in heavily-accented English – at which point Hafiz the fixer fell on his knees and began pleading in Arabic.

'We're from Channel Seven television in Australia,'

Nancy said, undaunted, indicating herself and Sheppard. The cameraman was still holding his camera.

'And them?' the Somali said, flicking his gun in the direction of the skiff.

Nancy grimaced. 'Why, that's the great Omar Raghib Abdulle. Isn't that so, Hafiz?' And as she spoke she put her boot into the fixer's backside and kicked him forward so he sprawled in the dirt.

The two Somalis looked at each other with astonishment, and for a moment it seemed they might even laugh.

'So who are you?' Nancy said.

'We are the Deadly Boys,' said the man with the Glock, and then, with a voice laden with menace, ordered her and the others into the back of his vehicle.

# 28

Sheba's body had been carried downstairs and placed on a stainless steel table in the galley, where it now lay under a clean white sheet. Soon it would be washed and wrapped in five pieces of linen according to the Muslim tradition – and Jouma knew that once that happened it would be off limits for good. He did not have much time.

Under normal circumstances, of course, there was a procedure for the post mortem examination of murder victims. Their bodies were taken to the morgue at Mombasa hospital where Mr Christie, the pathologist, used an array of hideous-looking apparatus to cut them open and scoop out their vital organs. But, again, these were not normal circumstances. Whatever evidence Jouma might be able to glean would be from a cursory external examination of the body only. Not for the first time, the Inspector felt he had been transported back to the seventeenth century. He really was on his own – and he could appreciate now why so many criminals were hanged in those days. It was a lot easier than trying to prove their guilt.

Carefully he pulled down the sheet covering Sheba's naked body and willed himself into the detached, almost inhuman mind of Dr Christie, a man who considered the dead to be nothing more than puzzles to be dissected, analysed, and then stitched back together again.

What would he make of this? *Where would he start?*

Normally, when Christie was conducting one of his autopsies, Jouma would be queasily clinging to the tiled room of his basement morgue, trying to think happy thoughts, desperately trying not to catch a glimpse of the blood and the viscera or hear the crack of bone and the slop of organs into metal dishes. Now he wished he'd paid more attention.

*The body. Christie always began with a once-over of the body.*

That, at least, was straightforward enough. The deceased was an eleven-year-old girl, of average height and more than average weight. Jouma knew about puppy fat, but there were large rolls of pocked flab around her middle and the tops of her thighs that could not be simply blamed on her age. Perhaps there was some underlying condition that had caused her weight problem; either that, or her Uncle Omar had been feeding her the choicest titbits from the meagre rations on board the *Kanshish*.

Gratefully, he turned his attention to the knife wound. The flesh was still stained with blood and at first he couldn't see it – then, by carefully prodding an area of puckered flesh to the left of the navel, he revealed a small incision in the skin. Jouma had been around enough autopsies to know that the natural elasticity of the skin could cause the wound to contract once the blade was removed. By gently stretching it between his fingers he was able to ascertain that it was perhaps an inch wide. This, at least, was consistent with the width of the blade on the gutting knife.

*Now what would Christie do?* he thought – although of course, he knew the answer. Sheba's abdomen would be unzipped with a scalpel and the internal damage caused by the knife assessed. Her organs would be removed for analysis, and the top of her skull would be sawn off so the pathologist could get to her brain.

As he pulled the sheet back over the body, Jouma couldn't help feeling that his examination had left him no better informed about Sheba's murder than before. In fact, the last few minutes had been an object lesson in futility.

He could almost hear Mr Christie's scornful laughter echoing all the way from the depths of his Mombasa morgue.

By the time Jake got back to Sheba's cabin the girl's body had gone and so had Jouma. He stood at the doorway and saw that the room had also been tidied. The bed was made, and the girl's toiletries were arranged neatly on the dresser. All that set it apart as a murder scene was the blackening pool on the carpet and the blood smears on the walls.

'Forgive me, sir.'

Maira had appeared in the corridor behind him. She was carrying a bowl of suds and a cloth.

'Forgive me,' she said again as she slipped into the room, her eyes averted.

He watched her as she knelt by the stain on the carpet and gently began dabbing it with a damp cloth.

'It's Maira, right?'

A sheepish nod.

'You're Sheba's nanny?'

'I have looked after her since the day she was born,' she said, scrubbing the carpet then wringing the cloth with her bony, calloused hands.

'What about her mother?'

'Her mother was killed. Murdered by Mr Mohammed's enemies.'

For a moment the old woman paused in her work, and Jake thought she was about to cry. But then she began again, a relentless, rhythmical scrubbing and wringing.

'Mr Mohammed is Omar's brother?'

'Yes.'

'Is that why he sent the girl to stay with Omar? Because of his enemies?'

'Mogadishu is a dangerous place,' Maira said. 'Mr Mohammed has many enemies. But then the only thing men are good for is making children and widows.'

'The boy, Jalil – you know that he has been accused of Sheba's murder?'

'I heard.'

'Where were you at the time?'

'Downstairs. In my quarters. She had lost her temper with me. When that happens I usually give her time to calm down before returning.'

'Did she often lose her temper?'

'She had a fiery streak.'

The way she said it suggested to Jake that the old woman had been on the receiving end of Sheba's fury more than once.

'Jalil was with her when you left?'

She nodded.

'Had they been fighting?'

'Sheba had said a few words to him. I can't remember what it was about.'

'The boy – what do you know of him?'

'Only that his mother was a whore,' Maira said matter-of-factly. 'She brought him to Omar when the ship was docked in Kismaayo. Said the men might be interested in using him.'

'*Using* him?'

She looked at him with sad eyes. 'She wanted a thousand US dollars.'

Jake felt his flesh creep. 'My God.'

'God has nothing to do with it. The boy was fortunate that Omar is not like that . . . '

There was a pause.

'Maira – did Jalil ever react to Sheba? I mean, did he ever *fight back*?'

'Not that I ever saw. I used to feel sorry for him.'

Jake thought about that piercing voice summoning Jalil to the wheelhouse, and the look of utter desolation on the boy's face at the prospect of another day in Sheba's company.

'Do you think that he was capable of killing Sheba?' he asked.

The old woman massaged her arthritic knuckles. 'Everyone has their breaking point,' she said, and then she turned back to her cleaning.

He eventually found Jouma in the galley, staring thoughtfully at the naked body on the stainless steel table. The inspector listened to what he had to say, running his fingers over the glinting patches of silvery stubble that had appeared on his chin. For such a fastidious man, Jake thought, being denied access to a razor must have been unbearable, on a par with having to wear these stinking pirate rags instead of a suit.

'He did it, didn't he?' he said presently.

'Jalil? Yes, there would appear to be little doubt that he stabbed her. But did he kill her? I am not so sure.'

'What are you talking about?'

'Look, Jake. See how overweight she is.'

'OK,' Jake said with a shudder. 'So she's fat.'

Jouma shook his head. 'Not just fat. *Obese.*'

'What's your point?'

'I am no medical expert – but I have seen plenty of stab victims, and I think I have a reasonable grasp of what it takes to kill someone with a knife. The fact is, my friend, it is an inexact science. Unless you know precisely what you're doing, you must rely on the blade either rupturing a major artery, or causing sufficient damage to a vital organ. Stab someone fifty times, the chances are you will kill them. Stab them once, the odds are shortened considerably.'

Jake thought about the scar across his own abdomen. It had been caused by a stiletto blade wielded by the assassin known as The Ghost. She was a professional killer, but during their fight on board *Yellowfin* she had only managed a single, wild jab into his stomach which had missed every artery and vital organ. The bitch had done plenty of damage, Jake reflected – but she hadn't killed him.

'If the blade is less than two inches long,' Jouma continued, 'then the odds are shortened even more.'

Jake looked at the body on the table and now he understood what the Inspector was trying to say. From his own experience in the fishing business he knew that in the right hands a gutting knife could fillet a good-sized fish with one slash. Why? Because under the skin they were a hundred percent muscle. But to get to Sheba's vital organs you'd have to plough through a thick layer of blubber. And unless the knife was driven into her belly with tremendous force – the force of a strong adult – there was no way it could have caused enough damage to kill her. The blade simply wasn't long enough to penetrate to the muscle layer.

'Jalil is an eight-year-old cripple,' Jouma said, reading

his thoughts. 'There is no way he could have had the strength needed to administer a fatal blow. Were we to cut the girl open, I would wager the blade never even penetrated the subcutaneous fat layer to the muscle beneath.'

'And even if he'd struck lucky and nicked an artery, that cabin would have been swimming in blood,' Jake said. He had seen the cabin, and a few smears and stains did not suggest Sheba had bled to death. 'So how did she die?'

'A heart attack brought on by the shock, maybe? Without a post mortem examination it's impossible to be certain.'

'So Jalil didn't kill her.'

Jouma sighed. 'I'm afraid that is very much a matter of personal interpretation. Even if the knife itself did not inflict the fatal blow, Omar could quite rightly argue that his niece would not be dead if Jalil had not stabbed her. Either way, the girl is dead.'

As the significance of the inspector's words hung heavy over the galley, Jake put his head in his hands. 'You know what this means, don't you?'

'Yes,' Jouma said. 'The boy is going to die – and I am to be his executioner.'

# 29

'He's a fine looking boy,' Kurt Anderssen said. 'How much do you pay him?'

Harry was deep in thought, watching the fragmented sun on the waves, and it took him a moment to realise who the Danish skipper was talking about.

'Who, Sammy? It depends. Jake takes care of that side of things.'

'I find you have to be careful,' Anderssen said. He was looking down from the *Osprey*'s flying bridge at the pulpit jutting from the prow of the boat, where Sammy the bait boy had been standing like a sentinel ever since they'd left Lamu that afternoon. 'You pay them too much, they fuck off and you never see them again. You have to feed it to them slowly. Drip, drip. No more than ten shillings a trip.'

'We've never had that problem.'

'No. I can tell he's faithful. His brother worked for Dennis Bentley, yes?'

'That's right.'

'That was a bad business.'

'A very bad business.'

Dennis Bentley was a skipper from Flamingo Creek who'd got mixed up with the wrong crowd and paid for it with his life. His bait boy, Sammy's elder brother Tigi, had been murdered by the same animals that killed Dennis.

'I will take him off your hands if you like,' Anderssen said.

'He's not a piece of furniture,' Harry said frostily.

'Just saying.'

'Thanks but no thanks, Kurt.'

Anderssen lit a cigarette and adjusted the boat's throttles. They were now thirty miles inside Somali waters, and had been hugging the coastline for the best part of an hour. 'OK,' he said, glancing at the GPS system on the dashboard. 'Round this headland and we're there.'

'Good.' Harry leaned over and called down to Mugo, who was keeping watch from the fighting chair bolted to the *Osprey*'s cockpit. A moment later she appeared at the top of the ladder.

'We're nearly there,' he told her.

'How long will this take?'

'Not long.'

'Good – we should get back before nightfall.'

'Absolutely.'

Anderssen had slowed the boat as they rounded the headland. Up ahead, in a shallow bay protected by a reef, was a small fishing village, a ramshackle collection of mud and stone huts congregated around a woodpile jetty. A handful of dhows were moored in the shallow water and, as the *Osprey* approached, gesticulating figures could be seen on the shore.

'You sure about this, Harry?' Anderssen said warily.

'Take me in,' Harry said. 'Wait here, and if I'm not back in an hour get the hell out of Dodge.'

The big Dane glanced at Mugo and rolled his eyes. 'He thinks he is James Bond, missy.'

'I know,' Mugo said. She could see now that a small skiff containing several men was coming towards them from the direction of the fishing village. 'That's why I am going with him.'

'Under the seat, missy – there's a box.'

Mugo reached under the banquette and pulled out a plastic coolbox.

'Slide it over, will you?'

Anderssen lifted the lid. Inside, instead of cold beer and sandwiches, was a sawn-off shotgun and a selection of handguns.

'I'll keep the sawn-off, you take one of the Glocks,' he said to Mugo. 'I take it they told you how to fire a gun in your police training?'

'I think we should take it easy, old man,' Harry said. 'There's no need for weapons.'

But Anderssen was staring at the approaching skiff. 'This is my boat, *old man*. If those thieving *kaffirs* want it, then they'll have to fight me for it.'

The skiff came alongside. It contained three men, each wearing *macawi* robes, their faces concealed beneath *keffiyeh* headscarves. They were armed with AK-47s. Up on the flying bridge, Kurt Anderssen slowly pushed two cartridges into the barrels of the shotgun, and beside him Mugo felt a rivulet of clammy sweat running down the back of her neck. She looked for Harry, but the Englishman was already clambering down the exterior ladder to the *Osprey*'s cockpit. As he did so, one of the men in the boat stood up and unhooked his *keffiyeh* so his face was exposed. And, to Mugo's astonishment, she saw that it was split by a huge, toothless smile.

'Harry?' the Somali exclaimed. 'Is it you?'

'Fraisal, you old dog!' Harry called back. 'Who did you think it was? The Kenyan navy?'

Now everyone, including the two Somalis in the skiff, was looking at each other with bemusement.

'You should be careful,' Fraisal chortled. 'You know what Somalis are like. Perhaps I will take you hostage.'

'Funny you should say that, Fraisal, old man,' Harry said, and as the skiff bumped *Osprey*'s side the two men reached across and shook each other by the hand. 'But that's just what I've come here to discuss.'

# 30

In Muslim culture the Imam is a spiritual leader, a man of unimpeachable Islamic faith who has been chosen to guide his community of followers in worship, in life, and through to the afterlife.

The Imam on board the *Kanshish* was nothing of the sort. He was a low-ranking Muslim cleric with gangland connections, who had fled his mosque in Mogadishu when the city was taken over by militant al-Shabaab fundamentalists who took exception to his own self-serving interpretation of the Koran. After fleeing north into Djibouti and eventually crossing the Bab al Mandab straits into Yemen, he had drifted for several months before washing up in the slums of Aden, where he had resigned himself to spending his remaining days preaching to the faithless and the damned, and partaking of the whores and the liquor. But the Prophet moved in mysterious ways – and when, through one of his few remaining Somali contacts, he had been offered a job working as a personal spiritual guide to the daughter of a Mogadishu warlord named Korfa Mohammed, the Imam had jumped at the opportunity to come home.

The job was based at Mohammed's fortified retreat south of the war-torn city – and while the money was good, the Imam soon discovered it was not the easy ride he had expected. The girl, Sheba, was intolerable – a fat, vain, bossy little whore who had been spoilt by her father to the extent that she regarded herself as some sort of minor royalty. She treated everyone like dirt, and made it abundantly clear that she had even less interest in the complexities of Islam than the Imam himself. To console himself, he had taken to regarding his position in terms of a lucrative short-term contract; a nest egg for his advancing years, if you like. And it was hardly taxing work. For three hours a day he was expected to read scripture with the girl, impress upon her the tenets of the book of divine guidance, and recite with her the teachings of the Prophet, peace be upon him. And while the girl was an insufferable little bitch, the money Korfa Mohammed paid him for his trouble more than made up for the abuse he received from Sheba.

Admittedly the Imam had been less than pleased when, due to certain unspecified threats, the girl and her entourage had been moved to stay with Mohammed's brother – and even less so when he discovered the brother in question was a pirate who was based on a ship in the middle of the Indian Ocean. But the substantial increase in his monthly stipend was most welcome, as were the assurances that his stay on board ship was only temporary until Mohammed got his affairs in order.

But now Sheba was dead. *Murdered by the cripple boy, no less!* It scarcely seemed credible. And while the Imam was thrilled that he would no longer have to endure the lash of her tongue, his joy was tempered by the fact that he was also out of a job. To compound matters there were also other more immediate inconveniences to deal with.

'I want her prepared in the traditional way,' Omar had told him – and the Imam, who had conducted plenty of funeral services but never stooped so low as to prepare a corpse for burial, had been obliged to scour the pages of the Holy Book for enlightenment on the precise nature of the *wudzu*, or ablution, ceremony. As he did so, he couldn't help thinking he was researching the preferred method of cooking the goose that laid his golden eggs.

It would not be a pleasant task. Although it was only a few hours since Sheba had been murdered, he was sure he could detect a greenish tinge to her deathly pallor – and that faint, sweet odour of decay in his nostrils could only be emanating from one source. But at least the body had already been cleaned. The old woman had seen to that, praise be. He had also heard that Omar's captive, the Kenyan detective, had instigated some sort of investigation into the girl's death. The Imam found that news to be extraordinary, not least because there was nothing to investigate. Hadn't the boy admitted stabbing her? Still, he wished the Inspector was here, if only for the moral support. He was a squeamish man and the sight of blood made him nauseous.

The ceremonial ablutions involved washing the body in strict order. First the private parts, then the hands, mouth, nostrils, face, right arm to the elbow, left arm to the elbow, the head, and finally the right and left foot to the ankle. After that the body had to be daubed with oil of camphor and then, because it was female, precisely wrapped in five strips of white cotton.

It was an arduous, fiddly process, and all the more galling was the knowledge that as soon as it was done the girl and his handiwork would be tossed over the side. Surely it would be easier to stitch her into an old rice sack and have done with it. But that, the Imam sighed, was the problem with religion. Nothing was easy.

*So, to work.*

★

In the ship's wardroom Omar Abdulle listened carefully to everything Jouma had to say. Then he sat back in his captain's chair, slammed his boots on the desk, and said, 'Have you killed a man before, Inspector?'

'No, Mr Abdulle. I have not.'

'It is not as difficult as you might think. In fact it is extremely easy. And killing a boy is even easier.'

Jouma opened his mouth to speak, but beside him Jake gasped with annoyance. 'Didn't you hear what he said, Abdulle? There *is* no proof that Jalil murdered the girl.'

Omar glanced at the Bani brothers, flanking him at the desk like a pair of vultures, and at Rafael looming implacably at the door. Then he sighed with an expression of quiet bemusement. 'You accuse me of being judge and executioner, gentlemen – but I would suggest that any court in the world would find the boy guilty.'

'Of manslaughter, perhaps—'

'Manslaughter, murder ... these are just words to describe the same terrible act.'

'Don't try to tell me there is any justice on this ship—' Jake began, but as he stepped forward angrily Jouma stopped him with his outstretched hand.

'You still intend to kill the boy?' he said.

'No, Inspector,' Omar said. 'I intend for *you* to kill him.'

'I am a policeman. I am not going to kill anyone. But I think you know that anyway, Mr Abdulle.'

Omar frowned. And then he spread his hands and grinned. 'Bravo, Inspector. A man of principle. And you are right – I should have known you would sacrifice your own freedom rather than kill the boy.'

'Sacrifice my freedom? I don't think so. The return of your imprisoned comrade is far too important. You talk about keeping your men entertained, Mr Abdulle – but I would suggest that your problems run far deeper than that.'

Jake saw that Omar's triumphal smile had frozen, and that the pirate leader was slowly leaning forward across the desk. An air of menace filled the wardroom.

But Jouma did not flinch.

'Twelve of your men are dead, and now your own niece has been murdered. What must your crew think? What do your lieutenants think? What do they think of the great Omar Abdulle now?'

Omar lunged for him, grabbing Jouma by the throat. Jake attempted to step in, but Rafael sprang forward with surprising speed to restrain him.

'You can kill the boy,' Jouma gasped, his eyes bulging in his head as the pirate leader's fingers tightened around his neck. 'But how long will that keep them amused?'

'Long enough,' Omar hissed. His hand opened and Jouma fell backwards onto the wardroom floor.

Grimacing behind a perfumed scarf, the Imam dipped a small square of cotton in a bowl of water and began delicately dabbing around the dead girl's exposed pudenda. Rapt in his task and in his own revulsion, he moved slowly up the body to the hands and face, avoiding the stippled knife wound, ceremonially washing the cold pale skin in the manner set down in the Holy Book. Having completed the face he gently moved the girl's head to one side in order to clean the ears and the neck. As he did so, he noticed something in among the whorls of gristle of the left ear; a thin rime of black, flaky dust around the entrance to the ear canal. He peered more intently and saw that more of the dust was visible now, coating the rim of the inner ear. And there was something else. In the canal itself, packed down so deeply that it would not be visible to any cursory examination, was what appeared to be a plug of material.

Puzzled now, he picked up a large sewing needle resting on the winding cloths. He carefully inserted the needle into the ear canal and, after a few moments, he was able to unpick a corner of the material. Several more seconds elapsed after which he emitted a grunt of satisfaction and withdrew the needle. From the ear itself came a sudden gout of thick black fluid, the consistency of mucus. The Imam squawked with dismay as the fluid filled the ear and then spilled down the side of the girl's neck.

They might have outstayed their welcome in the wardroom, Jake thought, but at least they were still alive. And there had been moments when he'd thought the chances of them coming out of Omar's *sanctum sanctorum* in one piece were remote. As it was Rafael was now escorting them without ceremony down to the storeroom where they had been incarcerated the previous day. The heady days of having their own cabin were over – Omar had withdrawn his hospitality.

But despite the imminent discomfort, Jake had nothing but admiration for Jouma. The little bastard had balls, of that there was no doubt, and never were they bigger and brassier than when he was standing up to someone he despised. And my God he despised Omar Abdulle. Jake could see it in his eyes. To Jouma, the great pirate leader was nothing more than a common street thug, a bully with a gun, the sort of ten-a-penny gangster the Inspector had been locking up for the last thirty years. Watching him stand up to Abdulle had been, for Jake, one of the most terrifying yet awe-inspiring things he had ever seen.

He just wished he had a fraction of the little detective's courage.

To get to the storeroom they had to go through the galley, and as they passed through the companionway they nearly collided with the Imam coming the other way.

The cleric seemed distracted, but his face brightened when he saw Jouma. 'Ah, detective. I was just coming to see—'

Behind them Rafael wheezed and grunted threateningly through his ruined throat, and the Imam froze – but Jouma, seeing what looked like blood on the cleric's fingers, ignored him.

'What is it?'

'Something . . . I don't know what. The girl—'

'Show me.'

They went through to the galley and into the small anteroom where Sheba's body was kept. The Imam had placed the wad of material, the size of a pea, on one of the metal benches running along the wall.

'It was in her ear,' he said, pointing at the body.

Jouma stooped and gazed at the wad. 'May I?' he asked, picking up the needle. Carefully he used the point of the needle to worry the material until it began to unravel. When he was finished he held up a narrow strip of bloodied linen measuring perhaps six inches in length.

'What the hell is it?' Jake asked.

'It looks like a strip torn from one of Sheba's dresses,' the detective said. 'Crude, but effective. Certainly enough to staunch the flow of blood.' He went over to the body and peered into the girl's ear. 'As I thought. There's something else in there.' He turned to the Imam. 'I don't suppose you have another needle I could borrow?'

The cleric nodded and, from a fold in his robes, produced a leather pouch containing a selection of sewing implements. Jouma crowed with delight as he saw a pair of narrow metal tweezers.

'Perfect,' he said.

With the tweezers he fished into Sheba's ear, cursing as the tips kept slipping from the object buried deep inside the girl's head. Finally he managed to make purchase and, with a sucking noise like a stick being hauled from thick mud, he pulled it out. It was wooden, two inches long, and tapered to a sharp point at one end. The end that was clamped in the tweezers was jagged, as if it had been snapped off.

'What is it?' the cleric asked.

'The murder weapon,' Jouma said, holding the object in front of his nose and staring at it with fascination. He stood and went across to Rafael, who had been watching the proceedings with as much interest and mystification as the other men in the room.

'Go and get Mr Abdulle,' the Inspector said. 'I think he will want to see this.'

# 31

Harry's reasoning was simple. If Jake had indeed been kidnapped by Somali cutthroats, then it was pointless just waiting for a ransom demand that might never come. The best person to ask about his whereabouts was a Somali cutthroat – and it just so happened that he knew one.

Fraisal Abduwali, by contrast, considered himself a respectable man. He was a thirty-five-year-old father of twelve who had worked as a mechanic at a yard on Flamingo Creek until four years ago when his wife's father had died, leaving him extensive fishing rights around a village in Somalia, forty miles north of the border. And all right, if he also supplemented his income running shipments of *bhang* and other contraband south to his friends in Kenya, so what? That did not make him a bad man. It certainly did not make him a cutthroat. Fraisal had no interest in piracy.

'Why are you here, Harry?' he asked.

They were sitting in Fraisal's house, which was the grandest in the village on account of the fact it was made from breezeblock and corrugated iron. Fraisal's wife, having served her husband's guests four bowls of pungent fish stew, had retreated outside, where she sat breastfeeding their youngest child.

'I've lost Jake,' Harry said.

Fraisal frowned, his face creasing into deep folds. 'Jake? Jake from London?'

'The very same.'

'I am sorry to hear that, my friend. Where did you lose him?'

Kurt Anderssen looked up from his bowl and snickered. Mugo, sitting cross-legged beside him, gave the Danish skipper an admonishing glare, and this time Sammy's shoulders began silently heaving.

Harry explained what had happened, and the Somali's face crumpled even further. For a man of thirty-five he looked more like ninety.

'You think because I am Somali I am on speaking terms with every pirate?' Fraisal said presently.

Harry sighed. 'No. But I don't like to think of the poor bugger tied up with a bag on his head. You might say I'm grasping at straws.'

'Yes. I rather think you are.'

'Mr Abduwali,' Mugo said, '*two* men are missing.'

'Yes, yes . . . the policeman.' Fraisal swiped a dribble of stew from his chin. 'I have to say, a fishing boat skipper and a Kenyan policeman would not be a valuable catch for the pirates who operate round here.'

'Who *does* operate round here?' Harry asked.

'There are a number of gangs. Small fry. But most of them work for the same man. His name is Garaad Islam.'

Fraisal explained that Garaad was the chief of a pirate gang known as the Coastal Volunteers, who in turn were made up of a loose confederation of smaller units operating along the southern coastline of Somalia from the city of Kismaayo a hundred miles south to the Kenyan border.

'Then it's possible that Garaad has our friends?' Mugo asked.

'Possible,' Fraisal said. 'But unlikely. Garaad prefers

ships. Human hostages are more trouble than they are worth.'

Harry's face fell.

'However,' the Somali continued, 'the gangs who work for him are not as astute as he is. It is quite possible that some low-ranking fool has taken it upon himself to make a name for himself. If Jake was in the vicinity of the border, he may have been the victim of an ill-advised raid into Kenyan waters.'

'I need to know, Fraisal,' Harry said.

'I will make inquiries. But it will take some time. I take it you will be staying here tonight?'

Anderssen spluttered. '*Stay* here? This man might be your friend, Harry – but this is fucking *Somalia*.'

Harry nodded. 'You go, Kurt. Take Sammy and Constable Mugo with you. I'll be all right here with Fraisal. He'll get me back to the border, won't you, old man?'

'You can take the boy, Mr Anderssen,' Mugo said firmly, 'but I am staying.'

'And so am I,' Sammy exclaimed.

Once again the big Dane found himself completely outnumbered. He fixed each of them with a withering stare, then nonchalantly checked his watch. 'I suppose it is getting late,' he said. 'It would be better to wait till morning.' Then he jabbed an accusatory finger at Fraisal. 'But I want your assurance that I won't get back to my boat to find it has been picked clean.'

Fraisal grinned. 'If there is any picking to be done, *effendi*, be assured that I will be the person doing it.'

# 32

Jake and Jouma stood beside the antique dressing table in Sheba's cabin. Arranged on the polished rosewood surface was a selection of utensils – a hairbrush, a comb, various shallow pots for cream and powder, a hand mirror – that were all clearly part of a set carved from the same wood and by the same delicate hand as the dresser itself.

The two men turned as Omar bustled into the cabin, followed by the Bani brothers and the lumbering presence of Rafael.

'What is the meaning of this?' he snapped irritably. 'What are you doing in here? Where is the Imam?'

'Tell me about this furniture,' Jouma said calmly.

The pirate's eyes bulged. '*What?*'

'Where did you get it from, Mr Abdulle?'

'It was part of a shipment in the hold of a vessel transporting luxury cars to Saudi Arabia,' Omar said, gesturing at the dresser. 'It is not really my style – but I thought Sheba would like it. Girls like to sit and look at themselves in mirrors, do they not?'

'And the accessories came with it?'

'Of course. I warn you, Inspector, this had better be relevant because I am losing my patience.'

Jouma reached over and picked up a rectangular wooden box from the dresser. It was lined with cork, lying open beneath the mirror. Inside it were three slim wooden hair batons, each fitted into its own holder, each measuring six inches. They were exquisitely turned to a tapered point and decorated with swirling inlays of gilt along their length.

'And these?'

Omar stared at the batons. 'Sheba wore them in her hair. Maybe she thought she was a geisha girl? How should I know?'

'There should be four of these sticks,' Jouma said, and his finger tapped at an empty holder. Then he nodded to Jake, who opened his hand. Lying on his palm was the needle-like fragment they had retrieved from Sheba's ear. Cleaned of the dark blood that had adhered to it, the same distinctive gilt patterns were now visible.

It was a perfect match to the other three.

Omar's mouth dropped open as Jouma explained where it had come from.

'What do you know about Maira?' Jake said.

'Maira?' There was a long pause, and when Omar spoke again his voice was dull. 'When my brother asked me to look after Sheba, I said no. What do I know about little girls, I asked him? He just laughed. "Omar," he said, "they are a mystery to me and to every grown man. That is why they have mothers." But Sheba's mother died when the girl was a baby. I said to him, how do you cope? And that is when he told me about Maira. "The old woman washes, feeds and clothes the girl." And then he put his hand on my shoulder and he said: "But you know what is the most astonishing thing about her, Omar? *That she hasn't killed her yet.* Because if anyone talked to me the way my daughter speaks to Maira, I would cut out their throat."'

Jake stared at the stump of wood in the palm of his hand.

'But everybody has their breaking point,' he murmured.

*Perhaps the boy is not even aware that he has the weapon in his hand until it is too late, and the razor-sharp blade slips easily into the buttery layer of flab beneath her thin cotton dress. She screams, and Jalil realises with horror what he has done. He sees the blood beginning to spread across the white cotton.*

*He does not know it is a superficial wound. In his mind he has killed her. He runs.*

*Where is Maira? She must be close by – close enough to come running when she hears the scream, the way she has done ever since Sheba was a baby. She finds the girl bleeding, but realises to her overwhelming relief that the wound is not fatal. She knows she must stop the bleeding. She gets to work, sitting the girl down at the dresser, calming her as she tends to the wound.*

*Is that when Sheba says it? Even as the old woman is helping her, as she has done every day of her life, dedicating her every waking moment to the well-being of the ungrateful little bitch, is this when Sheba finally utters the insult that pushes Maira over the edge?*

*The breaking point. Just as Jalil reached for his knife, Maira finds the wooden hair baton. Did she even know what she was doing when she plunged it into Sheba's ear? Murder only takes a momentary lapse of control. But once the act is done, it cannot be undone.*

*In her panic to remove the baton she pulls too hard and snaps it, leaving two incriminating inches still embedded in Sheba's ear. Blood pours out, covering the front of her robe as she tries in vain to revive the girl. But it is too late. Quickly, quickly! There is no time. Think, think!*

*And it is then that the realisation crystallises in her mind.*

*Sheba has already been murdered.*

*The old woman tries to dismiss the thought, the repercussions, but it is too strong. Her will – her reason – has been weakened by her own panic. She is controlled now by her own primitive instinct for self-preservation, an instinct that has lain dormant inside her for so many years.*

*And it makes perfect sense. Maira knows all too well how Sheba treats the boy. Her contempt for Jalil is matched only by her contempt for the old woman. Today it has driven them both to an act of madness – but there can be only one killer.*

*She knows she must conceal what she has done. She tears a strip from one of the girl's robes, rolls it in her arthritic fingers, jams it into the ear cavity to staunch the blood, pushing it far down with the end of the broken baton until it is no longer visible. When she sees the blood is no longer flowing she dabs the girl's facecloth in a bowl of warm, soapy water and carefully swabs away the blood from her face and neck, taking care to remove all traces from the crevices of the ear, from the soft skin below, from the fine strands of hair that have become matted and congealed.*

*Calmer now she thinks one, two steps ahead. The girl has been murdered, so she must think like a murderer. She begins to upset the furniture, spilling things on the floor, making it seem as if there has been an almighty struggle. Then she goes to the door. Composes herself. Turns. The room is as it should be. She goes downstairs to her room and waits until Omar returns.*

Maira's quarters were spartan, a metal-walled storage bulkhead down near the engine room. The door was slightly ajar, the tiny space beyond glowing dimly in the light of a solitary candle. Omar strode up, arm outstretched to barge in and apprehend Sheba's killer – but Jake stopped him.

'Let me,' he said.

For a moment Omar bristled, but then he shrugged. 'As you wish.'

Jake knocked lightly and pushed open the door.

He went in.

Saw the old woman on her knees, hanging from a loop of twisted material tied to a steam pipe running the length of the back wall, tongue lolling from her open mouth and her sightless, bulging eyes staring down at the floor.

'Oh, Maira,' he sighed.

# The Third Day

# 33

The notorious Somali pirate Qasim Fadir was a pathetic creature. Five feet tall, barely six stone, a mouthful of rotten teeth, grey-brown skin ravaged by malnutrition and juvenile affliction, and, to cap it all, a prosthetic wooden foot attached to the stump of his right shin that looked like it had been carved by a small child. He was, thought Captain Milton Mabuto, a typical example of a species that had no place on God's earth. If He had created man in His own likeness, then Somalis were an aberration, an early sketch that should have been erased instead of being allowed a precious space on His good Earth.

'You lost your foot on a landmine?' Mabuto asked.

The pirate nodded, his head bowed. That was in itself a good sign. It meant that his three weeks of interrogation had at least taught him respect. Mabuto wondered idly just how many hours of physical abuse it had taken to break the dog's spirit. Not many, he suspected.

'A pity. But do not despair, my Somali friend – soon you will be back among your own kind, where such deformity is commonplace.'

Another nod. Mabuto smiled grimly to himself. His hand was resting on the bars of a small metal cage, little bigger than a dog's kennel, where the prisoner had been kept overnight despite John Nola's instructions. One of Qasim's forefingers curled around the bars. With one lightning-quick move, Mabuto broke it with a single blow of his polished *rungu* club.

The Kenyan officer turned away and gestured to four of his men standing to attention by the cell door. The men hurried in and, between them, lifted the cage and took it upstairs. Mabuto followed them from the cell block and out into the compound. Dawn had only just broken, and there was a pleasant chill in the air that scoured the lungs when it was inhaled. He watched his men lug the prisoner across to a transport wagon, where a dozen more men were purposefully checking their weapons. He smiled to himself and strode to the bunkhouse.

John Nola was sitting in front of Mabuto's desk, sipping gingerly on a cup of blindingly strong coffee. It pleased the captain to see that his visitor from the Kenyan security service looked so wretchedly uncomfortable in his current surroundings. That is what came of spending your life behind a desk, getting soft when the real security work was being done here, at the sharp end, at the border, so close to the enemy that you could smell their stinking Islamic breath on the northerly wind. The agent was even wearing army fatigues, as if to give himself some legitimacy. Well, it simply didn't wash. As far as Mabuto was concerned it was utterly pathetic.

'The prisoner is in the truck,' the captain said, swinging easily into his leather chair. 'We will be leaving in ten minutes.'

'Good,' Nola said. 'What is our ETA at the rendezvous point?'

*ETA at the rendezvous point*, Mabuto scoffed inwardly. Precisely which American war movie had Nola been watching?

He checked his watch. '0930 hours.'

'Good.'

'More coffee?'

'No, thank you.'

Mabuto poured himself a cup from a nickel pot on his desk. 'May I ask you something, Mr Nola?'

Nola shrugged. 'Of course.'

'The prisoner – Qasim Fadir – he is regarded as something of a catch by you gentlemen of the intelligence community.'

'A catch?'

'I mean to say: he is relatively high up within the criminal organisation to which he belongs, is he not? He is not simply a footsoldier, like most of the dogs that are dragged through Mombasa port?'

'No,' Nola said. 'He is not, Captain. Why do you ask?'

'I am puzzled, that is all.'

'Really?'

'Yes, Mr Nola. Puzzled.'

'Why is that?'

'Because if he is so valuable, why are you letting him go?'

Nola glanced momentarily at the oily liquid in his cup, then placed it carefully on the desk beside the pot. Mabuto saw that it had barely been touched.

'Value comes in different forms,' he said.

*Typical Nairobi doublespeak*, the captain thought. 'I am still puzzled,' he said politely.

'It has been decided that at this point in time his value to the Kenyan state is greater by letting him go than by keeping him incarcerated.'

'But surely by keeping him incarcerated – by *interrogating* him – you stand to learn valuable information about his criminal network?'

'Possibly. But perhaps he has already given us all the information we need.'

Mabuto considered this for a moment, then dismissed it as yet more official nonsense. 'Or perhaps,' he said with a mirthless smile, 'the value of those he is to be exchanged for is greater.'

Nola looked at him. 'That, I am afraid, is classified information, Captain,' he said.

There was a pause, then Mabuto leaned forward. 'May I speak frankly, Mr Nola?'

'Of course.'

'It grieves me that loyal soldiers of the Kenyan army – *my men* – should be put in harm's way in order to secure the release of a Somali dog like Qasim Fadir, no matter how valuable you people may consider him.'

'I am sorry to hear that, Captain,' Nola said impassively. 'But if I may be frank, I don't give a damn what you think. You have your orders, and as a loyal soldier of the Kenyan army you will follow them to the letter.'

The two men's eyes met across the desk. Then Mabuto brought his coffee cup to his lips and slurped its contents noisily.

'Of course,' he said. 'In that case, we should be on our way. We do not want to be late.'

# 34

Shortly before dawn Harry emerged from his hut and, blearily suffering the after-effects of two lemonade bottles of liquor that Fraisal had claimed was distilled from sisal roots, staggered into the bushes to pee. He unzipped his pants, unleashed his stream, and it was only when he heard an outraged squawk from the undergrowth in front of him that he opened his sticky eyelids.

Mugo scampered into his line of vision, angrily pulling up her jeans, and for a moment they stared at each other in the half-light until Harry remembered to zip himself up.

'Don't you ever watch where you are going, Mr Philliskirk?' the young police officer snapped.

'Terribly sorry. Wasn't exactly expecting company.'

'I wasn't exactly expecting you to be awake, after all the alcohol you consumed last night,' Mugo said.

'Fraisal is an old friend. Old friends like a drink together.'

'It was disgusting to behold. You could barely speak. You certainly could not walk. Sammy and I had to put you to bed.'

Harry scratched at the bristles on his chin. 'Such are the labours of the righteous,' he said. 'Where is Sammy?'

'He is on the boat with Mr Anderssen.'

'Well, if *I* couldn't walk, I'm bloody sure Kurt couldn't.'

'He insisted on returning. He said he was worried he might be murdered in his sleep otherwise.'

'Don't tell me he swam?'

'No. Sammy and I had to carry him to the launch and row him across.'

Harry giggled. 'You really should have had a drink last night, Officer Mugo. It would have saved you a lot of exertion.'

'It is no laughing matter, Mr Philliskirk,' Mugo glowered. 'And I will remind you that although Fraisal is your friend, the rest of Somalia is not.'

'Calm down, Mugo.'

'You ask me to calm down. You ask me to calm *down*?'

And it was there, in the middle of a jungle in Somalia, far from anything they had ever before experienced and surrounded by several million people who would have happily slit their throats, that Harry realised that Mugo was scared – and, furthermore, so was he.

Nancy Griswold was scared too, although like Harry she would never admit it to anyone else. Certainly not to Red Sheppard – although deep down she suspected the cameraman knew. Red understood human nature. He could read the signs, the body language. It's what made him so damn good at his job.

*Well fuck you, Red – I defy anyone not to be scared right now.*

She was sitting with her back to the crumbling wall of a farm outbuilding, somewhere in the middle of a vast expanse of parched, godforsaken scrubland, its sheer bald monotony punctuated only occasionally by a gnarled tree thrusting from the dusty earth. Hanging from a bough of the nearest tree, forty yards from where she sat, was the man claiming to be the pirate leader Omar Abdulle. He was still alive, because the rope had been tied behind his back so that his head hung forward and his shoulder joints took the full force of his weight hanging ten feet in the air. Nancy had seen this form of torture before, on a grainy video shot in some Iranian prison and smuggled out by activists. It was variously known as *strappado*, *reverse hanging*, or *Palestinian hanging*, but the intended outcome was the same for the victim – the excruciatingly painful dislocation of the arms and the gradual tearing of the muscles, tendons and ligaments connecting them to the shoulder sockets.

Except the men doing the hanging had no interest in eliciting information. They were lounging on the ground, puffing reefers and laughing heartily at the plight of the screaming man dangling from the tree. And if things went to form Nancy knew that sooner or later – most likely when the victim fell unconscious – they would tire of their entertainment and cut him down. Then they would prop him against the tree and empty their AK-47s into him until all that was left was a tattered lump of meat with little or no distinguishing features at all.

Nancy knew this because that morning she had watched precisely the same thing happen to Omar's two henchmen. She also knew that once Omar was dead, the next in line was Hafiz the fixer, who was lying nearby with his hands bound to his ankles and his already filthy *dishdasha* fulsomely stained with the contents of his voided bowels and bladder.

*And when they'd finished with Hafiz . . .*

'What the fuck do they expect me to do with this?' Red muttered, his voice strained under his breath, his camera trained at the scene of slaughter playing out in front of him.

'Just keep filming,' Nancy hissed, reasoning that the fact they were a western news team might just be the only thing that was keeping them alive. But then Red was right: why had their captors insisted that everything was filmed? Did they expect it to appear on the six o'clock news? Even they couldn't be that dumb. No, the bastards probably wanted a memento of their grand day out, a video to show their friends and family at Christmas.

'I'm running out of battery,' Red said.

'Well don't fucking tell them that!'

Ah, Jesus – how the *fuck* had things come to this? Nancy glared at Hafiz, and despite the fixer's plight she had an almost uncontrollable urge to run over and kick him in the balls. Stupid little bastard. This was all his fault.

But as quickly as her anger boiled, it subsided again because deep down she knew that their predicament was *her* fault and hers alone. *Her* greed. *Her* impatience. *Her* insatiable bloody ambition. She had broken every rule in the book by swanning off into the great unknown with Hafiz. She hadn't checked his credentials, she hadn't verified his story – Christ, she hadn't even told her boss in Sydney where she was going.

'I'm sorry about this, Red,' she said.

'Ah, shut up, Nance,' Sheppard said, and the corner of his mouth curled slightly in a smile of solidarity.

One of their captors got up and sauntered across. It was the man who had been the front seat passenger in the technical yesterday. He was clearly the leader of this little cabal, the self-styled Deadly Boys – and if the weed had taken the edge off his aggression it had done nothing to dull the wild look in his eyes.

'Good film, yes?' he said. 'Good entertainment?'

'As snuff movies go, it's right up there with the best of them,' Nancy said.

The man laughed. 'One day maybe *I* am a movie star.' He clicked his fingers to attract Sheppard's attention, and when the camera was pointing at him he pulled his Glock from the waistband of his pants and began jabbing it at the lens. '*You looking at me? You looking at me? You fucking looking at me?*'

'Listen, mate,' Nancy said, trying to be as reasonable as possible. 'You know as well as I do there's been a big mistake here. You can't just go around kidnapping Australian nationals. Think of the consequences. Any minute now special forces are going to come flying over the horizon and then it's welcome to the real world – you know what I'm saying?'

For a moment the man stared at her. Then he pointed his gun directly at her head.

And then he said, '*You looking at me?*'

# 35

Things had happened fast that morning. Too fast, Jake thought – which struck him as crazy considering he'd been dreaming of this moment ever since he and Jouma had arrived on the *Kanshish*.

Shortly after dawn they had been roused by Rafael and marched down to the deck. Without ceremony they were bundled over the side of the ship and down the cargo netting ladders into two skiffs. Now, astonishingly, the rusting old coaster was far behind them and they were making good progress on a calm sea in the direction of the mainland. They had not seen Omar Abdulle that morning, or indeed the previous night. The pirate leader had locked himself away in his wardroom and was not entertaining visitors. Jake and Jouma's last hours on board the ship had been spent in a curious limbo, confined to quarters, counting the minutes.

Now that the moment had finally come Jake knew that he should have been feeling happy, excited that in a short time their ordeal would be over. But he was unable to shake the sick feeling in his gut that had stayed with him ever since he'd opened the door to Maira's quarters and found the old woman hanging there like some desiccated straw doll. At that moment, in the bowels of that hellish ship, he had felt despair – a *futility* – that was almost overwhelming. He knew Jouma felt the same, although the little detective was a genius at masking his emotions.

What surprised Jake was Omar's reaction. The belligerent, arrogant pirate seemed somehow shrunken when he saw Maira's body; as if in that moment he realised that for the first time on the *Kanshish* murder had been committed as a result of a human spirit being broken rather than out of cruelty or sheer bloodlust. But more than that he realised that now there was no one to punish for Sheba's murder. The ceremonial execution of Jalil would not be taking place today. The increasingly restless crew of the *Kanshish* would have to wait for their bread and circuses.

Omar had turned and walked away from the cabin without saying a word.

Jalil's reaction, when Jake told him what had happened, was equally dumbstruck. The boy sat blinking for several minutes on the floor of his cell as the news and its implications registered in his brain. When he finally spoke, it was with the distant, weary voice of someone emerging from a fitful sleep.

'Why did Maira kill her?' he said. 'Maira was the only person who *liked* her!'

Jake suspected that question would remain unanswered now. The only people who knew what had happened in those fateful few minutes in Sheba's cabin were dead.

'Come on,' he said to the boy. 'You must be hungry.'

Jake had taken the boy to the galley and sat him down at the table usually occupied by Omar and his cronies. In the storeroom he found slabs of salted meat, rice and vegetables fresh from the supply boat. He was no chef, but he knew how to whip up a wholesome meal. And anything would be wholesome compared to the oatmeal shit doled out to the likes of Jalil and the rest of the crew while Omar dined like a king.

He rinsed a hand-sized cut of meat and tossed it into a blackened skillet with some maize oil, and while it sizzled he boiled up rice and potatoes and greens in a large metal pot. After a few moments Omar's cook appeared in the doorway, his eyes bulging with outrage.

'What do you think you are doing?' he exclaimed.

'Fuck off,' Jake told him, and the cook did just that.

When the food was cooked, Jake put it on the best plate he could find and placed it in front of Jalil. The boy looked at it as if he had never seen food before, then fell on it ravenously while Jake sat and watched. When he was finished, the boy was so replete he looked dazed.

'My friend and I are leaving tomorrow,' Jake said.

There was a long pause. 'I know.'

'We are being exchanged for one of Omar's men on the mainland.'

'Take me with you,' Jalil said, an edge of desperation in his voice.

'I can't.'

'Please, Mr Jake!'

'I can't, Jalil. I wish to God I could – but . . . '

The boy's eyes fell, and at that moment Jake felt like the worst kind of bastard for even mentioning it.

'Listen – I'll make you a deal,' he said, reaching across the table and putting his fingers around Jalil's painfully thin wrist. 'Next time the ship docks at the mainland, I'll make sure there's someone waiting for you. Someone who will take you away from Omar, out of Somalia, to Kenya.'

'Omar will not let me go,' Jalil said sadly.

'Don't you worry about Omar. I'll speak to him.'

The boy's face brightened momentarily. 'Someone will be waiting?' Jake nodded. 'Who?'

'There are people – good people – who make it their business to look after young kids like you. As soon as I'm free I'll arrange for them to be there.'

'And they will bring me to Kenya?'

'First class ticket, old son.'

'Will *you* be there?'

'I'll be there all right. And the first thing we'll do is go fishing. How does that sound?'

From the expression on Jalil's face it sounded like the best thing in the world.

There were two skiffs, travelling at high speed abreast of each other in the direction of the mainland. Jake was in one, Jouma the other. Each boat had a rudder man, six heavily armed crewmen, and was commanded by one of the Bani brothers. In Jake's boat, staring out impassively from the bows, was Julius. In Jouma's, by contrast, Moses was hunched up against the gunwales with an expression of abject misery on his face.

'It seems strange that Mr Abdulle should not be present to welcome back his long-lost friend,' the Inspector called over the fizzing smash of spray and the jarring thump of the fibreglass hull on the swell.

Moses looked up at him. His skin was ashen, a state of affairs that pleased Jouma immensely. It was strangely invigorating to find someone who suffered from seasickness worse than himself.

'Mr Abdulle is a busy man,' the elder of the Bani brothers growled.

'I am aware of that,' Jouma said. Moses looked away, clearly unwilling to make conversation. But Jouma pushed him. 'I imagine that commanding a ship like the *Kanshish* is a difficult job. Keeping everybody on board content must be a constant worry.'

A noncommittal grunt.

'In fact I imagine the *Kanshish* is a dangerous place to be. Especially after recent events. I imagine the mood among the men could quickly turn mutinous.'

As the boat hit a wave, Moses gagged and put his hand to his mouth. Then he sighed. 'Do me the courtesy, Inspector Jouma, of saying what it is you wish to say. As you can see, I am no sailor.'

'Maybe not, Mr Bani – but you are an intelligent man. Indeed I would go so far as to say that Omar Abdulle relies upon your intelligence to run his business.'

'I am flattered,' Moses said sourly.

'Then let me ask you this: how long do you think his operation can continue? Sooner or later he will be caught, or he will be overthrown, or he will be superseded by someone younger and more ambitious and more bloodthirsty than he is. What then? Are you so devoted to him that you are prepared to die at his side?'

'So what do you suggest?'

'Omar and the others are career criminals – but surely you have more to offer your country.'

'My country?' Despite himself Moses laughed. 'You clearly don't know the first thing about Somalia, Inspector.'

'I know that it is crying out for people to make a stand against lawlessness and anarchy. To rebuild it from the roots upward.'

'And you think I am one of these people?'

'I *know* you are, Mr Bani.'

'Then you are mistaken,' Moses said. 'I have nothing to offer Somalia. Somalia can go to hell.'

As he spoke a cry went out from the prow, where one of the men was pointing at the low smudge of land that had appeared now on the horizon.

# 36

Other than his gift of the village, Fraisal's father had also bequeathed him the settlement's only mode of automated transport – a US army-issue jeep, dating back to the doomed Mogadishu expeditions of the 1990s, that had somehow made its way south from the capital intact and, even more remarkably, still worked. The vehicle had originally sported a utilitarian olive-green livery, but Fraisal, aware that certain of his more trigger-happy countrymen still harboured suspicions that the Americans would one day come back to Somalia to finish what they had started, had taken steps to disguise its origins. In other words he had got his hands on several tins of gloss paint and allowed his many children free rein to vandalise the exterior as they saw fit. Now, while the jeep still retained its distinctive outline, Harry felt like he was travelling in a Jackson Pollock painting on wheels.

He was sitting up front, next to Fraisal, with Mugo in the rear, the three occupants shaded from the morning sun by a woven canopy of banana and sisal leaves attached to the vehicle's body by bamboo stanchions. They had been travelling for an hour, heading inland from the village on a road that was little more than a dirt track hacked out of the jungle. Now, as the trees thinned,

Harry saw a vast plain of scrubland, punctuated by the occasional rocky outcrop, and beyond it, heavy with mist, a range of low hills.

'Where are we going, Fraisal?' he shouted over the rumble of the jeep's engine and the scream of its tortured suspension.

'My cousin Hemi,' the Somali replied.

'Why?'

'Because she knows everything about everything.'

Mugo leaned forward and rested her elbows on the back of Harry's seat. 'Where does she live?'

'There,' Fraisal said, pointing in the vague direction of the hills.

In fact Cousin Hemi's house was another fifteen miles. It was a comparatively well-kept farmhouse overlooking a modest grapefruit plantation on the side of a hill. As they drove up the track leading to the building they saw an old man in a straw hat tending the patch with a primitive-looking hoe. When Fraisal honked the horn he looked up and peered myopically, then waved uncertainly.

'Hemi's husband,' Fraisal told them.

Cousin Hemi was waiting at the door. She was a broad-beamed woman and she greeted them with a huge, toothless smile. When Fraisal jumped down from the jeep she waddled over and embraced him with such enthusiasm he was forced to extract himself before his ribs shattered.

'Do you understand Somali?' Harry asked Mugo.

'A little – but not when it is being spoken so rapidly.'

Hemi's smile dimmed a fraction when Fraisal explained who was in his jeep, but it was only a momentary lapse. Soon they were sitting at a wooden table in the shade drinking blood-temperature grapefruit juice freshly squeezed into what appeared to be bone cups.

'Cousin Hemi says she is fifty-six years old,' Fraisal said, and the woman grinned proudly. Harry smiled back, thinking that, in Somalia, that was probably the equivalent of getting a telegram from the Queen. He would have liked to have said she didn't look her age – but he would have been lying. Cousin Hemi looked about a hundred and forty, the skin on her face ravaged by hardship, as furrowed and rough as the dry earth of her plantation.

'This juice is very refreshing, madam,' Mugo said.

Cousin Hemi said something to Fraisal. 'She says you look like her first-born daughter.'

'I will take that as a compliment.'

'She says her daughter left one day to go to Mogadishu and seek her fortune, but never returned. She has not heard from her in more than twenty years.'

Mugo stared into the bottom of her cup, not knowing quite what to say.

'Kids, eh?' Harry chuckled unconvincingly. Then he gently kicked Fraisal under the table. 'I wonder if the lady has any information about the people we are looking for?' he said pointedly.

There was a prolonged, rapid-fire exchange in Somali – and, encouragingly, it was Cousin Hemi doing most of the talking. Presently Fraisal turned to Harry.

'Well?'

'She says she has not heard of your friends.' Harry's face fell. 'However, she says she was at the market only yesterday and overheard some gossip that might be relevant.'

'I'll take anything, Fraisal.'

'It seems one of the Deadly Boys was in town, bragging about a catch he intended to present to Garaad Islam as a tribute.'

Harry looked at his friend blankly. 'What the hell are you talking about? Deadly Boys?'

'A gang of young ne'er-do-wells and thugs. Local boys who think they are big-time hoodlums.'

'Garaad Islam,' Mugo said. 'You mentioned him yesterday.'

'Ah – well, now he really *is* a big-time hoodlum,' Fraisal said. 'He controls most of the coast south of Kismaayo. Piracy, drug smuggling, prostitution: you name it, Garaad runs it.'

'And the tribute?' Mugo said, staring at him intently. 'What is that?'

Fraisal sighed. 'Every young hoodlum around here aspires to be a member of Garaad's gang. But you don't just walk in – you have to prove yourself worthy first. In this case it would seem the Deadly Boys think they have something Garaad will appreciate.'

'You think the catch could be a couple of hostages?'

'It would not be unknown.'

'Then we'd better find these Deadly Boys,' Harry said.

The Somali's eyes widened. 'That, my friend, would be extremely dangerous. Not to mention foolhardy.'

'Fraisal is right,' Mugo exclaimed. 'And this is not what we discussed, Mr Philliskirk. It is time we returned to Kenya and reported our findings to the authorities.'

Harry's face hardened. 'Report what, Officer Mugo? Gossip from a market place? We need facts. Cold hard facts. And I for one don't intend leaving here until I have them.'

# 37

The skiffs had reached the narrow mouth of a coastal lagoon and were now idling in shallow water. Julius Bani put his foot on the gunwale and, through a pair of expensive binoculars, peered at the mangrove-fringed shore a hundred yards away.

Jake looked across at the other boat and his eye caught Jouma's. The Inspector looked tense. But then they all did, especially the men with the AK-47s – and that's what worried him. Omar Abdulle may have prided himself on his organisational prowess, but he was fifty miles away on his ship and it wouldn't take much for something to go wrong. *Why the hell wasn't he here?* The answer, Jake knew, was precisely *because* something might go wrong.

On the other boat, Moses Bani was checking his watch anxiously, like some harassed time-and-motion manager. He and his brother really were chalk and cheese; the fastidious logistician and the cold-blooded military man. Ever since they had left the *Kanshish* Jake had studied both men, wondering who was in overall charge of this particular mission, and now he hoped fervently that the Banis had reached a firm agreement on the chain of command because this was no time for fraternal strife.

Currently it looked like they were working in tandem, at least as far as what happened next was concerned. Julius lowered his binoculars and looked over at his brother, who raised five fingers. This was clearly intended to be a highly co-ordinated and choreographed rendezvous, and Jake wondered exactly how it would pan out. The only hostage exchanges Jake had ever seen were in movies, and involved Cold War spies being walked across some remote bridge in East Berlin.

Had he not been so inextricably involved in this one, he might have found it exciting. Right now, though, the only thing he felt was sick with apprehension.

'What have we here?' Captain Mabuto murmured to himself. The Kenyan army captain was standing at the tree line, watching the pirate skiffs negotiate the entrance to the lagoon and approach the shore. Through his binoculars he counted fourteen pirates in all, all with their faces covered by *keffiyeh* headscarves – as if *he* cared about the identities of the cowardly Somali scum.

*But who were the others?* Nola, the security agent from Nairobi, had mentioned hostages – but had been less than forthcoming about who they actually were. Now, unless he was very much mistaken, Mabuto could see two men, one in either skiff, one of them white, the other black. He did not recognise them, nor did he expect to. Ever since he'd received his orders he had known that this was some sort of covert operation that had gone wrong. In his mind he had convinced himself that the hostages were agents, Nola's colleagues, who had been captured while attempting to infiltrate the stronghold of the Somali pirates.

This was the only possible reason a prisoner as valuable as Qasim Fadir was being handed back.

His knowledge did not make him feel any better about the situation. To Mabuto, a man who had devoted his life to safeguarding the borders of his country, the idea of any sort of deal with the Somali vermin was repellent – and made even more so by the involvement of the men in suits from Nairobi, men who would gladly exchange their own grandmothers in the name of political expediency.

'Is that them?'

Mabuto glanced at Nola, who had appeared at his elbow – although the sickly smell of the agent's cologne had betrayed his arrival several minutes earlier.

'Right on time,' said Mabuto. 'I am surprised.'

'Why?'

'I was not aware Somalis were capable of telling the time.'

'Report, Captain,' Nola snapped.

Mabuto scowled. 'I see two hostages. Male. An African and a European.'

He said it in such a way as to elicit some sort of explanation from Nola as to the identity of the men in the boats. But the agent just snatched the binoculars from him and took a look for himself.

'Very well, Captain Mabuto,' Nola said. 'Let's get ready.'

Mabuto smiled to himself. *Oh, he was ready all right. More than Agent Nola would ever know.*

'Sergeant Kalami!' he snapped.

'Yes, sir.'

'Get the prisoner ready.'

The skiffs nudged the shale and their armed crews jumped out. Guided by Julius they fanned across the narrow beach in almost military order. When he was satisfied, Julius signalled to his brother.

'Shall we, Inspector?' Moses said.

Jouma shrugged. 'Why not, Mr Bani?'

The two men stood up unsteadily and for a moment were obliged to grab each other – and in that moment their eyes met and Jouma saw the weariness of a man who wished he was coming with them to the other side.

They stepped from the boat into the warm, shin-high water and was now wading ashore followed at close quarters by one of the pirates. Looking back, Jouma noted that the ruddermen had remained with their respective boats, no doubt in preparation for a quick getaway.

'Good trip?' Jake asked when he reached the shale beach. The Englishman had disembarked with a lot more confidence and was now waiting with Julius and a phalanx of twelve gunmen.

'That is officially the *last* time I will be setting foot on a boat of any description,' Jouma said.

Jake smiled. 'Amen to that.'

The Bani brothers exchanged brief words, and then Julius gave orders. An advance column of six men moved quickly from the beach to a position on a low bluff by the tree line. The rest followed and as they crested the bluff Jake saw they were in a shallow clearing bisected by a red dirt track leading inland through the imposing mangroves. At the far end of the track, maybe a hundred yards away, was an olive-coloured transport wagon, and positioned in front of it were a row of five uniformed soldiers, their rifles trained on them.

Captain Mabuto checked his men. They were standing in formation in front of the wagon, nervously fingering their rifles. He gave the order and Sergeant Kalami brought Qasim Fadir forward. The prisoner had been released from his cage, but his hands were bound in front of him and his posture was still stooped and uncomfortable.

'Stand by, Sergeant,' Mabuto said. Then he turned to Nola. 'The men and prisoner are ready, sir,' he said deferentially.

Nola did not take his eyes off the pirates a hundred yards away.

'Very well, Captain Mabuto. You may proceed.'

Mabuto saluted, and straightened his combat tunic and beret to the correct angle. He jammed his heavy wooden *rungu* club under his arm and walked purposefully towards the pirates.

The overhanging branches of the mangroves blocked out the sun, and the gloom was such that the soldier appeared to materialise out of thin air. He was a short, dapper African with a worm of a moustache on his top lip and an officious gait that suggested he was in charge. At precisely the midway point between his men and the pirates he stopped smartly.

'My name is Captain Milton Mabuto of the Army of the Republic of Kenya,' he announced. 'I have been instructed by my government to facilitate the exchange of illegally held hostages for the suspected pirate and criminal Qasim Fadir. Who am I addressing?'

Moses stepped forward and unhooked the *keffiyeh* from in front of his mouth. 'You are addressing me.'

'You have the hostages?'

'As you can see.' Moses signalled to his brother, who brusquely shoved Jake and Jouma forward. 'You have Qasim?'

'That was the arrangement.'

'Then shall we get started?'

'By all means,' Mabuto said. With that he executed an

immaculate drill-square turn and marched back to his men.

'Kenyan?' Jake said under his breath.

Jouma nodded.

'Then that's a good thing, right?'

'I hope so, my friend.'

The Inspector felt an insistent prodding between his shoulder blades and he looked round to see Julius's dead eyes staring at him over the rough cotton of his *keffiyeh*. He glanced at Jake beside him, and the two men shared a weary smile that said: *here we go again*.

'Goodbye, gentlemen,' Moses said. 'And good luck.'

It was muggy in the mangroves, oppressively so to a man like John Nola who was used to the cooler air of Nairobi and an air-conditioned office in the heat of summer. Even so, he shivered. He could not wait to be out of this hellhole and back on the plane back to the capital. Back to civilisation.

He glanced at Mabuto. The captain seemed unaffected by the heat or by the circumstances. Then again he was a soldier and he had been trained to deal with extremes. He stood with his arms folded behind his back, gripping the handle of his *rungu* and slapping it rhythmically into the palm of his hand, a faint smile visible beneath the clipped moustache. Nola knew what Mabuto thought of him, of all suit-wearing pen pushers – and the loathing was mutual. He wondered, though, what the captain would think if he knew that on this particular issue the pen pusher agreed with him. In Nola's opinion, the decision to release Qasim Fadir was little short of criminal negligence on behalf of the government.

And he had good reason to feel aggrieved at what was

about to take place before his very eyes. Qasim Fadir was *his* case. For the last three weeks, round the clock, he, John Nola, had supervised the pirate's very specific interrogation. It had been arduous, sapping work because Fadir was stubborn. But every man has his breaking point, given time, and after three weeks in a basement in Nairobi, subjected to all manner of physical and psychological persuasion, Fadir was on the point of reaching his.

Now this. All that work in flames because a superfluous Mombasa policeman and a reckless foreign national had got themselves kidnapped by the very pirate gang Nola was on the verge of cracking; and because a cowardly, glad-handing politician was more interested in advancing his own cause than that of his country.

Inwardly Nola seethed. But he was also astute enough to appreciate his own ambitions. To rock the boat over Qasim Fadir would achieve nothing except that which was detrimental to his own career. His eyes were firmly on the top job in the National Security Intelligence Service. When that goal was achieved he would be better positioned to stand up to the venal and temporary politicians.

Twenty yards along the track, the prisoner was being escorted to the exchange point by one of Mabuto's men, a tall ebony-skinned sergeant named Kalami. From here Qasim appeared tiny and cowed-looking, hobbling painfully on his prosthetic foot – but Nola had no doubt that there would be a satisfied smirk on his face as he neared his comrades approaching from the other end of the track. It was just as well, he thought, that he could not see it.

From here he could now make out the hostages. *Jouma and Moore.* The detective and the fishing boat skipper. They were being pressed forward towards Qasim by two pirates with Kalashnikovs. The rest of the gang were in position behind them, watching warily.

'When this is over, I want to be on the road immediately,' Nola said.

'As you wish, sir,' Mabuto said.

And it was at that moment that Sergeant Kalami reached to the small of his back, produced a handgun concealed in the waistband of his combat trousers and fired it at point-blank range into the top of Qasim Fadir's skull. There was a puff of smoke and instantaneously the prisoner's head dissolved in a spray of red.

'*Wha—*' Nola said, and this incoherent expression of shock and confusion was his last. Mabuto turned and calmly shot him between the eyes with his service handgun, and as he lay on the dirt, already dead, the captain calmly shot him twice more.

The crossfire came initially from the trees on either side of the track, where Mabuto had positioned four two-man machine gun units; but soon the bullets were coming from all directions as the startled pirates returned fire. One round, aimed at Jake's head, snipped the top of his ear and hit the crewman directly behind him in the throat. He threw himself to the dirt and scrambled on his hands and knees to the side of the path, rolling into a ditch as fizzing tracers criss-crossed just a few feet above his head like something out of a war movie. He could *hear* the fucking things humming through the air even though the noise of carbines mingled with the shouts and screams of men was deafening. Branches and leaves were falling in slow motion all around, and a mangrove trunk exploded beside him.

He peered over the lip of the ditch, not quite believing that he wasn't already dead, a sick feeling in the pit of his stomach as he thought about Jouma, who had been standing right beside him when the shooting had started. But the little detective was not among the dead men – at least Jake couldn't see him among the tangle of limbs. At the end of the track the bodies of the pirates were piled up where they had fallen, most of them cut down in the first few seconds. Those that had survived the initial onslaught were now using their own dead as cover as they blindly returned fire. Except they *weren't* simply blasting away at shadows in the trees; they were providing covering fire for Julius Bani, who was scrambling back towards the boats with one arm locked around the almost doll-like figure of Jouma. The Inspector's eyes were wide with fear as the two men tumbled back through the surf – but at least he did not appear to be hit. Jake cursed his impotence, but found himself urging the pirate on as bullets churned the water around them.

One of the ruddermen was already dead; the other was frantically yanking at the ripcord to start the engines. With a loud cough and a burst of oily smoke it came to life; bullets plucked at the water as Julius leapt forward and, grasping the slippery fibreglass hull, threw himself over the side of the craft as it pulled away.

From his position hidden in the ditch Jake looked back at the track. The remaining pirates were continuing to fire, but they were hopelessly exposed and outnumbered. A couple of them turned and ran for the abandoned skiff, but were picked off before they even reached the beach. The last two realised the game was up and threw their weapons onto the ground in front of them – and as they did so the deafening gunfire abruptly ceased. There were angry shouts and the two men gingerly stood from behind their protective shield of corpses, their hands behind their heads. Now soldiers were beginning to materialise from the trees and presently, from the far end of the track, Captain Mabuto appeared, picking his way deliberately around the bodies of the pirates, pausing briefly over that of Sergeant Kalami who had stood no chance in the initial volley. Mabuto said something to his men, and they carried Kalami back to the truck.

By now the two surviving pirates were on their knees, and as the *keffiyehs* were ripped from their faces Jake saw that one of them was the hijacker he'd hit with the fire extinguisher on *Yellowfin* what seemed like a lifetime ago. Mabuto stood in front of them, staring at the rapidly receding skiff containing the Inspector and Julius Bani – and as the boat finally disappeared behind the headland he shook his head slowly. He said something to the pirate from *Yellowfin*, who spat on his gleaming boots. Mabuto hit him hard across the face with the bolus of his *rungu* and then brought the club down on the pirate's skull so the noise of splintering bone echoed across the glade.

Jake had seen enough. This was not a hostage exchange that had gone wrong, it was a carefully planned slaughter. And while he might have survived the firefight, he knew it was more by accident than design. There were not supposed to be any witnesses, and once they saw he was not among the dead they would hunt him down.

Slowly, silently, he crawled away from the ditch and back into the mangrove forest. After a hundred feet, when he felt it was safe, he got to his feet and started running – and as he did so, a single gunshot from a Kenyan army service handgun rang out through the trees.

# 38

Harry Philliskirk was many things: impulsive, reckless, some would say downright dangerous. But he was not mad. Moreover he had a finely tuned instinct for self-preservation. He would not be wandering blithely up to a gang of Somali hoodlums with questions about two missing men from Kenya. Even Harry understood this was a very bad idea.

The news had come as a great relief to Mugo, who had been convinced that this was precisely what he intended. Indeed she had been wondering just when it would be appropriate to assert the authority vested in her by the Kenyan police force, put the Englishman in cuffs, and force him back to Kurt Anderssen's boat.

Instead it was Harry who announced they were heading back to the village, where the only imminent danger to life was from Anderssen himself. The Danish skipper was apoplectic at having woken that morning to find Harry and Mugo had left without him.

'Why the hell didn't you tell me where you were going?' the Danish skipper raged. 'You think I don't have better things to do than wait around here? This is fucking Somalia, Harry – it is a dangerous place.'

'I thought you'd appreciate the lie-in,' Harry said.

'That hooch of Fraisal's is potent stuff.'

'Dah – you are a maniac.'

'Maybe so. But at least I may have a lead where Jake and Jouma are being held.'

They were in the *Osprey*'s cabin. Spread across the central fold-down table was a sea chart of the southern coastline and a large-scale atlas open at the relevant sector of mainland. Marked in pen were asterisks denoting the location of Fraisal's village and the small town where Cousin Hemi did her shopping at the market. Northwest of it, indicated with a circle, was an unmarked area that, according to the map, was only a short distance from a main highway leading to the coastal town of Kismaayo.

'Here,' Harry said, tapping the atlas.

Anderssen exploded again. 'There's nothing there!'

'Because this map isn't detailed enough, Kurt. According to Cousin Hemi there's an old sisal plantation here that the Deadly Boys use as a headquarters.'

'*That*'s your idea of a lead?' Anderssen roared. 'The ramblings of some old woman on a grapefruit farm? Why am I listening to this? Why did I ever listen to you in the first place?'

'What do you plan to do with this information, Mr Philliskirk?' Mugo said. She was determined to remain calm, even though privately she agreed with Anderssen's assessment. Harry had taken a snippet of gossip overheard in a Somali marketplace and extrapolated it into hard fact. And while she was just as keen as Harry to locate the missing men, this was not a lead. It was just gossip.

'I'm going to take a trip up there. Scout around a bit, see what I can see. Don't worry – I won't be knocking at the door. But if I can at least confirm that Jake and Jouma are being held by these Deadly Boys then it's a job well done.'

'And what then?' Anderssen demanded. 'You plan to call in an air strike?'

'I'll be coming straight back. We're only forty miles from the Kenya navy base at Manda Island. We'll go there, give them co-ordinates – they can have a rescue team scrambled and in place in a couple of hours. We have to act fast, though. If Cousin Hemi is right, these bastards will be getting ready to deliver Jake and Jouma to the great warlord in Kismaayo.'

Anderssen stared at Mugo incredulously. 'Are you listening to this, missy? Are you hearing what this madman is saying?'

'Mr Philliskirk – Mr Anderssen is right. You cannot go out there on your own.'

'Somebody has to,' Harry pointed out.

Anderssen threw up his hands in despair.

'We should return to Manda, as you suggest,' Mugo suggested diplomatically. 'But we should go now. Tell them what we have learned and let them decide what to do.'

'There's no bloody *time*!' Harry exclaimed, banging the table with his fist. 'Don't you get it?'

Anderssen stood up. 'To hell with you, Harry. I've had enough of this bullshit.'

'Where are you going?'

'I'm going home.'

He pushed past towards the cabin door.

'What about you?' Harry asked Mugo.

'Mr Anderssen is right. We have done all we can. The longer we stay here the more we are in danger.'

Harry glared at them defiantly. 'Very well. Have it your way. But it's not the English way. I'm not in the habit of leaving unfinished business.'

'Bravo, Churchill,' Anderssen cackled. 'But you're coming with us.'

'I'm afraid Mr Anderssen is right, Harry,' Mugo said, sliding from the banquette and stepping out onto the cockpit. 'I am sorry, but this is for the best.'

She nodded to Anderssen who slammed the cabin door and locked it with a key – and before Harry knew what had just happened, he was trapped.

# 39

Jake had no idea how long he had been running blindly through the sapping undergrowth of the mangrove forest. Time had long ceased to be important. The only thought going through his head was: *don't stop running and don't look back*. All that mattered was that every desperate step took him further away from the carnage and the soldiers who would soon be on his trail. It was only when he finally fell to the forest floor, sobbing for breath, his clothes sodden and muddy and his skin shredded by thorns, that he thought about Jouma, and the expression of utter terror on the detective's face as he was dragged to the skiff by Julius Bani.

*Jouma . . . Ah, Christ . . . .*

Then he froze. Something was moving in the undergrowth nearby. Footfalls. Careful, deliberate movements designed to minimise sound. And had the forest been alive with the usual sounds of birds and wildlife they would have remained silent. But the birds and wildlife were silent too.

Jake pressed himself against a tree and tried to control his breathing. Ahead the undergrowth was moving; the fat green leaves swishing as if tickled by a faint breeze. A figure emerged, less than a yard from where he stood.

Instinctively, knowing that any delay could be his last, Jake launched himself, using his superior weight and build to bring the other man down. He heard a squawk and felt hot breath on his face, but his fists were already pummelling as he wrestled himself on top. Now his forearm came down hard on his opponent's neck, and the man emitted a feeble gurgle – but Jake was in another place now, and the feeling that surged through his body was an almost ecstatic release of anger and fear. He was killing a man but he didn't care because it felt good. Suddenly it was the best damned feeling in the world.

'*Waittt . . .*'

The single word came out as a barely audible hiss, but it stopped Jake cold.

Moses Bani stared up at him.

'Give me one good reason why I shouldn't kill you,' Jake said, releasing the pressure slightly on his throat.

The pirate blinked. 'Because I am already dead,' he said – and as he pulled away Jake saw to his horror that the front of Moses's shirt was soaked in blood.

'Jesus,' he said, and manhandled him into a sitting position against a tree. 'Where are you hit?'

'It doesn't matter,' Moses wheezed, and then he coughed and flecks of blood appeared on his lips. 'The damage is done.' He looked up. 'You should get out of here. If those soldiers catch you they will kill you.'

'What the hell happened back there?'

'This was never a hostage exchange, Mr Moore. It was a state-sponsored execution.'

Jake stared into Moses's dark eyes. Burst capillaries had turned them red, and they appeared to be drifting in and out of focus.

'They can't get away with that,' he said, lamely.

Moses smiled thinly. 'If they had been anyone other

than incompetent Kenyan soldiers, that is precisely what would have happened. Anyone but incompetent Kenyan soldiers would have ensured that there were no witnesses. But you are still alive.'

'Don't forget your brother,' Jake said.

Moses's face twitched slightly. 'Julius is alive?'

'He managed to get to one of the skiffs. Jouma was with him.'

Moses cleared his throat and spat a red gobbet on the ground, and his face twisted with pain. 'Then the Kenyans were even more incompetent than I thought,' he said presently. 'Killing you and your detective friend should have been a priority.'

'Why?'

'Because nobody would believe the word of a Somali pirate – but a Mombasa policeman? That is a different matter.'

Jake suddenly realised that Moses had answered the question that had been preying on his mind ever since he'd watched Jouma being wrestled onto the skiff.

'Then Omar will keep him alive?'

Moses smiled sadly, exposing bloody teeth. 'If I were in a position to advise Omar, I would suggest the inspector was kept alive, yes. But as you see, I am not in a position to advise him.'

'Surely to God Omar isn't that stupid.'

'Stupid? No. Unpredictable? Very much so. I suspect he will not take this latest setback at all well.'

'What do you mean? What will he do?'

'I don't know, Mr Moore.'

The two men fell silent as, through the trees, they heard the distant shouting of men.

'You should go now,' Moses said. 'It would appear your absence among the corpses has been noted.'

'*Where?*'

'Head for the coast. If you are lucky you will find a fisherman who will take you to the border.'

'And if I'm not?'

But Moses did not reply. He was already dead.

# 40

Sammy the bait boy did not like Kurt Anderssen. He did not like being on his boat and he did not like the way the big white skipper kept looking at him appraisingly, like he was a carcass hanging in a market stall. Moreover he did not like the way Anderssen kept asking Harry how much Sammy was worth, because the very last thing Sammy wanted was to work as a bait boy – or any other sort of boy – for Kurt Anderssen.

What Sammy liked least about Anderssen, however, was the way he shouted and swore and threw things around when he was angry. Like when he'd discovered Harry and Mugo had left the village without telling him this morning. Like now that he'd discovered *Osprey*'s propellers were fouled with seaweed and her engine intakes clogged with silt. Sammy had heard swearing before – Jake and Harry swore all the time – but never anything like this. Standing up to his waist in the water beside the stern of the boat, ripping at the accretions with his bare hands, Anderssen had been issuing a more or less constant stream of foul-mouthed invective for the last twenty minutes.

So far Anderssen hadn't asked for Sammy's assistance – and the boy hoped he wouldn't. At least not until he had done what he had to do.

He looked up at the flying bridge, where Mugo was somehow managing to doze in the captain's chair. He looked to the locked cabin door. Making sure Anderssen didn't see him, he stepped onto the port rail and scampered along to one of the reinforced glass portholes and peered in. Harry was lying on one of the banquettes, frowning up at the ceiling. Sammy tapped at the glass and Harry, seeing who it was, jumped up and came across.

*OK?* he mimed, raising his thumb hopefully.

Sammy made the actions of a madman clearing seaweed from the propellers.

*And Mugo?*

Sammy rested his head on his hands and closed his eyes. This time Harry raised both thumbs, then urgently tapped his watch. Sammy nodded and, with a single athletic movement, swung himself up onto the bridge.

Mugo was sitting with her arms folded, her head slumped on her chest, snoring lightly. How on earth she could sleep with Anderssen's racket was a mystery, but the noise made the bait boy's job much easier. He scanned the dashboard of the powerful boat and there, still hanging from the ignition, was a bunch of keys. Holding his breath, Sammy reached across and snatched them. A moment later he had shinned down the connecting ladder and landed like a cat on the polished deck of the cockpit.

'Even the cocksucking *weeds* are bastards!' Anderssen was shouting, but his head was down below the stern rail and Sammy was able to creep unnoticed to the cabin door. He recognised the right key immediately – *Yellowfin* might have been a poor second to *Osprey* in terms of specifications and cost, but they shared the same locksmith. Hands shaking slightly, he nosed the key into the lock and turned.

Harry squeezed through the half-opened door. He nodded his gratitude to the boy and squeezed his shoulder meaningfully. Then he turned and moved quickly to the rail, edging along the exterior wall of the cabin towards the bows.

'You, boy! What the fucking hell are you doing?'

Kurt Anderssen was staring at him, his hands on the stern rail, both of them filled with slimy seaweed.

Sammy needed no second bidding. He leapt onto the rail and ran along it with the expertise of an acrobat until he reached the blunted bows where Harry was frantically unfastening the *Osprey*'s rubber launch from a deck cleat.

'Go,' the boy said, half pushing Harry into the launch while he swiftly unpicked the rope knot and freed the mooring. 'Find Mr Jake.'

From the other side of the superstructure he could hear Anderssen bellowing, and above him he saw Mugo staring down at them from the bridge with a look of bleary incomprehension that quickly sharpened into open-mouthed disbelief.

There was a high-pitched rasp as the launch's 50cc engine kicked into life, and as Sammy felt the mooring rope chasing through his fingers.

'A pay rise for you when we get home, Sammy boy!' Harry called back at him as he swung the craft around and aimed it towards the village a hundred yards away, from where woodsmoke was rising beyond the furthest branches of the trees.

# 41

*Incompetent Kenyan soldiers.* Moses Bani's phrase kept revolving in Jake's mind as he hurried quickly through the mangrove forest. And it sent a shiver down his spine because he knew that if the men on their tail *hadn't* made such a botched job of the ambush – if they'd had just a fraction of the ruthlessness and training of, say, the SAS or some other special forces unit – then it would have been a very different story that morning. As it was, he was alive when by all accounts he should he dead.

His plan was to keep it that way – and here again the ineptitude of the soldiers was to his advantage. Jake might have been prey, but the hunters had not been schooled in the art of stealth. The soldiers, blundering around in the undergrowth, shouting, cursing and occasionally unloosing a jittery round or two, could be heard a mile away. And while Jake had no idea where he was heading, he could at least be confident of avoiding his pursuers.

He'd been running for maybe fifteen minutes when the trees suddenly thinned and, without warning, he emerged into bright, hot sunlight at the edge of the forest. Ahead of him now was a dirt road. It was straight and bisected several hundred square miles of largely featureless bush terrain in the direction of some low hills in the far distance.

*Which way?* Moses had told him to head for the coast and hope to get lucky. Jake's instinct was to find the nearest outpost of civilisation – a farm, perhaps – and steal a vehicle. By his calculations he could not have been more than fifty miles from the Kenyan border. He could probably *walk* it in a couple of days.

Yet the sobering fact remained that Kenyan soldiers had just tried to kill him, and were still intent on completing the job.

Deep in the forest behind him came a series of gunshots.

Jake headed east, towards the coast.

He had not gone far when a cloud of dust had appeared on the road about two miles away, moving slowly towards him from the west. Jake jumped down a shallow embankment into a dried-out irrigation ditch.

Soon, through the dust and the heat haze, he saw it was a battered pick-up truck. There were goats in the back of it, and as the vehicle bumped over the pot-holed surface the scrawny animals were being thrown up and down like some crazy version of whack-a-mole.

But at least they were goats, not gunmen. And that was good enough for Jake. He scrambled back up to the road and began waving his hands in the air.

The pick-up was travelling at such a leisurely pace the driver had plenty of time to stop. He was an elderly Somali with scribbles of white hair clinging to the base of his skull and perhaps three teeth in his head. He stared through the cab window with an expression of bemusement on his face as Jake ran over to the truck, his shirt smeared with Moses Bani's blood.

'*Unaongea Swahili, saaxiib?*' he said, asking the man if he spoke Swahili.

'Little.'

Jake told him that he was English, needed a lift to the coast, and would pay the man handsomely if he would help. The man nodded and smiled, but it was clear that in fact he spoke very little Swahili at all. Eventually Jake was reduced to crude hand signals, aware all the time that the longer he stood around in the middle of the road the more chance there was of being caught by the soldiers on his trail. Eventually the man seemed to get the drift. He gestured with his thumb to the back of the pick-up.

'Thank you,' Jake said, reaching in through the open window to shake the man's hand. The man reached across to the passenger seat and handed him a heavy wooden stick.

'What's this for?'

The man pointed at the goats and brought the stick down with a slap into the palm of his hand.

'Goats get angry,' he said. 'You hit.'

# 42

Of the fourteen crewmen who had left for the mainland that morning, only Julius and the rudderman were still alive when the remaining skiff finally limped back to the *Kanshish*. There had been a third who had escaped the ambush, but a bullet had torn his femoral artery and Julius had thrown him over the side before he bled to death in the bottom of the boat.

The men on deck watched dumbly as the bloodied survivors came aboard. Omar watched too, from the bridge gantry, Rafael looming over him like an obsidian boulder. His face was impassive, and he watched only briefly before turning away and going into the bridge.

Jouma was dragged to the brig where, despite the gloomy claustrophobia, he found it blissfully calm after the deafening chaos of the ambush and the pell-mell escape from the lagoon.

He knew it wouldn't last, though. Omar's expression had told him as much. Or rather his eyes had, because in them Jouma had seen profound shock, *bewilderment* even, at how events were uncontrollably unravelling around him. Soon, Jouma knew, that shock would be consumed by a terrible fury followed by retribution, and he had no doubt at all that more blood would be spilled on this ship before long. But what happened after that? Omar had laughingly described the killing of Karim in terms of bread and circuses to appease the mob; but since then twelve more members of the mob had been wiped out in the service of their leader.

Would more killing be enough to pacify them this time?

Even if, this time, the victim was Jouma himself?

In the wardroom Julius Bani waited patiently until Omar had stopped smashing furniture and instead slumped at his desk with his head in his hands. There had been something strangely pathetic about the display and Julius was glad it was over. In fact it struck him that there was something strangely pathetic about Omar all of a sudden. He seemed diminished somehow, as if someone had pricked him with a pin and allowed the hot air to gradually escape.

'What do I do, Julius?'

'It's over. We must make arrangements.'

Omar's head dipped into his hands again. 'Who is doing this? The Korean tanker and now the exchange – who has betrayed me?'

Julius stared at him with contempt. Was he so stupid? Did he not see that the rot had set in the day Qasim Fadir was captured? Qasim – Omar's second-in-command and a man even more fastidious in his planning than Moses – would have resisted torture for as long as possible. But eventually he would have talked. And Julius could just imagine the reaction of the Kenyan security agents when they discovered how Omar Abdulle and his merry men had been leading them and the international protective convoys on a merry dance these last few months.

The ambush by the men on the Korean ship? That made

sense if you thought of it in terms of a deal Qasim had struck with the Kenyans. *'Bring something to the table, Qasim, and we will see about your release. Tell us Omar's next target and we will make things happen for you.'*

The ambush today? Well, that was the Kenyans making a point. They didn't do deals with Somali pirates. And if making that point also meant a couple of hostages died, then so be it. The report of whoever was in charge of the soldiers would be quite insistent that it was the Somalis that had started shooting.

And it would have been a perfect plan were it not for one small oversight.

'We still have the Kenyan detective,' Julius said.

Omar's eyes widened. 'I will kill him!'

'*No!*' For the first time Julius allowed his irritation to break through. 'Don't you see? We can use him.'

'How?'

Julius explained his plan. It seemed to take a painfully long time for its significance to register, but eventually Omar looked up.

'What about the crew – ?'

'Forget about the crew. They think you are cursed. As soon as word spreads about what happened on the mainland today, there will be mutiny.'

'But I am their leader. Their *father*.'

'A father does not send his children out to be slaughtered.'

Omar stood and rested his knuckles on the desk.

'You know what you have to do,' he said to Rafael, who had been standing by the door. The bodyguard nodded once and left the room. Omar went to one of the maps on the wall. 'Tell the bridge to make the necessary course alterations and to start the engines. I will go and see Jouma.'

'You know it is the only alternative,' Julius said.

Omar nodded sadly. 'I only wish I was going to be here to see it.'

# 43

The Deadly Boys hadn't killed Hafiz the fixer. Or at least they hadn't got round to it just yet. And that was something that made Nancy Griswold very happy indeed; because for the first time since they had been kidnapped by the Somali hoodlums and brought to this godforsaken farm she did not feel she was in imminent danger of prolonged and agonising death.

Far from it. Right now her captors were distracted by the wonders of Red Sheppard's camera, especially the leader of the gang, who called himself Jazi and who fancied himself as Robert De Niro and was therefore thrilled that Red had a small portable monitor in his case on which he could watch his Travis Bickle impersonations.

When Nancy had casually let slip that she had been a TV actress in a previous life it had given her almost deified status – and for the last hour or so she had been obliged to hold an impromptu acting masterclass.

While doing so she and Sheppard were also collecting priceless footage of Somali pirates in their natural habitat – which, after all, was what they had come for in the first place. And if Jazi was not exactly the top-ranking pirate overlord she'd been promised, in many ways he and his

Deadly Boys were even better value for money. Footsoldiers, as De Niro had himself proved in *Goodfellas*, very often made for better copy than the *capi* and the *consiglieri*.

'That's good, Jazi,' she said, coaxing him towards the camera. 'Now tell me, what is it you plan to do with me and Red? Say it like De Niro would, Jazi.'

'I go take you to fuckin' Garaad,' Jazi said in a very vague approximation of a New York accent.

'Garaad?'

'He the big boss, lady. He going take care of you.'

Nancy glanced up at Sheppard, who shrugged behind his camera lens. 'Garaad is a pirate?'

'He the biggest pirate, lady. He going make Deadly Boys in his organisation when we bring you to him.'

'Where does he live, Jazi?'

'Kismaayo.'

'Is that far from here?'

Jazi was about to reply when one of his men came hurrying round the corner of one of the farm buildings, shouting something in Somali. At once Jazi's demeanour changed and his impish De Niro grin evaporated. His men, who had been sitting nearby njoying the show with hoots of laughter, sprang to their feet and clutched their weapons.

'What is it, Jazi?' Nancy asked.

'Someone is coming,' the leader of the Deadly Boys growled. 'You better hope it's not for you.'

The pick-up had travelled a little over five miles when the driver pulled off the road and onto an even rougher track. Presently it arrived at a crumbling adobe building, with greasy black smoke coiling from a bonfire somewhere nearby.

*Nice place*, Jake thought caustically, using the farmer's

stick to rap the nose of a goat that was nibbling at his clothes. Still, beggars could not be choosers and if this was where the old man lived then he was in no position to complain. Maybe there would be food and water here. In any case, he had his eye on the pick-up – and while the prospect of stealing it from the old man made him feel uneasy, it was a guilt that he could live with.

But then it struck him that something was not right. If this was a farm, then it clearly hadn't been used for some time. There were no working fields, just a wide open expanse of rocky wasteland, and the only animals within miles of the place were the goats in the back of the pick-up. Close up, the main farmhouse itself appeared derelict – in fact part of it looked as if it had been damaged by fire.

The farmer sounded his horn and a few moments later three young Somalis in designer sportswear, wraparound shades and baseball caps emerged from around the corner of the building.

'Oh, shit,' Jake groaned when he saw they were toting AK-47s.

He sank back onto the hard metal floor of the pick-up as the farmer climbed stiffly from the cab and engaged in a short conversation with the men. Presently they came over to the truck, weapons sported loosely in the crook of their arms, and peered at the new arrival as if he was an exhibit in a zoo.

They seemed highly delighted by what they saw.

'You know that you are a madman, Harry,' Fraisal said. 'You know that if they find you they will kill you.'

'It's like I said, old chum – I don't intend being found. It's purely a reconnaissance mission. Now if you'll just lend me the keys to your jeep ...'

The two men were standing at the edge of the village,

on the only road in or out. Fraisal looked sadly at his multi-coloured vehicle, then shook his head. 'I can't let you go,' he said.

'People keep saying this to me,' Harry said. 'They don't seem to appreciate that they really don't have any choice in the matter. My friend Jake is out there somewhere, and I intend to find him. So you either lend me the jeep, Fraisal, or I shall be forced to steal it.'

The two men stared at each other, then Fraisal burst out laughing. 'You and whose army?'

Harry raised his hands, karate style. 'These are lethal weapons.'

'Get in the jeep, Harry,' Fraisal said. 'If I give you a lift at least I know I'll see it again.'

Jake was taken at gunpoint to the other side of the farm buildings, where the sight that greeted him was one of bloody carnage. Two bodies lay sprawled on the ground, a third was hanging by the wrists from a tree, the grotesquely extended arms suggesting that they had popped from their sockets.

He reeled, wondering just how much more of this he could take. Ever since he and Jouma had been abducted from Kenyan waters violent death had been a constant companion; casual bloodshed and murder as much a part of Somali life as eating and sleeping. Jake found it perversely reassuring that he still found it repulsive, because it meant he still had a sliver of humanity. It seemed everyone else in this godforsaken land had lost theirs years ago.

A man was approaching, and by his rolling gait and swaggering demeanour he was clearly the leader – indeed he reminded Jake of a younger version of Omar Abdulle.

'What have we here?' he announced.

'Listen,' Jake said, suddenly weary of tin-pot gangsters. 'I've had a long day and I'm sick of people pointing guns at me. I don't know who you are, but if you can get me to the border I will make it very worth your while.'

'I am Jazi, leader of the Deadly Boys – the most feared gangsters in all of Somalia. And you will kneel down when you speak to me.'

Jake braced himself for the inevitable whack behind the knees, and when it came his legs were already bent. He stared up at Jazi and shook his head. How old was he? Nineteen, twenty? He'd seen wide boys like this from the sink estates of east London to the slums of Mombasa.

'Do you see what happens to enemies of the Deadly Boys?' Jazi was saying, pointing with pride at the body hanging from the tree.

'I'm not your enemy. I'm just a fishing boat skipper who is a long way from home.'

Jazi puffed out his chest in readiness for his next pronouncement – but his thunder was stolen by a sharp cry from behind him; and peering round the gangster's legs Jake saw, obscured by the low branches of the tree, the remains of what had once been a breezeblock and corrugated steel cattle shed. Two figures were walking towards him from the shed and both of them, Jake realised to his astonishment, were white. The man was pot-bellied and bearded, and with him was a woman, short and slightly bedraggled looking. They were staring at him with the same blinking disbelief – although the expression on the woman's face soon transformed into something less than welcoming.

'Who the hell are you?' she demanded, stomping across the compound towards Jake with such ferocity that for a moment even the Deadly Boys were taken aback. 'Where are you from and what are you doing here?'

'I think I'm a prisoner,' Jake said. 'But you'd better ask our friend here.'

Nancy Griswold cocked her head slightly. 'You're not CNN? BBC?'

'No. I'm a fishing boat skipper. Now who the hell are you?'

# 44

The vehicle was a 1970s VW camper van with Idaho plates. In it were six women belonging to an evangelist group called the New Life Children's Refuge who, despite warnings, had crossed the border into Somalia in order to rescue children orphaned in the ongoing civil war and take them back to the US. They had form for this: just over a year earlier, members of the same sect had tried the same thing in the aftermath of the Haiti earthquake and been jailed on suspicion of child abduction. This time there would be no mistake, though. The group had acquired the relevant paperwork and accreditation, and when they reached Kismaayo – the first stop on their tour – they had arranged to meet the missionaries who ran the city's main orphanage. They were, of course, aware of the dangers of travelling through bandit country. But they were also confident that, with God on their side, they would overcome any obstacle that came in their way.

Dust-streaked and dented, the van was now less than twenty miles from Kismaayo and the occupants had been gripped by a profoundly joyful sense of achievement. They had been singing hymns to keep up their spirits ever since crossing the Kenyan border; now their renditions of

*How Great Thou Art* and *Dear Lord and Father of Mankind* were delivered with extra gusto. More than one of the women was in tears.

They were about to burst into *Guide Me, O Thou Great Redeemer* when they came to a crossroads. Standing in the middle of the junction was a man. He was wearing army fatigues and he was pointing his rifle directly at the approaching van.

'Don't worry, Claudine,' one of the women said to the driver. Her name was Karen, she was from Little Rock, Arkansas, and she was the leader of the expedition. 'He's military. We got nothing to worry about. Just stop the vehicle nice and easy and I'll go see what he wants.'

'Be careful, Karen,' the women called as Karen jumped down from the cab and confidently approached the soldier.

'Hi, honey,' she said. 'We're headed for the orphanage in Kismaayo. Can we help you at all?'

There was a momentary pause, then the soldier fired his rifle and shot Karen between the eyes at close range. She flew backwards and had barely hit the ground before half a dozen soldiers climbed out of the roadside ditch and surrounded the VW.

Captain Milton Mabuto appeared from a stand of trees on the other side of the road and made his way down, pausing briefly to examine Karen's body and the stump of collapsed bone and hair that was all that remained of her head.

'I told you not to shoot her,' he said to the soldier.

'Sorry, sir. My finger slipped.'

Mabuto took a deep breath and calmed himself. Now was not the time to lose control – even if he'd had a lifetime's provocation in the last hour. *Onward Christian Soldiers* . . . the reassuring words of his favourite hymn scrolled across his mind and he thought about the suffering of Our Lord Jesus Christ, and how his own trials were nothing in comparison to His.

By the time he reached the van, the women had been ordered out and were standing in a terrified line at the side of the road, facing the ditch.

'Good afternoon, ladies,' Mabuto said. 'Regretfully my men and I must requisition your van in the name of the army of Ethiopia. We hope you have a pleasant day.'

As the van drove away the men were still giggling among themselves at their new-found status as Ethiopians, but Mabuto himself found nothing amusing about the situation. And when they eventually returned to their base, the men would not be laughing either – because Mabuto intended to go through them like a dose of salts. Those who weren't transferred upcountry would find their previously indulged existence at Kiunga radically overhauled to one of a living hell. That would be their punishment for betraying their country, for letting their commanding officer down so badly, and for sullying the ultimate sacrifice of Sergeant Kalami.

Poor Kalami. If only there had been more like him – a fine, competent, and loyal soldier able and willing to carry out his orders to the letter – Mabuto would not be in this present mess. But Kalami was dead in the back of the transport truck heading for the border, while his captain and six hand-picked men – the best of a very poor bunch, admittedly – were on a salvage operation deep inside Somali territory.

Their mission? To hunt down and eliminate the surviving hostage. The same hostage who should have been eliminated at the scene of the ambush as a matter of the highest priority, along with his policeman friend from

Mombasa – the one who had last been seen heading out to sea in a pirate skiff.

*How could it have come to this?* It had been such a simple plan, Mabuto thought sadly. His entire life and career had been forged with an overriding patriotism; the idea of doing business with pirates was anathema to him. Instead, he had decided to take the opportunity presented by John Nola and the rest of the besuited Nairobi liberals to discredit the Somali scum entirely.

So confident was he that his scheme would be successful, he had already written the report he intended to present to his superiors upon his return to base. It was in his desk drawer, and he could remember every word.

*. . . as Sergeant Kalami brought the prisoner forward for exchange, his opposite number on the Somali side produced a weapon and shot him. This was the signal for heavy enfilading gunfire from concealed Somali positions in the trees, during which both hostages were targeted and killed immediately. Despite the suddenness of the ambush, my men responded in exemplary fashion, returning fire and killing a number of Somalis. Casualties on our side were light. However, I regret to inform you that NSIS agent John Nola was mortally wounded in the firefight . . . It is my view that the entire hostage exchange was used as an excuse by the Somalis to inflict maximum possible casualties on not only Kenya army personnel, but innocent hostages including one foreign national.*

If that wasn't enough to warrant an open declaration of war on the Somali scum, then Mabuto didn't know what was.

Or at least it would have been, had his men not completely forgotten their prime objective and instead of gunning down the hostages become embroiled in a running gun battle with the admittedly tenacious pirates instead. By the time it was all over, the English hostage had already escaped into the jungle and the ensuing manhunt had been unable to find him. All they'd found was one of the pirates, and he was already dead.

Now, when he should be on his way back to base, Mabuto was obliged to play an infuriating game of damage limitation. The fate of one of the hostages was out of his hands, but he was confident that even if he was still alive the policeman would not last long in the pirates' lair. As for the Englishman – well, that was a different matter. The road they were on led only two ways: to the wastelands in the west and what was laughingly called civilisation, the city of Kismaayo, in the east. A man on the run would instinctively head for the latter, perhaps desperate enough to delude himself that he would somehow be safe in such a place.

Mabuto would find him before then. And when he did, he would kill him.

# 45

The *Kanshish* had been on the move for an hour now and although he knew next to nothing about such things the Inspector could tell from the great shuddering vibrations that down below her turbines were being pushed to the maximum.

It meant only one thing: Omar Abdulle, the great pirate, was on the run.

It did not surprise him. After what had happened that morning, Omar was entitled to feel like a hunted animal. His men had walked into an ambush and it was little short of a miracle that any of them had survived it. Ironically Jouma knew that he owed his life to Julius Bani, one of the pirates he so despised; but his relief was tempered by the knowledge that Jake was most probably dead.

Alone in the brig it had not taken long for his grief to turn to anger. But neither had it taken long for his anger to be consumed by deep unease. The soldiers who had been firing at them were Kenyan, or so it seemed. Yet the ambush was not directed exclusively at the Somalis. Instead they were firing at everyone, hostages included. And although it now seemed like a dream, *had he not seen the Kenyan army sergeant shoot the pirate captive in the head?*

The cell door opened and Omar came in.

'Well, Inspector,' he said. 'Perhaps it is time to reconsider the moral superiority of your countrymen, is it not?'

'Your crew must be upset, Mr Abdulle,' Jouma said calmly. 'Do you plan to kill me to appease them?'

'It was my first reaction, I admit. You are, after all, a Kenyan. But reason has prevailed. And we have both lost friends today.'

'Indeed. So what now, then?'

'You will come with me, Inspector. It is time the bloodshed ended.'

At the aft of the *Kanshish*'s hold, hidden from view by bulkheads, was the entrance to a long-forgotten maintenance access shaft leading by means of a badly-corroded metal ladder to the turbine housings in the bowels of the ship. The shaft bypassed the engine room, widening sufficiently at this point to allow a man to stand with a certain degree of comfort. A dusty ventilation grille provided a little light, and also a view of the engine room itself, where the ship's engineer – a survivor of the original Nigerian crew by dint of his knowledge of the vessel's innermost workings – spent his days in a cramped control booth under a headache-inducing fluorescent striplight.

Jalil had discovered the shaft quite by accident one day when he was playing hide and seek with Sheba, and sometimes he would go there in order to avoid her shrieking orders. Nobody else knew about it and, despite its proximity to the turbines, the boy found it a peaceful place for solitude and contemplation.

Now that Sheba was dead, Jalil had spent most of his time down here. The atmosphere had changed on the

*Kanshish*; there was a brooding undercurrent that scared him, and the return of the shore party that morning – or rather what scraps remained of it – had thickened the discontent to almost tangible proportions. The crew were mutinous. Jalil had heard them talking openly about how the ship was cursed and how, by logical extension, so was Omar. Jalil had wanted to warn Omar about what was being said; but whereas before the pirate leader had treated him like a son, now he was distant to the point of brusqueness. Jalil had not murdered Sheba, but it was as if Omar regarded him as part of the same conspiracy that was out to undermine him.

Jalil wished Jake was still here. At least Jake listened to him.

But from what he had heard, the Englishman was dead.

And down in the maintenance shaft, Jalil the cripple boy wept.

In his office overlooking the blunted skyscrapers of downtown Nairobi, the head of the Internal Division of the National Security Intelligence Service was eating a lunch of spiced chickpeas when the phone buzzed on his desk. Cursing, N'Kuma threw his plastic fork into the Tupperware box and jabbed one of the buttons.

'I told you, Mary – no calls while I am eating my lunch,' he said.

His secretary apologised profusely but told him he had an urgent call from a Superintendent Elizabeth Simba of Coast Province CID in Mombasa.

'Who?' The name rang a bell, but N'Kuma couldn't for the life of him remember why.

'The lady insists it is a matter of the highest possible importance, sir,' Mary said.

N'Kuma sighed and pushed his chickpeas to one side.

It was just as well his wife had prepared him a cold lunch that day. 'Very well, put her through.'

Jalil's lunch consisted of a hunk of bread so stale it was virtually solid. He had salvaged it from the deck galley and now he removed it from the pocket of his shorts. He was about to begin nibbling when he heard a strange noise echoing from the far end of the engine room: grunts of exertion, punctuated by the boom and shudder of something heavy being dropped onto the metal deck.

The boy peered through the grille and gasped as he saw two familiar figures appear next to the control booth normally occupied by the Nigerian engineer.

*Rafael and Julius.*

But what were they doing? Between them they were manhandling a blue barrel from the wheelhouse access staircase. The barrel was extremely heavy. Julius was sweating profusely. On his command, Rafael began rolling the barrel on its rim past the booth and behind the boiler housing. Julius followed him and a few moments later came the noise of hammering. Presently the two men emerged into the light. Julius was smiling with grim satisfaction.

*A job well done.*

The two men left the engine room and went upstairs. Jalil waited until he heard the top connecting door slam shut. He kept waiting, listening intently for any sound other than the mechanical buzzing and ticking of the engine control panels. But there was nothing.

'We have a problem,' N'Kuma said addressing the eight men seated at a polished mahogany boardroom table. They consisted of high-ranking agents, military personnel and government representatives, all of whom had been dragged from whatever they had been doing to attend this emergency meeting at immediate notice. And to emphasise the gravity of the situation, N'Kuma was flanked at the top of the table by the overall head of the NSIS and the Minister for the Interior.

'About an hour ago a detective superintendent in Mombasa received a call, made via satellite telephone, from one of her senior detectives. The detective's name was Daniel Jouma.'

The name prompted a round of muttering and glances.

The division chief nodded. 'As you know, Jouma was one of two hostages held captive by the Somali pirate Omar Abdulle. As you also know, the hostages were due to be exchanged this morning for the prisoner Qasim Fadir at a prearranged location about fifty miles north of the border. The operation was under the supervision of John Nola.'

The Minister for the Interior shifted impatiently in his chair. 'As you say, we know all this. Get to the point.'

'Jouma was calling from a ship, somewhere in the Indian Ocean, off the Somali mainland.'

'A ship?' the Minister exclaimed. 'What the devil is he doing on board a ship?'

'The ship is Omar Abdulle's base of operations, sir.'

'What happened to the hostage exchange?'

'It would appear things did not go according to plan. According to Jouma there was an ambush, in which Qasim Fadir, and, it is thought, the second hostage – the British fishing boat skipper – were killed.'

'Treacherous Somali dogs,' grumbled a senior-ranking army officer from the other end of the table.

'According to Jouma,' N'Kuma continued, 'the ambush was instigated by Kenyan troops.' At this there was uproar, which the division chief allowed to die away before continuing in the same measured tone. 'He distinctly saw one of our soldiers execute Qasim Fadir before machine gun emplacements in the trees opened fire on the pirates. He says around a dozen Somalis were gunned down, and he only managed to escape with the help of one of Abdulle's senior lieutenants.'

'What about Nola?' said the NSIS head.

'We have been unable to contact him.'

'What about the officer in charge of the army unit?' asked one of the army generals.

'The same.'

'Who is he?' asked the Minister.

'His name is Captain Mabuto,' N'Kuma told him. 'He runs the coastal border garrison at Kiunga, north of Malindi.'

'Do you know this man, General?' the Minister said.

At the other end of the table the general shrugged. 'I know of him,' he said unconvincingly. 'From what I understand he is a first class officer.'

'There was more,' N'Kuma said. 'Jouma says the pirates are willing to hand him over unharmed, in return for immunity.'

More uproar.

The general leaned forward and stared up the table at N'Kuma. 'My question to you is this: you say this Mombasa detective was on board the Somali ship?'

'That is correct, General.'

'Then who's to say he didn't have a gun at his head when he was on the telephone?'

N'Kuma shrugged. It was a fair point.

The NSIS head nodded. 'The general is right. We can't be sure that Jouma was not being coerced into saying what he did. And my concern is that we have not heard from Agent Nola or Captain Mabuto. We need to get to the bottom of what actually happened at the exchange before we start cutting deals with these people.'

'Then what do you suggest we do about it?' the Minister demanded. 'This has the potential to be very embarrassing for the government.'

*Yes,* N'Kuma thought, *especially when his government had sanctioned the release of a high-value prisoner in order to protect its own public image.*

A slight Eurasian man in a white naval uniform cleared his throat. He had remained thoughtful throughout the meeting, but until now had kept his thoughts to himself. His name was General Choi and he was, despite his unprepossessing demeanour, the man in overall charge of the Kenyan navy.

'You say this rendezvous point was what, twenty miles inside Somali territory?' he said.

'That is correct, sir.'

'Then I can arrange to have an aerial reconnaissance team in the area inside thirty minutes.'

The army general gave a contemptuous snort. It was well known that the army regarded the navy as its junior counterparts in the Kenyan military machine – and in terms of numbers and resources, the fact was not in doubt.

'Might I ask, *General* Choi,' he said, making sarcastic emphasis of Choi's rank, which was a result of the navy's peculiar decision to adopt army designations, 'how he proposes to do this? Even if he sails one of his gunboats into Somali waters and fires a reconnaissance team out of one of its cannons, it will still take several hours. This is a job for the air force.'

Choi smiled to himself as the table broke into sycophantic laughter. 'The general seems to have forgotten that the bulk of the air force is currently on manoeuvres along the Ethiopian border. I believe the only aircraft they have in range is a transport plane. Hardly appropriate for reconnaissance work.'

'Then what do you suggest?'

'A Royal Navy Type 22 Frigate, the *Winchester*, is currently docked at Manda Island for maintenance,' Choi said. 'It is equipped with a Lynx helicopter.'

The army general's face was a mask of humiliated fury.

'Yes, but will the Royal Navy co-operate?' N'Kuma asked.

'Ordinarily it would take a great deal of to-ing and fro-ing between here and the Admiralty in Whitehall to get clearance,' Choi admitted.

'Time we don't have,' the Minister pointed out.

'However, the commander of the *Winchester* and I were at naval college in Dartmouth together.'

The army general's jaw dropped and Choi smiled sweetly across the table at him.

# 46

The derelict farm where the Deadly Boys had made their headquarters was twenty miles south of Cousin Hemi's grapefruit plantation, and a further five miles beyond the town where she did her market shopping.

'Keep your head down,' Fraisal warned as the jeep approached the outskirts of the town. Harry needed no second bidding; he could tell by Fraisal's voice that they were reaching the business end of this particular adventure. For a white European this was deep inside enemy territory, a place run by trigger-happy militias, where he would not only be spotted a mile off but most probably killed if he was identified. He ducked down into the footwell of the passenger seat and pulled a blanket over himself.

'We are coming into the marketplace now,' Fraisal said, and Harry felt the vehicle slow to a crawl. He could hear voices, shouts, the bray of a donkey, the impatient toot of a horn. He heard Fraisal cheerily bidding good afternoon to people and marvelled at his cool; in a place like this, having a white man as a passenger was tantamount to a death sentence.

Then the jeep stopped. Harry screwed shut his eyes as he listened to Fraisal and another man in animated conversation. *What the hell were they talking about?* Under the blanket, with sweat pouring down his face, it was easy to become paranoid. And now he could feel the first twinges of cramp in his legs. He tried not to move. He tried not to *breathe*. Then he felt something heavy land on his shoulder and it felt for all the world like an accusatory hand – but then the jeep moved off again and seemed to be picking up speed.

After what seemed an eternity, the blanket was whipped from him and he looked up from the footwell to see Fraisal grinning down at him.

'Are you all right, my friend? You can come out now – the coast is clear.'

'Bloody hell, Fraisal,' Harry said, extending his lanky frame painfully into the seat. 'I felt something on my back and I thought I was a goner.'

Fraisal laughed and reached into the rear seat. In his hand was a bunch of bananas. 'When you go to the market you are expected to buy something,' he said. He ripped one of the fruit from its fibrous stem and handed it to Harry. 'Eat it,' he said. 'Who knows when you will get the chance again?'

There was something about the dishevelled Arab slumped against the wall that seemed familiar to Jake, a vague feeling that he had seen him before. The Arab clearly thought the same. In the gloom of the cattle shed, where they had retreated from the heat of the midday sun, he sensed he was being watched.

'*You were on the boat*,' the Arab said finally.

Nancy Griswold looked from one man to the other. 'You *know* each other?' she said.

'My name is Hafiz. I deliver supplies to the *Kanshish*. *You were on the boat!*'

'Boat? What the hell are you talking about, Hafiz?' Nancy said. 'The Pommie told me he was some sort of hostage. Isn't that right?'

'I was being held on a ship,' Jake said. 'An old coastal freighter operated by a pirate named Omar Abdulle.'

From another corner of the shed, Red Sheppard chuckled darkly. 'Omar Abdulle? It's a fucking small world.'

'What do you mean?'

'We just watched those bastards hang him from that tree out there.'

Nancy described how they'd paid Hafiz thirty grand for an interview with Omar Abdulle, only for the legendary Somali pirate to turn out to be one of the fixer's friends. When she'd finished she glowered at the Arab, who physically recoiled into his soiled *dishdasha*.

Despite their predicament Jake laughed and shook his head. 'Well, Omar's real enough, you can take my word for it. And right now I think I'd rather be back on the *Kanshish* than stuck here. These guys—'

'The Deadly Boys,' Nancy said disparagingly.

'—have they given any indication of what they plan to do with us?'

'Apart from hang us?' Sheppard said.

'Jazi – the leader – mentioned something about taking us to see a bloke called Garaad,' Nancy said.

Hafiz groaned miserably. 'Garaad Islam,' he said. 'He is in charge of the Coastal Volunteers. Pirates in Kismaayo.'

'Taking us to see him?' Jake spat. 'And what then?'

'He may sell you on. Or he will probably kill you. White hostages are very dangerous to a man like Garaad. They attract too much attention.'

'That's reassuring to know. Don't you think we should tell Jazi this? If he's wasting his time, maybe he'll let us go.'

'What Garaad does with you makes no difference to Jazi,' Hafiz said. 'All he cares about is the respect of Garaad Islam for capturing three white prisoners. He will be hoping that Garaad will invite the Deadly Boys to join his organisation.'

'Either way it looks as if you'll get to meet a real-life pirate leader,' Jake said to Nancy, reading her thoughts.

'So what's he waiting for?' Sheppard said. 'Why is Jazi keeping us hanging around here?'

'Garaad Islam is a very busy man,' Hafiz said. 'You must make an appointment to see him.'

Not far from the crossroads where they had hijacked the VW Combi, Mabuto and his men came across a small-holding where the owner, an elderly man with a bald head framed with a frizz of white hair, kept a handful of scrawny-looking goats.

Mabuto was of the opinion that a fugitive in a foreign land would automatically head in the direction of the coast, where at least there was a chance of finding a boat. But he also knew that the first priority for any fugitive was finding provisions – and that, out of necessity, meant finding the nearest habitation.

The old man had seen enough in his life not to be fazed by the arrival of a dozen armed soldiers. He even offered them a jug of faintly rancid-smelling goat's milk as a gesture of neighbourliness. But unfortunately he had not seen any white man in the vicinity. Had they tried the woman who lived a mile further down the road? They really should, if for no other reason than to try her home-baked corn crisps, which were absolutely delicious.

The soldiers were clambering back into the van when Mabuto noticed a dark red smear down the flanks of one of the goats in the paddock. At first he thought it was some sort of marking paint – but when he touched it he discovered it was fresh and wet.

It did not take much persuasion – a few slaps about the head and a rifle butt in the stomach – to make the old man talk. Yes, he had picked up a white man on the road to Kismaayo; and yes, he had driven him directly to the lair of the Deadly Boys, who were a group of local hoodlums who were prepared to pay for such things. But he was just a poor goatherd and he meant no trouble, and if they wanted any more milk to take with them then all they had to do was ask.

Mabuto shot him through the head, partly so he wouldn't talk but mainly because he was a lying Somali dog who had cost them valuable time and, had Mabuto himself not been so observant, could have allowed the fugitive to escape.

There was a subdued atmosphere on board the *Osprey* as the sleek fishing boat headed south towards Kenyan waters. Even Kurt Anderssen appeared to have blown himself out, and he had said little since the decision had been taken to leave Fraisal's village and head home without Harry.

*It was his own damn fault,* Anderssen reasoned. *They were doing him a favour by heading to the navy base at Manda, because Mugo was right – this was a job for the professionals, not some half-cocked English vigilante. If Harry made it back to Fraisal's village then all well and good. But the chances are he was already up to his neck in trouble.*

Down in the cockpit Mugo and Sammy sat pensively, staring back at the boat's wake and at the looming mass of the Somali mainland receding off their starboard rail. The bait boy in particular seemed preoccupied, and

Mugo could tell he was feeling guilty about his part in Harry's escape.

'Mr Philliskirk is a force of nature, Sammy,' she said. 'When he makes up his mind to do something, he will do it. You are very loyal to him – and to Jake.'

Sammy nodded sadly. 'Will he be all right?'

'He will be fine.'

Mugo knew how lame she sounded, and her own overriding feeling was also guilt. It was her weakness that had led them to this situation, her inability to act on what she instinctively knew to be right. Her only excuse was, of course, her loyalty to Jouma – but what would Jouma say if he knew that her actions had indirectly put another life in danger? She knew what Superintendent Simba would say. And if there was one certainty ahead it was that her career as a police officer was over before it had even started.

But maybe that was for the best.

She went up to the flying bridge.

'Chiamboni headland up ahead,' Anderssen said, gesturing at a fist-shaped outcrop of land reaching into the sea. 'That's the border. And I think we've got company.'

In the distance, circling slowly in the water, was a squat white vessel bristling with antennae. It was a Kenya navy border patrol gunboat from the base at Manda Island.

'This is where the shit really hits the fan,' Anderssen said.

As he spoke a helicopter appeared in the sky above the headland, moving fast towards them as it swooped down to within touching distance of the ocean's surface.

'Christ,' Anderssen said. 'They're really preparing a welcome for us.'

The chopper was heading north, headed almost

directly for them. But it showed no sign of slowing; instead it roared overhead so close that they could see the helmeted face of the man in the open side door and the snout of his pivot-mounted machine gun. Sammy waved but there was no response, and in an instant the chopper had gone.

# 47

It had been strange to hear Simba's voice over the crackling satphone. The superintendent had sounded different somehow, yet familiar; like speaking to an old acquaintance after many years.

But she was still the same old Simba.

'What the devil do you think you are playing at, Daniel? Kidnapped by Somalis? At *your* age?'

'I assure you it was not my intention, ma'am.'

He had told her what had happened, and what Omar had proposed, and after that there was a long silence as Simba processed the information.

'Ma'am?'

'I'm still here, Daniel.'

'Mr Abdulle is most insistent that you relay this information to the relevant authorities in Nairobi. He is anxious that his men are not held responsible for what happened.'

Another silence. 'Can he hear me?'

'No, ma'am.'

'Yes or no, Daniel. Is this true?'

'Yes, ma'am.'

'You are not being pressured to say this?'

'No, ma'am.'

'Very well. I will do as you ask.'

'Thank you, ma'am. One thing I would ask of you—'

'Don't worry, Daniel. I will call her.'

A melancholic mood had settled over Jouma after he had made the call. He had been trying not to think of Winifred, deliberately forcing all thoughts of his wife from his head, concentrating only on the circumstances of his captivity and how best to deal with them. But today had been difficult. Freedom had been so close that to have it so brutally snatched away was almost too much to bear. The self-protective barrier he had erected in his mind could no longer cope and now dark thoughts spilled through the cracks.

*Winifred . . . Jake . . .*

As he tried to rebuild his defences he found the only way he could do so was to find someone to blame. And while it would be easy to condemn Omar, Jouma instead found his anger directed at the reckless murderous duplicity of his own government. He had dedicated his life to the protection of his countrymen, yet at the moment he needed them most they had let him down with shocking disregard.

Lost in his private turmoil he had been standing on the quarterdeck for some time when he was joined at the rail by Omar.

'I am sorry for your friend,' the pirate said.

'I am sorry for your men.'

They stared out at the horizon. Over it, maybe a hundred miles away, was Kenya. It was receding fast.

'What now, Mr Abdulle?'

The pirate sighed. 'Now? Now, Inspector Jouma, it is every man for himself.'

Jouma nodded. 'I understand.'

'The ship is on a course for Kismaayo. It will be there

in two hours, maybe three. This will soon be over for you.'

'And you?'

'You are an intelligent man, Inspector. I do not need to tell you that my position here has been fatally undermined by recent events. When a captain loses the confidence of his crew, there is no place for him aboard his ship. Soon I will be leaving, and you will never see me again. It saddens me, because I think, deep down, we are very similar you and I.'

'You are a criminal, Mr Abdulle. There is no similarity between us.'

'Look into your heart, Inspector. Tell me that you do not see the same anger that is in mine. Yes, I operate outside your laws. But they are still your laws, not mine. And is not betrayal a greater crime? Is not injustice?'

Jouma said nothing. He did not trust himself to speak in case he found himself agreeing with the pirate leader.

Winifred Jouma was ironing her husband's shirt when the telephone rang. She stared at it for a long time, because it was the first time it had rung since Daniel had disappeared. And she knew it was not her sister in Lake Turkana, because she'd expressly told Mary not to call in case someone was trying to get through.

Five rings. Six.

She placed the iron in the cage at the end of the board and carefully threaded a wire hanger into the sleeves of the shirt. She buttoned the shirt and hung it on the back of the living-room door, next to the three identical white shirts that made up her husband's collection. She had lost count of the number of times she had ironed them in the last two days. The room was heavy with the smell of spray-on starch.

Eight rings. Nine.

Winifred went across to the sideboard where the phone was. She clicked off the ancient Roberts radio that was tuned to Radio Kenya.

Eleven rings.

She picked up the phone.

'Mombasa four-one-seven?'

'Mrs Jouma?'

'Speaking.'

'This is Elizabeth Simba.'

'Good evening, Superintendent. How may I help you?'

'I have some news about your husband.'

# 48

Fifty minutes after it left Nairobi, a Gulfstream jet touched down at a small airstrip on the outskirts of Garsen, twenty miles north of Malindi. The stairs hissed open and N'Kuma hurried to a car waiting on the tarmac. It was unusual for the head of the Internal Division to personally head up an operation – but these were most unusual circumstances and he had his orders from the very top.

Their driver was an NSIS field officer from Mombasa. His name was Toby Okeyo, and while his boss strapped himself into the rear seats he screeched away towards the exit, then turned onto the main highway.

'What is the latest?' N'Kuma demanded.

'The Lynx took off from Manda fifteen minutes ago. By the time we reach the base the first images of the exchange site should have been transmitted.'

'Good.'

They crossed the bridge over the Tana River in the direction of Lamu. 'There is something else, sir.'

'What?'

'A navy gunboat intercepted a game fishing vessel heading south from Somali waters about an hour ago. The boat is registered to a Danish national named Kurt

Anderssen, based in Watamu. Anderssen was on board, along with a Mombasa police constable named Mugo and a bait boy employed by Jake Moore.'

N'Kuma's eyes narrowed. 'The British hostage?'

'Yes, sir. It seems they were part of an unofficial search party looking for the hostages.'

'And?'

'There was another member of the party, sir,' Okeyo said, glancing into his rear-view mirror. 'Name of Philliskirk. He runs the fishing business with Mr Moore. Apparently Mr Philliskirk is still in Somalia. It seems he has information as to where the hostages are being held.'

'My God,' the chief groaned. 'A foreign national on a personal crusade in the middle of Somalia. That's all we need.'

The Kenya navy base at Manda, one of the islands making up the Lamu archipelago, is a small outpost consisting of a few whitewashed buildings overlooking the bay. The base is home to a handful of gunboats and light border patrol vessels, but on the other side of the island is a deep-water port capable of handling larger ships.

The Royal Navy frigate HMS *Winchester* was moored to a snug concrete jetty, and with men crawling over her exterior armed with paintbrushes and oxy-acetylene torches she looked more like a building site than a modern fighting ship. On the bridge, however, there was activity of a different type. In the cramped control room, the commanding officer was peering at a screen which was displaying high resolution images beamed directly from the ship's Lynx helicopter.

He looked up as N'Kuma arrived. Their handshake was brief, and there were no pleasantries. The images on the screen did not lend themselves to joviality. They showed aerial shots of the lagoon where the hostage transaction had taken place that morning. Bodies were clearly visible floating in the water and strewn across the red dirt of the track leading inland from the beach.

'Looks like there was a bit of a firefight,' the commander said.

'Yes,' N'Kuma said darkly. 'But I don't see many of our men.'

It was true. The dead were almost all dressed in jeans and T-shirts. Many of them were wearing *keffiyeh* head-scarves. N'Kuma could see only one body wearing military fatigues. He was lying on his back at the inland side of the track, but from this distance it was impossible to see his face.

'Can they get in any closer?' N'Kuma said. 'This one in particular interests me.'

The commander relayed an order to a communications officer sitting in front of the screen.

'Three-Zero, requesting a close up of the body in grid sixteen, over?'

'Roger that, control,' came a disembodied voice through a speaker on the wall.

Mugo sat in one of two chairs in a windowless, cinderblock interrogation room. The only other furniture was a plastic table. She had been waiting for nearly thirty minutes when the door to the room opened and a young man in a crumpled suit came in.

'Good afternoon, Constable Mugo. My name is Toby Okeyo.'

'You are with the government?'

'In a manner of speaking.' He put a slim folder on the desk in front of him. 'I hope you are well; I understand you have been on quite an adventure.'

'I was foolish,' Mugo said.

'On the contrary, Constable Mugo. From what I hear you and your friends have shown admirable initiative.'

'Thank you, sir. But I don't think my superintendent would agree with you.'

'But surely you knew what your superintendent would say long before you set off for Somalia? So why does it worry you now?'

Mugo shrugged. 'You don't know my superintendent.'

Okeyo chuckled. 'Then you must accept the painful truth that your life will be punctuated at regular intervals by reprimands from your senior officers. If it makes you feel any better, I received the mother of all reprimands from my own boss just this morning.'

'Yes, sir.'

'Another thing that might cheer you up, Mugo.'

'Yes, sir?'

'Inspector Jouma is alive and well.'

Mugo's face lit up. 'He is safe? I mean – he is here?'

'Sadly not,' Okeyo said. 'He is still being held captive. But he has been in communication with us, and we are doing everything in our power to secure his release.'

'Thank you, sir!' Mugo said. Then: 'And his friend, Mr Moore?'

'Mr Moore's precise circumstances are not so clear at this point.'

'I see.'

Suddenly businesslike, Okeyo opened the file. 'I want to talk to you about Mr Philliskirk. I understand he is still in Somalia.'

'Yes, sir.'

'Do you know where?'

Mugo told him about Fraisal's village, and their trip to Cousin Hemi's plantation. When she mentioned the

Deadly Boys Okeyo began writing something on the inside cover of the file with a pencil.

'And you think this is where Mr Philliskirk has gone?' he said.

'I am sure of it.'

'If I was to provide you with a map of the area, do you think you might be able to pinpoint the vicinity of their headquarters?'

'Mr Anderssen knows where Fraisal's village is. If you show me that, then I think I may be able to assist you.' She sighed. 'I am sorry, sir.'

'Sorry for what?'

'I should never have allowed Mr Philliskirk to go off by himself. I should never have allowed him to go to Somalia.'

'On the contrary, Officer Mugo. Our job is to monitor any activity that poses a threat to Kenyan security and any intelligence is welcome – however unorthodox the method by which it is gathered. There have been a number of kidnappings involving foreign nationals in this area over the last few months. Missionaries, mainly. They tend to think their belief in God makes them immune from criminal gangs. Your friend Mr Philliskirk may have inadvertently led us to one of those gangs.'

'What will you do?'

'We will make inquiries,' Okeyo said obtusely. 'In the meantime we must hope that Mr Philliskirk has not become the latest hostage.'

It did not take long for the image to arrive.

'Is that him?' the commander of the *Winchester* asked.

N'Kuma stared at the face on the screen. 'Poor John,' he said.

'What now?'

'Well, from what I can see, we are still missing a hostage and Captain Mabuto. There is also a platoon of Kenyan soldiers unaccounted for. It would be very helpful, Commander, if you could ask your aircrew to reconnoitre the area around the exchange point.'

'Of course. But you'll understand when I tell you I don't want them hanging around bandit country too long, sir.'

'Of course,' N'Kuma said. As he spoke he felt his Blackberry vibrating in the inside pocket of his jacket. He peered at the message that had just arrived in his in-box. 'Were you and General Choi good friends when you were at naval college, Commander?' he asked, slipping the phone back into his jacket.

The commander smiled. 'We shared a room.'

'Then on his behalf I would ask you for one more small favour before you order your helicopter back to base.'

# 49

Ten miles outside the market town Fraisal turned off the highway and followed a track into a thick forest of casuarinas. When he was out of sight of the road he swung into the trees and stopped the engine.

'The plantation is about a hundred yards further along the main road,' he said. 'If you cut through the trees it will bring you out at the top of a hill overlooking the area. It's exposed. You will have to be extremely careful.'

'I will,' Harry said. 'I don't intend being there long. Just a quick peek, that's all.'

'I'll wait for you here.'

The two men shook hands. 'You're a good man, Fraisal.'

'And you are a damned fool, Harry. Now be careful.'

Harry set off through the trees, following an animal trail through the undergrowth that gradually began to ascend. To his right was the highway and he made a point of keeping it in sight as long as possible in order to keep his bearings. But it wasn't long before his route took him away from the road and into deeper, thicker vegetation that in sections threatened to swallow him up.

As a result he did not see the ageing VW Combi

driving slowly past. Nor did he see it turn left onto the track leading to the farm.

'*You fuckin' looking at meee-eeee?*'

The prisoners in the cattle shed hadn't seen much of Jazi for a while. In fact if it wasn't for the two Deadly Boys guarding the door – or rather lounging on the ground, smoking joints, with their AK-47s slung across their knees – they might have thought their captors had left.

What they didn't know was that Jazi had been waiting for a call on his cell phone. And just a few moments ago it had finally come through. As a result Jazi was in an extremely good mood as he burst into the shed, filling it with blindingly bright sunshine.

'Get up, my friends, and make yourselves presentable!' he said, beaming. 'The great Garaad wishes to see you.'

Jake, who had been dozing in the thick heat, opened his eyes and winced. In his fitful dream he had been back in the grey, cold northeast of England where he had grown up – and leaving it for the sweltering reality of his Somali prison was almost heartbreaking.

'It's about bloody time,' Nancy Griswold said, collecting her things and giving Red Sheppard an impatient nudge. 'How long will it take to get there?'

'Not long,' Jazi said. Then he looked at Hafiz. 'Not you.'

The fixer looked like a small child who was about to burst into tears. 'But . . . why?'

Jazi laughed. 'Why the fuck would Garaad want to see an Arab dog like you?'

Hafiz looked imploringly at Nancy. 'Madam – *please*. Tell the gentleman that I am with you. Surely you won't leave me here? You will need a translator. Someone who knows the lay of the land.'

Nancy put her hands on her hips. 'You're a bloody piece of work, Hafiz, you really are. And after the way you stitched us up back there I ought to wash my hands of you.' She looked at Jazi. 'He's coming too.'

The fixer fell at her feet in abject gratitude, and she kicked him away as if he was an over-amorous dog.

'A shame,' Jazi said. 'I was looking forward to killing him. But perhaps Garaad will appreciate it more.'

Jake got to his feet. 'If we're going, let's go.'

They walked out into the compound and past the flyblown bodies of the men Jazi and his comrades had tortured and executed earlier that day. Jake wondered if a similar fate awaited him at the hands of Garaad Islam, who by all accounts sounded like yet another psychopathic Somali gangster. There was a part of him that had, by now, had enough of kowtowing to thugs and murderers. He thought back to how pleasurable it had felt to smash Omar's crewman in the face with a fire extinguisher, and it suddenly annoyed the hell out of him if this single act of resistance was to be his last.

As they walked towards the ruined farm building the seed in his mind grew with frightening speed. *What did he have to lose?* Things weren't going to get any better once they were in the charge of Garaad Islam, and if these headline-hungry Aussies thought their nationality and status as international news reporters was going to buy them special treatment then they were sorely mistaken. If there was one thing he had learned from his experiences on board the *Kanshish* it was that, like all effective gangsters, pirates were not interested in publicity. All that concerned them was making a profit and staying alive.

No, he thought, their little jaunt to Kismaayo could

only ever end one of two ways: hanging from a tree, or else locked in some stinking cellar for months on end while the politicians back home refused to act.

They were being led to a technical parked in the shade of a tree next to the farmhouse, Jazi in front, the two guards bringing up the rear. Four men were slouching in the back of the vehicle, smoking *bhang*. Fifty yards, no more.

Either way, Jake thought, life as he knew it was over. He was already as good as dead.

He slowed then pretended to stumble on the rough ground. He fell momentarily onto one knee and then, with every last ounce of power, he sprang up and backwards and smashed one of the guards in the face with his elbow. The AK-47 dropped to the dirt and Jake pounced on it. But even as he attempted to scramble to his feet he felt a heavy blow to the side of his head and he pitched forward, his vision exploding into a single white light. More blows rained in, and then he was aware of rough hands grabbing him – and when he opened his eyes he was looking straight down the barrel of Jazi's handgun.

'That was very *stupid*!' Jazi shouted, his nostrils wide.

'Are you fucking crazy?' Nancy Griswold was screaming. 'Are you trying to get us all fucking *killed?*'

'Fuck you,' Jake said and spat a mouthful of blood. Then to Jazi he said: 'Why don't you kill me, you jumped up little bastard?'

Later Jake would think back to that moment and wonder whether Jazi would have actually pulled the trigger. But he would never know, because just then the Deadly Boy standing beside him was hit in the neck by a bullet fired from somewhere off to the right – and as he fell down dead, the second guard was hit in the chest.

Jazi screamed something and ran towards the farmhouse. The men in the technical, doped up to the eyeballs, seemed to take an age to react. One of them went down almost immediately, but another grabbed the general-purpose machine gun and began firing indiscriminately.

Jake grabbed Nancy by the arm and, together with Hafiz, they ran back to the cattle shed and flung themselves through the door as the gunfire crackled around them.

'Everyone all right?' Jake shouted.

'Red!' Nancy cried. 'Red's still out there!'

During his long and distinguished career, Red Sheppard had never run from a story. It was in his blood, and like all great news cameramen he was instinctively able to snap into a zone of professional detachment in which he was merely an observer of the action rather than a part of it.

If it hadn't been for his instinct Sheppard would have hit the dirt or started running like everyone else when the firing started. Instead he calmly raised his camera onto his shoulder and, standing his ground in the compound, began recording the unfolding drama, just as he had done since he was a five-dollar-a-week junior snapper on the *Murwillumbah Weekly Gazette* back in Australia.

Through his viewfinder he saw men in military uniform moving quickly through the outbuildings – stopping, firing, moving again like they were in an exercise; then he panned to the technical where three of the Deadly Boys were sprawled over the side, and the fourth seemed to be laughing maniacally as he blasted away with the .50 Cal on its welded tripod; and then, out of nowhere, Jazi appeared with a rocket launcher over his shoulder and Sheppard saw him fire at a group of soldiers huddled down by the farmhouse; and then there was an almighty explosion as the rocket hit the supply of diesel oil the Deadly Boys kept handy to fuel their vehicles, and Sheppard cursed as the flash threatened to burn out his retina; and he was still standing there, doing his job, when a bullet smashed through the camera lens and blew out the back of his skull.

Five miles away and at an altitude of 1,000 metres Flight Commander Phil Passingham, at the controls of an RAF Lynx helicopter, saw a flash of light in his peripheral vision off to the east.

'Did you see that?' he said.

Behind him, manning the chopper's door-mounted heavy machine gun, Airman Chris Gatenby was scouring the horizon. 'Roger that, sir,' he said. 'Looked like an explosion to me.'

'Looks like it was from that sector control wanted us to take a look at.'

Passingham, a 38-year-old veteran of both the Iraq and Afghanistan conflicts, considered his next move. He was under strict instructions to proceed with caution and observe only, and he was all too aware that the Lynx, while hugely manoeuvrable, was also susceptible to surface-to-air fire.

'What do you think?'

'I think we should take a look,' Gatenby said.

Passingham smiled to himself. 'That's the spirit.'

Gatenby had already loaded the weapon's ammo belts and was now making a last check of its spindle mount.

'Firing,' he said, and the Lynx shook as he unleashed a

short burst at the empty scrubland below. 'Operational,' he said.

'Hang on to your hat, Airman – we're going in.'

'We have to get out of here,' Jake said urgently.

'They shot Red,' Nancy moaned, staring through the door of the shed at the cameraman's body on the ground.

'They're going to shoot us all unless we get out of here, Nancy – so snap out of it.'

'Who *are* they?'

'Kenyan soldiers,' Jake said.

'*Kenyan?* But—'

'Trust me, our paths have already crossed today.'

He pulled Nancy away from the door and pushed her to the far end of the shed.

'There is a window,' Hafiz said hopefully, pointing up at a foot square hole in the wall above their heads.

'Too small,' Jake said. 'We don't have time.'

He took two paces back and planted a firm kick on the breezeblocks. As he thought, the blocks were brittle and the mortar holding them together was rotten and flaking. Two of the blocks shifted outwards, and when he kicked them again he saw daylight.

'Don't just bloody stand there, Hafiz – get kicking!'

The two men had soon dislodged three slabs, and a firm push was all it took to remove them entirely.

Outside the gunfire suddenly stopped.

'Shit,' Jake said.

Nancy looked at him. 'What is it? Why have they stopped?'

'Because there are no Deadly Boys left to kill. Come on, let's go.'

First Nancy, then Hafiz and finally Jake squeezed through the hole in the shed wall. They emerged into a small paddock of baked earth. Beyond was a rusted wire perimeter fence and then a gentle two hundred yard slope to a rocky ridge. Their only possible option, Jake knew, was to reach the ridge and hope there was something on the other side – a road, another farm, a fast car with a full tank of petrol perhaps.

They could hear shouts from the compound behind them, and a single shot rang out as presumably one of the Deadly Boys was finished off by the soldiers.

'I hope you can run, Nancy,' he said.

She smiled grimly. 'Like the bloody wind, mate.'

They set off for the perimeter and found a gap where the wire had rusted away. Now they were out in the open and brutally exposed. Any second now the soldiers would appear – but there was no point in looking back, they just had to keep running.

And it was then that a figure appeared on the crest of the ridge, waving frantically at them. It was nothing more than a thin silhouette at this distance, but there was something terribly familiar about it – so much so that Jake almost burst out laughing at the tricks his mind was playing on him.

Then he heard a voice calling his name, and he realised that it was no hallucination, that the figure on the ridge really was . . .

*Harry?*

'I'll be damned,' Passingham said. He jabbed a button that patched him through to the control room of HMS *Winchester*.

'Control, we have a situation here. Requesting advice, over.'

The comms operator's voice said: 'Go ahead, Three-Zero, over.'

'Ah, control – I think it would be easier if I switched on forward cam, over.'

'Roger that, Three-Zero.'

Passingham activated the remote camera slung beneath the Lynx's nose. It was one of two cameras fitted to the chopper, the other being a stationary unit in the belly used for taking high-resolution digital stills. The forward cam had a limited field of movement operated by the pilot or co-pilot and was able to transmit lower-quality live-action images via a satellite comms link.

In the control room of the *Winchester* N'Kuma watched what looked like a grainy home movie of tiny running figures.

'This is the area you asked us to reconnoitre,' the commander said. 'Where your agent thought there might be hostages?'

'It looks like he was right,' N'Kuma muttered.

*But who were they?*

The commander grabbed the mike. 'Three-Zero, what is your position, over?'

'One mile from target and closing, over.'

'Can you increase magnitude in the forward cam, over?'

'Roger that, control.'

The screen went blurry for a moment, and when it resolved itself the figures were much clearer.

'Who the hell *are* those people?' the commander said.

'I don't know,' N'Kuma said. 'But those are Kenyan soldiers.'

Passingham's voice interjected over the speaker. 'Be advised, control, I have bodies in the farm compound. Repeat, I have bodies in the compound and there would appear to be a live situation underway. Request advice, over.'

N'Kuma looked at the commander. Everybody in the control room looked at the commander.

'It's your call,' the commander said to the NSIS chief.

N'Kuma looked at the screen. He thought about what Jouma had said about Kenyan troops opening fire at the hostage exchange. He thought about a gun at Jouma's head as he said it. He thought about John Nola lying dead at one end of the track and around a dozen dead pirates at the other.

*He thought about the fact that there were no dead Kenyan soldiers.*

'You should consider the soldiers to be hostile,' he said.

Captain Mabuto did not see the Lynx until it suddenly appeared three hundred yards to his right and barely fifteen feet off the ground.

*What was this?*

He was standing by the cattle shed, with blood pouring from a shrapnel wound that had rendered his right arm useless. Two of his men were dead, killed in the explosion from the rocket launcher. The remaining four were in pursuit of the British hostage and his companions. He did not know who the others were, just as he had no idea who the dead white man with the video camera was. His ears were ringing and there was a strange buzzing inside his head and he was getting increasingly *irritated* by things not going to plan.

And now this? An attack helicopter? Who . . . ? *What . . . ?*

Hefting an assault rifle with his one good arm, Captain Milton Mabuto, a man who regarded himself as Kenya's most loyal patriot, was shouting the words to *Onward Christian Soldiers* as he opened fire at the rapidly approaching chopper.

⋆

The Lynx is one of the most agile helicopters in military service, but it still needs a top pilot to perform at its best. The joystick was like an extension of Passingham's hand as he coaxed the aircraft into a sickening climb to three hundred metres and then brought it round in a tight, steep banking manoeuvre.

'Hold on,' he said. But the words were barely out of his mouth when a series of dull metallic bangs on the Lynx's reinforced underbelly and an insistent red flashing light on his instrument panel told him that they were under fire. Glancing up Passingham saw the men in uniform staring up at him with open mouths.

*But if they weren't shooting . . .*

'I see him, sir,' Gatenby shouted. 'Single shooter on your three o'clock.'

Passingham executed a perfect evasive manoeuvre and eased the Lynx round the back of the farm buildings.

'Lining you up, Mr Gatenby.'

'Roger that, sir.'

As the Lynx roared over the top of the cattle shed, Gatenby immediately opened up with the chuntering .50 Cal, directing a controlled field of fire at Mabuto, who simply disintegrated in a cloud of dust and splintered masonry.

'Target secured, sir,' Gatenby reported.

'Roger that,' Passingham said, circling the remaining soldiers and noting to his satisfaction that they had all dropped their weapons and raised their hands. 'Good boys,' he said.

He had no desire to engage in a turkey shoot today.

It was all over in a matter of seconds. Jake looked up from the dirt and shielded his eyes as the Lynx landed in a blizzard of dust.

'Friends of yours, Harry?' he shouted over the din of the engines.

Harry Philliskirk grinned under the bill of his greasy baseball cap. 'Do you think I would leave you dying when there's room on my horse for two?' he said.

# 50

Sheba's body, washed and sewn into a white cotton winding sheet, was brought on deck with all due reverence. It was carried on the shoulders of four crewmen, and the bearers were followed by the Imam who was dressed in his ceremonial robes and carried a copy of the Koran.

The procession made its way from the superstructure across to the bows of the *Kanshish*, where a makeshift platform had been constructed from the galley table and covered in a tablecloth taken from Omar's dining room. The crew stood in respectful silence and watched as the girl's body was laid on the platform. High above them, Omar and Jouma watched from the bridge gantry.

It was a scene, Jouma thought, that would have almost been touching had it not been for the fact that at that moment, at the stern of the ship and hidden from prying eyes by the wheelhouse, Rafael and Julius were making preparations of their own. In contrast to the solemn funeral ceremony, theirs involved carefully lowering a rigid inflatable motor launch over the side and securing it to the stern deck cleats with mooring ropes.

'My brother once told me that of all his children he liked Sheba the least,' Omar said. 'He said she reminded him of his wife.'

'Did you ever meet his wife?'

'Just once.'

'What was she like?'

'Like Sheba. But heavier and bossier.'

'Why did he marry her?'

'Because he owed her father a great deal of money.'

'I see. I would not have thought that was a good basis for marriage.'

'No. It wasn't.'

Below, the Imam turned to face the crew. He said something which was caught by the wind and carried away from Jouma's ears, but the crew responded by getting down on their knees and prostrating themselves.

'Are you a religious man, Inspector?'

Jouma shrugged. 'I do not attend church, if that is what you mean. But if you mean do I believe in God—?'

'Every man must believe in God,' Omar said. 'Whatever his own particular God happens to be.' He turned and offered his hand. 'I must go now. But before I do I have been meaning to thank you.'

'For what?'

'For your professionalism. I am an impulsive man and I would never have thought to look beyond Jalil for the murder of Sheba. Because of you, his life has been spared and for that I am grateful. You have taught me a valuable lesson.'

Jouma looked at the pirate's outstretched hand.

'You know I cannot take it,' he said.

Omar nodded. 'Yes,' he said. 'I do.'

And with that he turned and went into the bridge.

To his great relief the Imam completed the funerary rites without anyone appearing to notice that he had made most of it up. The only lines of the *Janaza Salah*, the Muslim prayer service, he could remember were the general purpose, '*Glory be to Thee, O Allah, and I praise Thee. Blessed is Thy name and Thou art exalted. Thy praise is glorified, and there is no god other than Thee.*'

*Thank God for the Koran*, he thought. The real miracle of the Holy Book was that you could open it at any page and find a passage that, on the face of it, had some relevance to whichever ceremony you happened to be presiding over. It also helped that virtually none of the crew had read it, mainly because virtually none of them could read.

His service complete, all that now remained was to commit the girl's body to the deep with enough mumbo-jumbo to disguise the fact that they were essentially tipping it into the sea. *Some big shark was going to have a feast tonight*, the Imam thought and was forced to bring his hand to his mouth in order to stifle a bout of wholly inappropriate laughter.

Jouma wondered what would happen if he was to interrupt the funeral service to tell the crew of the *Kanshish* that their great leader was deserting them. Dumb incomprehension, most probably. Then the inevitable violence. He had seen it before, during the elections of 2007, when tribal warfare had erupted and his own countrymen had turned on each other for no other reason than they could think of no better way to express their anger.

It was such an easy, yet misguided solution – like sticking a Band Aid over a spurting artery.

He could see now why someone with the charisma and wilfulness of Omar Abdulle had been able to command these men. It was because they were sheep. Had they had an ounce of resourcefulness between them they would not have been on board the *Kanshish* in the first place.

Omar called himself their father, and he was right. They *needed* him.

But now he was gone, and it struck Jouma that the crew had got precisely what they deserved.

The four bearers gently picked up Sheba's body and brought it to the bow rail. The Imam flipped a few pages of the Koran and jabbed his finger onto one of the verses. It had absolutely no relevance whatsoever to the matter in hand, but he read it anyway. When he had finished, he closed the Holy Book and, on his signal, the bearers tossed the corpse into the sea.

The mooring ropes securing the rigid inflatable to the stern of the *Kanshish* had been used to suspend a makeshift zip line, and Omar laughed at the sight of Julius clinging like a monkey to the loop of rope as he slid down into the launch. Now only Rafael was left on board the ship. Over his shoulder was a large canvas bag containing weapons, money and supplies. The bodyguard grabbed the rope and the mooring cable sagged alarmingly under his weight as he made his way across the gap.

Omar signalled to Julius on the flying bridge, and the boat's outboards fired up, the noise drowned out by the churning of the *Kanshish*'s props and the rumble of its engines. Rafael hacked through the ropes and the launch pulled away, maintaining a steady course designed to keep the ship's superstructure between them and any prying eyes on board.

Omar watched the rusting freighter recede into the distance and felt a pang of sadness that he would never see her again. The *Kanshish* had been a good mistress, and a profitable one. But all things had to end, and Omar had not made a success of his life as a businessman without knowing when to move on.

'Rafael – pass me the phone.'

It was time to call in some favours on the mainland. People who would help him to continue his business. It was always the case that when one door closed, another one opened.

'Rafael,' he said irritably. 'The phone!'

But when he turned he saw that his trusted bodyguard was sitting by the rudder and had not moved. Beside him, Julius was holding a handgun.

'What is the meaning of this?' Omar demanded.

Julius raised the gun and pointed it at Omar's head. 'Rafael and I have decided that it would not be beneficial to remain as your subordinates,' he said. 'We feel it is time we went our separate ways.'

Omar's face turned ashen. 'But why? Julius – this is our great opportunity! Together we can rule Somalia, we can—'

But Julius shook his head. 'Like I said, Omar – it's over.'

Jouma went through to the bridge, where the two Nigerian helmsmen were diligently maintaining the ship's course to Kismaayo, unaware that Omar was already on his way to another destination on the mainland.

As he passed the wardroom he noticed the door was slightly ajar. He pushed it open and went inside. It stank of cigars, and a swath of smoke still hung around the light fittings like the ghosts of its previous occupants. It reminded him of a crime scene, a moment frozen in time. His instinct was to look for evidence – but for what? And what possible purpose would it serve? The only thing that might have been helpful was the satphone, but the cradle on the desk was empty. Omar had either taken the handset with him or, more likely, tossed it over the side.

He left the wardroom and went downstairs. He felt strangely dislocated, as if he was wandering around a hotel whose guests had all vanished into thin air. The cabin doors were open, but the cupboards and wardrobes were still filled with clothes and other non-essential belongings. Pillows still bore the impression of the heads that had recently slept on them.

Further down he went, past the galley and the mess hall and the storage cupboard that had been his prison. And it was then that he truly felt alone, despite the fact that on the other side of the thin metal walls was an entire crew of violent men who at any minute were going to realise that they had been betrayed by the only man they trusted.

'Inspector!'

Jouma turned. 'Jalil?' It seemed the boy had materialised from thin air. 'What are you doing here?'

'Omar has gone, hasn't he?'

'Yes – yes, he has gone. But the ship will soon be in Kismaayo.'

Jalil's expression was fearful. 'Please. Come with me.'

'Where?'

'Come with me, Inspector. There is something you must see.'

# 51

The Lynx came in low over the Chiamboni headland and swept south to Manda naval base.

'Looks like we're going to make it on fumes,' Passingham said lightly – but from two of his three passengers there was no response. Jake and Nancy Griswold had been asleep almost from the moment the chopper took off from the plantation.

The third passenger, however, was wide awake. Harry Philliskirk had spent most of the short journey talking about rugby with Gatenby, and admiring the .50 Cal door-mounted heavy machine gun.

Passingham smiled to himself. Old Harry was quite a character, that was for sure. The sort of eccentric expat Brit that would not have looked out of place at the height of Kenya's crazy colonial invasion. It was somehow reassuring to see people like that still existed – although having listened to Harry's account of how he had risked life and limb to find his friend in Somalia, Passingham wasn't sure where eccentricity ended and certifiable insanity began.

This particular story would take some unravelling, that was for sure – and Passingham did not envy the suits and the brassnecks whose job it would be to piece together just how Jake, Nancy and Harry had ended up in the back of his helicopter, and how a captain in the Kenyan army should have found himself on the receiving end of Airman Gatenby's unerringly accurate machine-gun fire.

Pirates, gangsters, hostages, security agents, vigilante soldiers – it made his head spin just to think about it. The only thing that was certain was there were a hell of a lot of dead bodies lying on the red Somali dirt.

'How far to the base, Flight Commander?' Harry asked.

Passingham checked his equipment. 'Five minutes, sir.'

'Better brace myself then. I have no doubt I'll be in deep shit with the powers that be.'

'I'm sure they'll be gentle with you.'

*Mugo and Kurt Anderssen won't be, though,* Harry thought. Assuming they had returned safely to Kenya, it might be prudent to avoid his shipmates for a while.

He looked at Jake. The temptation to wake his friend and demand the details of his ordeal was powerful – but so was the knowledge that what Jake had been through in the last forty-eight hours had been just that: an ordeal. And what made it worse was that his little detective friend was still out there somewhere, held captive by pirates, with no imminent prospect of freedom – assuming, of course, that he was still alive. Harry was a man who treasured his freedom more than any single thing in his life, and even the very idea of being forcibly stripped of it brought him out in a cold sweat.

Nancy Griswold was slumped with her head on Jake's shoulder. Her mouth was open and a thin stream of drool had spilled from her slack lips. From the little he had seen of her, she was something of a force of nature too. 'Headstrong Aussie' was how Jake had introduced her, and judging by the way she had browbeaten Passingham into transporting Red Sheppard back to Manda base it was no mean description. The cameraman had been duly wrapped in tarpaulin and his body was now secured to one of the helicopter's external stanchions. As soon as they landed, it would be taken to the morgue at Malindi hospital. Right now a Kenya air force transport chopper was en route to Somalia to collect the rest of the dead.

'It's been quite a day,' he said.

'You might say that,' said Passingham.

'I expect you'll have a nice cold beer waiting for you when you get back.'

'Chance would be a fine thing, sir. I expect I'll have to make do with a nice cup of tea and a debriefing with my commanding officer.'

'That's bad luck,' Harry said. 'Listen – I don't suppose you know a bar in Lamu called Gunther's? Does the best seafood on the entire coast, and the manager is a personal friend of mine.'

'I'm afraid I don't, sir.'

'Well, what I was going to suggest is you drop me off there, rather than back at the base. I'm gagging for a beer, and I'm not sure I can be bothered with all this red tape business.'

Passingham laughed. 'Love to, Mr Philliskirk. But I'm afraid that's Manda up ahead.'

The Lynx swept into the bay, and as it did so Harry could see the sleek outline of Kurt Anderssen's boat moored in the turquoise shallows. *Oh, shit. So the old bastard had beaten him to it after all.* And then he saw another boat moored nearby – and his heart skipped a beat.

This time there was no time for sympathy. He reached over and violently shook Jake awake.

'Harry – what the hell is it?'

'Down there, old man,' Harry said excitably. 'Isn't that the best sight you ever saw in your life?'

Jake blinked to clear his sleep-fuzzed vision and looked down.

'Oh, yes,' he murmured appreciatively as he saw the unmistakeable lines of *Yellowfin*. 'That's just beautiful.'

The Lynx touched down on the *Winchester*'s landing pad, and even before its rotors had stopped turning its passengers were being shepherded in different directions by various officious-looking men in suits.

Jake found himself in a small cabin with a headache-inducing centrally-positioned light. Presently N'Kuma came in. The NSIS Internal Division chief introduced himself but dispensed with the pleasantries before getting down to business. Jake would, he said, be fully debriefed about his kidnapping and the abortive hostage exchange. But for the moment there were more pressing matters to attend to. He told Jake about the satphone communication from Jouma earlier that day.

'He is on board Abdulle's ship and appears to be in good health.'

Jake felt a huge weight lifting from his shoulders. 'What did he say?'

'He gave us a set of co-ordinates where the *Kanshish* will be at 1700 hours today. He says Abdulle is prepared to let him go in return for immunity from prosecution.'

'What are the co-ordinates?'

'A position ten miles south of Kismaayo. Abdulle is giving us permission to pick him up.'

Jake looked at his watch. Astonishingly it was only three o'clock. Already it felt like this day had lasted a thousand years.

'Then what are you waiting for?' he exclaimed.

'As per Abdulle's instructions a US Navy frigate from the international fleet is already en route to the rendezvous. They will pick up Jouma and Abdulle and transport them to Mombasa.'

Jake smiled to himself. 'A frigate? Abdulle always did have an over-inflated sense of his own importance. So when do I leave?'

N'Kuma blinked. 'With respect, Mr Moore, I assure you there is no need for you to go. The Americans are quite capable of dealing with the situation.'

'With respect, Mr N'Kuma, you can go to hell. I got Jouma into this mess and I fully intend to be there when he is released. And I don't suppose Abdulle included someone called Jalil on his list of passengers, did he?'

'Jalil? Who is Jalil?'

'Someone I made a promise to,' Jake said. 'And that's another reason why I'm going.'

# 52

Sheba was gone and, as with every funeral, the mourners had gathered for the wake. But while the traditional Muslim wake would have been sober, respectful and reflective, few of the *Kanshish* crew were devout and those that were weren't going to miss out on a rare opportunity to let their hair down. No sooner had the girl's body been pitched over the side than a huge vat of distilled sorghum liquor, known as *chang'aa*, was hauled on deck from the cargo hold and liberally distributed among the crew. Mixed with industrial quantities of *bhang* this made for a potent combination, and soon the sound of raucous laughter and singing could be heard over the rush of the ocean as the *Kanshish* ploughed inexorably north.

It would not be long before the first fights broke out, Jouma thought to himself as he followed Jalil down the steep metal steps to the engine room. But that was no bad thing. As long as they were at each other's throats it meant they weren't at his.

'What are we doing here, Jalil?' he said as they reached the bottom of the stairs.

'Look . . . '

Opposite were the valves and dials of the engine

control panels, and tucked away in the corner was a small booth where the engineer sat. The door of the booth was open, and the engineer, an original member of the ship's Nigerian crew, was lying in a pool of his own blood, his throat sawed through to the bone.

Jalil gestured to him to follow and limped round to the back of the engine housing, where it connected to the turbine chambers and the diesel tanks. Stacked in a neat pyramid and roped securely to the boiler were four large plastic barrels with the letters $NH_4$ $NO_3$ stencilled on the side. Jouma had seen them before, on the quarterdeck. It was the ammonium nitrate shipment that had washed up near Rafael's mother's village. But what was it doing here?

He went closer and saw that the barrels had been tampered with. Some sort of metal pin had been punched into each, and each pin was connected to the others by wire.

It was then that Jouma realised what he was looking at.

Ammonium nitrate was, as Omar had said, commonly used as an agricultural fertiliser. But Jouma had also paid attention during the mandatory terrorism seminars introduced in the wake of the al-Qaeda attacks on hotels along the Kenya coast back in the days when the fundamentalists were not such a household name. He knew that the chemical could also be used as a base ingredient for a devastating improvised explosive device. All it needed was a little plastic explosive and a supply of fuel oil to make sure everything went with a bang. The pins were blasting caps, presumably smothered in Semtex, so that was one part of the equation completed. And under the deck were fuel tanks capable of storing more than eighty tons of diesel, so that was the second. The ship would be running low, but it didn't matter; with this much ammonium nitrate there was more than enough to blow the *Kanshish* and everybody on it to kingdom come.

Jouma followed the connector wires from the blasting caps round to the engine consoles. As he expected, they were hotwired to the electrical circuits of the control panels themselves. He scanned indicator dials – there were a dozen of them, ranging from temperature and capacity gauges to turbine rev counters and speed limiters. The device could be connected to any of them, and set to detonate at any given point. Jouma was no electrician. To his untrained eye the mass of wires spilling from the access dock of the control panel looked like multicoloured spaghetti. Nor did he have the first clue about bomb disposal; the only way he could think of to disable the device was to cut the connector wires – but what if there was some sort of failsafe in the mechanism that would trigger the blasting caps anyway?

'What is it, Inspector?'

'It's nothing,' Jouma said breezily. 'But I want you to go up to the bridge and tell one of the helmsmen to come down here immediately. Tell him I think there may be a problem with one of the engines.'

# 53

Within an hour of Jouma's phone call to Simba the USS *New Orleans*, a mid-range frigate assigned to pirate patrol duties in the Indian Ocean south of the Horn, had detached itself from its small fleet of international vessels and set off at top speed for the Somali port of Kismaayo.

By the time the *Winchester*'s Lynx helicopter had been serviced and refuelled and was ready to go again, the American ship was less than thirty miles from the rendezvous point with the *Kanshish*.

'You must be a glutton for punishment,' Gatenby, the door-gunner, grinned as Jake jumped aboard.

'I'm only here because I like the kit,' he said, gesturing sheepishly at the flight suit and helmet they'd given him to wear.

'Very debonair,' said Flight Commander Passingham, and as he spoke the Lynx's engines started to whine and the rotors began revolving. 'Now strap yourself in, please.'

As the Lynx took off, twenty miles to the south another military aircraft was landing on a hastily-marked field at the back of Malindi hospital. It was an air force transport helicopter, and in its belly was a grim cargo of bodybags.

Out of sight of the main building the bodies were loaded onto two ambulances and driven the short distance to the mortuary where they were sorted according to priorities and stacked in the freezer. The majority of corpses were those of Somali pirates, and in all likelihood would remain there for several weeks before someone got round to dealing with them.

One corpse retrieved that day had been given priority treatment upon its arrival at the hospital, however.

'Madam – you can come through now.'

Nancy Griswold looked up and saw security agent Toby Okeyo, who had driven her to the hospital from Manda base, standing in the waiting room door. She took a deep breath and followed him to the morgue.

The hospital mortician had done his best to make Red Sheppard look presentable, but his was a small and under-funded unit and the cameraman's head was really in quite a state of disrepair. As a stopgap measure, he had placed a heavy gauze bandage over the right eye socket and packed the shattered skull with polystyrene chips from a recent shipment of syringes. Then he had covered the top half of Sheppard's head with a folded sheet and wheeled the corpse into the small chapel of rest attached to the mortuary.

Nancy gave a little exclamation and put her hand to her mouth – and even though she'd promised herself she wouldn't cry she wept hot tears now.

*Red . . . Ah, Christ, Red . . .*

Then she angrily swiped them away. Get a grip, you silly bitch, she chided herself. You're not some dippy model parachuted into Africa for a celebrity show, you're Nancy Griswold of Channel Seven News. You have reported from war zones. You have interviewed warlords, dictators and mass murderers. It's a dangerous job, and these things happen. Red knew it as well as you did.

*That's the spirit, Nance!* she heard Red's familiar voice in her head.

Yeah, but spirit's all very well, you great galah – but what am I going to do without you?

*You'll be fine.*

You think so?

*You're a ball-breaker, Nance. I just took the pictures.*

Yeah, and if you hadn't been such a bloody idiot and ducked like everyone else you'd still be here.

*Yeah – but check out the footage. The bastards might have shot out my lens but they missed the bloody hard drive and the memory. I'm telling you, the stuff on there will win you a Walkley Award. This is the biggest story of your career!*

But we never got to speak to a pirate.

*Bugger the pirates – what about Kenyan army's shoot-to-kill policy?*

Christ, you're right, Red.

*When was I not?*

Behind her, Okeyo cleared his throat. 'Take your time, madam,' he said.

'It's him,' she said, her voice hoarse.

The agent nodded and the mortician pushed the gurney out of the room.

'Where will they take him?' Nancy asked.

'There will be an autopsy to determine cause of death—'

'I would have thought that was bloody obvious!'

'Purely procedural, madam. Then arrangements will be made with your consulate in Nairobi to have the body repatriated. I understand a member of the consulate staff is on their way as we speak.'

'I see.'

'In the meantime, if there is anything else I can do—'

'As a matter of fact there is,' Nancy said. 'Red's camera.'

'I believe it was brought back with his personal effects.'

'Good. Because I want it. There's something on there he wanted me to see.'

The crew of the *Osprey* had experienced an awkward reunion at the naval base, largely because Kurt Anderssen had refused to even as much as acknowledge Harry's presence in the room. Harry, meanwhile, wasn't speaking to Kurt because Kurt had locked him in the cabin – and Mugo wasn't speaking to either of them because she thought they were behaving like little children. Instead she played cards with Sammy and tried to put out of her mind the news that Superintendent Simba was on her way from Mombasa.

Two hours passed. Then the rattan ceiling fan that had been lazily circulating the warm air emitted a small puff of smoke and stopped working.

'Fuck this, Harry,' Anderssen announced, getting to his feet. 'I need a beer.'

'Agreed,' Harry said. 'Come on, Sammy. And you, Officer Mugo.'

'But my superintendent is coming,' Mugo said.

'Then what possible excuse do you need?'

They had been told that they were not allowed to leave the base until they had been fully debriefed. There had also been thinly-veiled threats about revoked licences and even prosecution. But escape proved easier than they'd expected. The door to the mess hall was unlocked and there appeared to be nobody around. Ensuring the coast was clear, they crept round to the rear of the building and followed a barbed wire perimeter fence to its furthest extent two hundred yards from the main compound. Here they found a service road with a barrier manned by a sentry half asleep in a wooden guardhouse. Next to the guardhouse were some half-dug foundations and a portable concrete mixer. Harry and Kurt grabbed the mixer and pulled it round to the front of the guardhouse, followed by Sammy and Mugo who were carrying a bag of concrete mix between them.

'That's us finished, chief,' Harry called to the sentry, who blinked awake. 'See you same time tomorrow.'

The sentry nodded dopily but the two men had already pulled the mixer under the barrier and were making their way out of the base with their accomplices trotting happily after them.

Half an hour later, with the mixer abandoned in a roadside ditch, they hitched a lift on a fishing dhow to Lamu Island, and within the hour all four were enjoying a cold Tusker in the bar of Gunther's fish restaurant overlooking the harbour.

For Constable Lucie Mugo, who drank rarely if at all, the beer was the best thing she had ever tasted in her life. All she needed now, she concluded, was a cigarette.

# 54

The Nigerian helmsman was a thin, wiry man with a studious demeanour and it took him several minutes of close-quarters examination before he was ready to give his opinion on the massive ammonium nitrate bomb wired to the engineering console.

'I have absolutely no idea,' he said. 'I am not an engineer.'

'But surely you must have *some* clue as to how this equipment works?' Jouma said.

'*Ye-es.* But having a clue is a very different matter to understanding fully. You see this bomb could be set to detonate depending on the turbine speed, or the engine temperature, or it could simply be wired to a timer. I do not know.'

'How long before we reach Kismaayo?'

'Two hours.'

'How far offshore are we?'

'Ten miles.'

'How near to the mainland can you bring the ship?'

The helmsman shrugged. 'It depends.'

'*Give me an estimation,*' Jouma said, coming perilously close to losing his temper. What the helmsman didn't seem to realise was that the bomb less than six feet from where he now stood could go off at any minute.

'The ship is fairly high in the water. The fuel levels are low. I'd say maybe a quarter of a mile.'

Jouma nodded. 'Good. Then do it.'

'Why?'

'Because there are more than a hundred souls on this ship and only two working skiffs.'

The helmsman looked staggered. 'You are evacuating the ship?'

'Do have a better idea?' Jouma said.

Thirty miles from the target Flight Commander Passingham checked his on-board data readouts and made a slight adjustment to the Lynx's heading. The navy chopper was travelling at two hundred miles an hour and at an altitude of fifteen feet above the ocean's surface.

'Ten minutes to contact,' he said.

Jake gripped the door handle until his knuckles were white. It was not just the thrill of the ultra-low-level approach that had set his nerves jangling, it was the sudden realisation of what he was doing. When he had watched the *Kanshish* disappear over the horizon that morning, he had firmly believed that it would be the last time he would see either it or Omar Abdulle. Yet he was now just ten minutes away from confronting his nightmare again.

'You all right, sir?' Gatenby asked. 'You look a bit peaky.'

'I'm fine. Just not used to travelling by helicopter, that's all.'

'Don't worry – we'll soon have you back on the ground again.'

As far as Jake was concerned, that moment could not come soon enough.

⋆

The Imam enjoyed a drink as much as the next man, and while dangerously toxic *chang'aa* would not ordinarily be his tipple of choice he had drunk enough of it that day to be pleasantly drunk.

But that was before he had been told there was a bomb on board the ship.

News like that could sober a man up in an instant.

Ashen-faced he stepped out onto the bridge gantry. Below on the foredeck the revelry continued apace. Many of the crew were now so far gone they had not even noticed the ship had changed course and that the Somali mainland was now visible as a hazy black swipe along the horizon.

He turned and looked at Jouma, who nodded encouragement. Above him, Jalil began clanging the alarm bell on the wheelhouse roof.

Bleary eyes looked at him and gradually the crew fell silent.

'My brothers and sisters,' the Imam shouted. 'I have some important news for you.'

'Strange,' said Passingham.

'What is it?' Jake said, leaning forward towards the flight deck.

'We should have had a visual by now.'

Through the tinted windscreen of the Lynx Jake could see only empty ocean. The jangling sensation began to coalesce into a general feeling of unease in the pit of his stomach.

'You sure you've got the right co-ordinates?' he asked, and immediately knew it was a stupid question to ask a Royal Marine pilot.

'Oh, we're in the right place all right,' Passingham said.

'It would appear that the pirate ship isn't, though. Unless—'

Ahead now Jake could see what Passingham had noticed: a subtle disturbance on the surface of the ocean.

'They've changed course,' he exclaimed. 'It looks like they're headed for the mainland.'

Passingham nodded. 'Then we'll do the same. I'd better tell our American friends that there appears to have been a change of plan.'

'Why would he do this?' the Imam wailed. 'To his own *people*!'

'Because they are *not* his people,' Jouma said. 'They have never been anything other than animals to do his bidding.'

The two men were watching as the crew, snapped by necessity from their drunken stupors, were frantically making preparations to abandon ship. The two remaining skiffs, which had been stored in the bows, were being made ready and decisions were being made as to who would go in them. But there was no concept of women or children first here. Far from it. This was a case of the survival of the fittest – which meant those who were male and able-bodied received priority treatment. The rest were a burden who would have to take their chances.

'But this – this is an *abomination.* It is cold-blooded murder.'

'No,' Jouma said. 'It is Omar's vengeance.'

'Vengeance?'

'Against the foreign persecutors who systematically destroyed him. He wants to kill them the same way they killed him in the eyes of his men. A rendezvous. An ambush. I understand now: the bomb is set to go off at the same time as my rescuers arrive.'

'Can't you warn them?'

'How? Omar has taken the satphone and the radio does not work.'

The Imam looked at a loss. 'When do your friends arrive?'

Jouma looked to the horizon for any sign of an American frigate. 'That depends if we can outrun them.'

Jake's heart was racing as the *Kanshish* appeared on Passingham's cockpit radar system as a fuzzy blue blob. But his unease was also ramping up, because something was clearly not right about the situation. The freighter was already far too close to the mainland, yet appeared to be on a heading that would take it directly into the shallow waters near the coast.

'Inspector!' Jalil shouted.

The boy's eyesight was infinitely sharper than Jouma's, and it took the Inspector an embarrassingly long time to see what he was pointing at off the starboard side: a tiny speck, no bigger than an insect at this distance – but undoubtedly closing on them.

Jouma checked his watch. 1655 hours. The cavalry were depressingly on time.

'I'll be damned,' Passingham said. 'What the hell are they doing?'

Even at the distance of two miles Jake could see that all around the ship small splashes were appearing in the water, as if someone was throwing stones over the side.

'They're jumping overboard,' Jake said incredulously. '*They're abandoning ship.*'

'This is all very wrong,' Passingham said. Then he

nodded, as if some momentous decision had been made. 'Stand by, Mr Gatenby – we're going to take a closer look.'

Gatenby needed no second bidding. He was already strapped to his .50 Cal in the doorway as the Lynx, travelling at its maximum speed, lurched upwards and swooped low over the deck of the *Kanshish*.

'They're giving us a good look, sir, but I don't see anything incoming,' Gatenby reported, as less than fifty feet below him the men on the deck flattened like wheat in a field.

'Roger that,' said Passingham. Reducing speed, he gained two hundred feet of altitude and came round in order to sweep the length of the freighter from its bows to its superstructure. 'You've got one chance, Mr Moore. If you see your pal Jouma, let me know because I'm not at all happy about this.'

'*There!*' Jake yelled as the chopper swooped past the superstructure. 'On the bridge gantry.'

The Lynx climbed out of range of any small-arms fire and, hovering above, they saw two small figures waving from the gantry.

'You sure that's your man?'

'That's Jouma all right,' Jake said. *And he's got the boy with him.* But where was Abdulle? And why the hell was the crew abandoning ship in such a panic? Scenarios began to play across his mind, and none of them were good.

'We're going to have to make it quick,' Passingham said. 'Mr Gatenby will lower the winch. You'll have to help him get our people aboard.'

As Jake got into position by the door Passingham brought the Lynx into position just a few feet from the roof of the superstructure.

'They're certainly in a hurry to get off,' Passingham remarked calmly, as from all sides of the deck the remaining crew were flinging themselves from the rail. As he spoke Gatenby was remotely lowering a winch and harness from a spool above the door.

*Don't think about that now. Just do what you have to do.*

Jake peered down and saw the Inspector and Jalil looking up at him. Jouma was frantically waving his hands, but the gesture seemed one of urgency – as if he was telling them to back off.

*Just get them off the ship and ask questions later.*

Jake removed his helmet and for a split second Jouma was stunned. But then the gesturing started again with even more urgency, and this time it looked like the detective was trying to shout something.

*For Christ's sake, stop flapping and grab the fucking harness.*

'How are we doing, Mr Gatenby?'

'He's got the harness, sir. He's attached it to himself and the boy.'

'OK – then let's get them up.'

'Roger that, sir.'

The chopper remained dead still in the air as the harness line began hauling Jouma and Jalil upwards to the open door. In just a few seconds Jake and Gatenby were able to reach down and grab them – yet even as he was dragged into the aircraft's belly Jouma was still gesticulating crazily.

'What the hell is it, Inspector?'

'*Bomb!*' Jouma screamed.

And at that moment the *Kanshish* was torn apart.

Ten miles away the commander of the USS *New Orleans* said, 'Jesus Christ – what was that?'

Beside him on the frigate's bridge, his first officer said:

'I'll be damned,' because away on the eastern horizon it looked as if the sun had come up. 'Missile launch?'

The commander considered this for a moment. There were plenty of US subs lurking in the Indian Ocean, and it was not beyond the realms of possibility that the President had run out of patience with Iran.

But the glow on the horizon had not faded like the burners of a missile. It was just *there*, lighting up the purple sky like a forest fire.

'What do you think?'

The first officer shrugged. 'As long as we can charge Uncle Sam for the overtime, sir.'

The commander grinned. 'Feel free to be creative with your invoice.'

The initial explosion ripped a huge hole in the side of the *Kanshish* and then, with nowhere else to go, the blast fired upwards and through the cargo holds and foredeck. Like an insect swatted by a rolled up newspaper, the Lynx was flung violently sideways by the shockwave and was then peppered by shards of wood and metal. Three huge holes suddenly appeared in the aircraft's fuselage close to the open door where Gatenby was sitting. A fist-sized piece of shrapnel passed harmlessly through the cabin. The second ripped into Gatenby's right leg below the knee. The third smashed through the roof and into the rotor mechanism – and suddenly every warning light on Passingham's flight console flashed red.

'Brace yourselves,' the pilot said, his voice almost ethereally calm as the chopper began spinning dizzyingly out of control. 'I'm afraid we're going down.'

In the control room of the *Winchester* all hell broke loose.

'Sir – I've lost contact with Three-Zero—'

'Sir – I'm getting an intercept from the *New Orleans* about some sort of explosion off the Somali mainland—'

'Sir – long range radar is confirming an explosion—'

# 55

He should have been dead. Every scintilla of common sense told him that.

But he wasn't. He was looking up at the sky, listening to the steady rain of minute debris falling onto the water all around him.

He was alive.

He sat up. Two hundred yards away the disfigured corpse of the *Kanshish* belched thick black smoke into the sky. The explosion had ripped her in half. The stern section was lying on its side, the torn remains of the wheelhouse half underwater. Beyond it the bows were jutting out of the sea at an angle of thirty degrees. The midsection, where the main deck and the hold had been, had disappeared. The men who had been standing there, those that had not been instantly shredded in the blast, were now oil-covered debris floating on the surface.

'If I was a cat I'd say that counted as five lives down at least,' Passingham said.

The pilot was sitting on the other side of the Lynx's inflatable life raft. He had a broken leg and lacerations to his face, sustained when the chopper hit the water. Next to him were Jouma and Jalil, who had cuts and bruises, and Gatenby, the gunner, whose badly mangled leg was oozing blood through a wholly inadequate field dressing.

Jake himself had emerged from the wreckage virtually unscathed – which he still found hard to believe. But then the reason they were still alive was because the Lynx had struck the surface of the water like a skimming stone, propelled sideways by the blast wave as if by a giant sweeping hand; and while its rotors and tail had been ripped off it had come to rest with its central section relatively intact.

But the main reason they had survived was that the *Kanshish* was pitifully low on diesel oil. The main tanks beneath the wheelhouse were empty; it was the reserves under the cargo hold that had fuelled the blast. If the freighter had been fully laden, she would have simply ceased to exist and every living thing within a half-mile radius would have been instantly vaporised.

'Are you OK?' Jake asked Jalil.

The boy nodded, staring at the wreck, the flames reflected in his wide dark eyes.

'Where's Abdulle?' The question was directed at Jouma, although he already knew the answer.

'Gone a long time ago.'

Something nudged against the raft. It was a body, naked and charred, glistening with thick black oil. Yet five hundred yards away dozens of exhausted survivors were dragging themselves ashore. One of them was the Imam, who had been among the last of those who had jumped from the ship. As he crawled from the surf, he kissed the wet sand and thanked Allah profusely.

'It is very strange,' Jouma said distantly. 'But up until a couple of days ago I was terrified of the ocean. Now I rather like it.'

# 56

The moon was full and low in the night sky and the Chiamboni headland cast a long and deep shadow across the ocean.

'This is the border,' Jake said. 'We'll be at Manda base in an hour.'

Jouma nodded. 'Good. But I suspect it will be some time before they let us go home.'

The two men were standing on the forward observation deck of a Kenyan navy gunboat that had picked them up twenty miles inside Somali territory an hour earlier. They had been transported to the rendezvous by the USS *New Orleans*, which had reached the *Kanshish* just as the last of the ageing coaster was disappearing into the oily water.

'Excuse me, sir.' The gunboat's skipper poked his head out of the bridge door. 'Your call is ready.'

'Thank you,' Jouma said.

Jake smiled. 'I'll go and check on Jalil. Last I saw he was flat out in the crew's quarters.'

'He has had a very busy day.'

When Jake had gone, Jouma stood by himself for a while, feeling the warm breeze on his face. Then he turned and went to the bridge where the skipper was waiting with the ship-to-shore handset.

He took a deep breath. 'Hello?'

'Daniel?'

Her voice sounded strange, as if he was hearing it for the first time.

'Hello, Winifred.'

A pause. 'Superintendent Simba said you were back. Are you well?'

'I am fine, thank you. And you?'

'Fine.'

'How was your trip to Lake Turkana?'

'It was fine.'

'How is your sister?'

'She is well.'

'I am sorry I was not at the airport to pick you up.'

'That is all right. I got a cab.'

'It was not too expensive, I hope.'

'No.' Another pause. 'How is the weather in Lamu?'

'Winifred, I—'

'Will you be home tonight?'

'Possibly.'

'I will put some supper in the oven for you.'

'Thank you.'

'Will you be going to work tomorrow?'

'I don't know.'

'Well, if you do, I have ironed you a shirt.'

'Winifred—'

'Yes, Daniel?'

' . . . Goodnight.'

*

*The storm came to that part of the mainland quickly and violently, and the wind bent the trees and the waves pounded the coast with an exquisite savagery. The next morning all that remained was the evidence of its rage: the destroyed shanty houses, the upended palms, and the detritus of the ocean scattered across the shore as far as the eye could see.*

*The two boys were up early, with the sun, anxious to get down to the beach before the professional scavengers moved in, the cold-eyed men who regarded anything the sea regurgitated as their own. Barefoot they raced down the track from their village and they gasped at what they saw. It was as if a huge garbage scow had been scooped up and its contents tipped onto the sand.*

*The boys ran down to the surf, whooping with excitement. There would be rich pickings here today; their special collection would be swollen by many more exotic items, that was for sure.*

*It did not take them long to start finding things: plastic shopping bags, polystyrene food containers, a genuine McDonald's soft drink cup complete with lid and straw, cooking oil canisters with strange writing on the sides, beer cans from America, coffee jars, empty chemical vats, and, best of all, a laptop computer with a large tear in the screen.*

*It was always the same after a storm. Sometimes the boys wondered just how much stuff was out there, just waiting to be brought ashore.*

*All too soon, though, the cold-eyed scavengers began to materialise on the beach and the boys knew it was time to go. With their treasure trove collected in one of the plastic shopping bags they reluctantly made their way back along the shore towards the village.*

*And it was then that they discovered the body.*

*It was a man, lying face down and half-covered with seaweed. He was wearing an army uniform and a fine-looking leather belt. There was a gold chain around his neck and an expensive-looking watch on his wrist. The boys looked at each other. Whoever he was, he looked very important.*

*Ensuring that the scavengers weren't looking, the boys quickly removed the watch and the necklace and put them in their bag.*

*'If he is a soldier, maybe he has medals?' one of them suggested.*

*Giggling with excitement they rolled him over onto his back.*

*There were no medals – but there was a hole in his forehead. His mouth and eyes were open and there was an expression of utter surprise on his face.*

*But wait: there was something in the breast pocket of his shirt. The boys gasped. It was a cell phone – or at least it looked like a cell phone. Had they been able to read the words along the top they would have known that it was, in fact, an Inmarsat Fleet Phone used to make ship-to-shore calls via satellite. No matter – it did not work now. Now it was good only for their collection of curious artefacts.*

*'Look!'*

*The man had gold teeth!*

*There was a sharp whistle and they saw one of the scavengers hurrying towards them. The boys shouted abuse at him and started sprinting for the village. The scavenger could keep the gold teeth – most of them carried pliers specifically for that purpose. The boys had what they wanted, and when the next storm came they would come back for more.*

Missed Nick Brownlee's previous novels?
Turn the page for a peek
at Nick Brownlee's gripping novel
*Bait*
Available now from Piatkus

# Day One

# Chapter One

As a boy, George Malewe had gutted thousands of fish for the white men who came to catch game off the coast of Mombasa. But, as he plunged the blade of his favourite teak-handled filleting knife into the soft underbelly and eased it upwards through the stomach wall with a smooth, practised sawing movement, it struck him that he had never before gutted a white man.

A man, George concluded, was not so different from a large karambesi or marlin. The guts spilled out on to the cockpit deck with the same moist splash. And the pool of blood that hissed between his bare toes had the same warm tacky consistency as that of a big game fish.

Admittedly, there was more of it. It would take him a lot longer to swab down the deck and hose the entrails out through the scuppers in the stern of the boat when he was done.

And, George reflected, he had never before gutted a game fish that had been bound to the fighting chair with fishing line.

Nor one that screamed as he eviscerated it.

'George – move your arse, will you?'

He jumped suddenly at the harsh voice from above. 'Yes, Boss.'

The scrawny African moved to one side, so that instead

of hunkering between the bound man's knees he now leaned against the outside of his immobilised left thigh.

'Smile!'

George turned and looked up into the lens of a camera pointing down at him from the flying bridge. He knew all about cameras, and this one was top of the range. Very expensive. He beamed, revealing a decimated set of yellow teeth beneath the peak of his New York Yankees baseball cap.

The Boss Man holding the expensive camera pulled away from the eyepiece with a snarl of annoyance.

'Not you, you stupid *kaffir. Him.* You get on with your work.'

George's face fell and he turned silently back to the gaping abdomen of the man who sat bound by his wrists, forearms, ankles, upper thighs and knees to the steel struts of the fighting chair.

'Come on, Dennis!' the Boss Man said cheerfully. 'Say cheese!' Again he snorted with annoyance. 'George – lift up his head, will you?'

George went behind the fighting chair and wrenched the bound man's head off his chest by a hank of silvery hair.

'Up a bit, up a bit ...'

From his position on the tarpaulin-covered flying bridge, overlooking the cockpit and the stern of the boat, the Boss Man wobbled on his feet slightly as he adjusted the focus on his camera.

'He don't look too clever, does he, George?'

George glanced down at the grey upturned face. The mouth hung slackly and the open eyes had rolled upwards.

'He look dead to me, Boss.'

'Mmm.'

The Boss Man put down the camera and clambered gingerly down a set of iron ladders connecting the superstructure to the cockpit. He was thickset and the way he staggered drunkenly as the boat pitched and rolled on the swell indicated that he was no sailor.

But then George had known that anyway. The skippers who worked these fishing grounds for a livelihood knew every inch of the reef, knew precisely where the snag-toothed coral lay near enough to the surface to rip the bowels out of a thirty-foot twin-engined game-fisher like *Martha B* as easy as tearing paper.

The Boss Man didn't have a clue.

George did; but then you didn't crew fishing boats from the age of eleven without learning how to navigate into open sea, how to read the currents and how to anticipate the waves that could pick you up and smash you into matchsticks.

That was why he was here.

That and the five hundred dollars the Boss Man had promised him for navigating *Martha B* through the reef, gutting the white man in the chair and asking no questions.

George felt a flutter of excitement as he thought about the money. Five hundred dollars was a fortune in a country where the average monthly wage was less than ten. With five hundred dollars, he could *be* someone. There would be no more scraping a living on the streets of Mombasa, no more stealing from white tourists just to put food on the table for Agnes and little Benjamin. With five hundred dollars, he could set himself up in business, be one of the smartly dressed *tausi* like Mr Kili who drove around in expensive cars and could order things done simply by snapping his fingers.

'Yep. He's dead all right,' the Boss Man said, a hint of disappointment in his voice. 'Cut the line, George.'

*Five hundred dollars.*

Gutting the white man had not been as hard as George had imagined. Once the Boss Man had smashed him over the head with the metal claw of the grappling hook, the rest had been relatively straightforward. In fact, he had quite enjoyed it. It certainly beat stealing wallets, cameras and cell phones. Of course, George had been puzzled as to who this white man was, and what he had done to deserve such a fate. But the Boss Man seemed to know him, so that was OK.

*Ask no questions.*

As the last of the fishing line was cut from the dead man's wrists, George looked at his face and shuddered.

'Right. Get him to the back of the boat.'

The Boss Man was back on the flying bridge now, issuing his orders against the increasingly excited cawking of the seagulls circling overhead.

George manhandled the body out of the fighting chair to the stern rail.

'OK. Get rid of him.'

The body splashed into the ocean. It floated face-up for a moment, but only until the empty abdominal cavity filled with water and sent it swiftly beneath the surface.

'Right,' the Boss Man said. 'Now get that shit cleared up.'

As he got to work with the hosepipe and the stiff brush, George reflected that the body would not last long in these waters. The blood and entrails siphoning from the scuppers would soon attract a hammerhead or a bull shark, and tuna or sailfish would consume what was left.

As he worked he hummed a tune, 'Wana Baraka',

which was a traditional folk song he used to sing with his mother in the shanty church of Likoni when he was a boy. It was about how those who pray will always be blessed, because Jesus himself said so. Nowadays George sang it to his own son, Benjamin, and just the thought of his little boy brought a broad smile of joy to his face. There were not many things in George's wretched life that he was proud of, but Benjamin was one. Today was his third birthday, and five hundred dollars would buy him a present he would never forget.

But, suddenly, George's beatific expression turned to one of puzzlement. Putting his hand to the peak of his cap, he stared out across the grey water towards the western horizon. A boat was approaching, low in the water, and, judging by the cascades of spray it threw up as it smashed against the swell, it was travelling fast.

George looked up to the flying bridge, but the Boss Man was hunched over, fiddling with something under the steering console.

'Boss!'

'What is it, George?'

'Boat coming.'

The Boss Man appeared at the rail, squinting through his sunglasses at the rapidly approaching vessel. He smiled. 'Right on the money,' he said, and turned back to the wheel again. 'Get on with your work.'

As he swabbed the deck, George watched the other boat out of the corner of his eye until it drew near enough for him to identify it as a high-powered speedboat, the kind he sometimes saw moored near the rich tourist resorts at Kikambala, Bamburi and Watamu. There was a white man at the wheel, hunched down behind the Perspex windshield. George did not recognise him. As the boat drew alongside *Martha B*, the man tossed a mooring rope across. George took the rope and secured it to one of the deck cleats.

'Right, Georgie-boy,' said the Boss Man, 'I'm afraid this is where I'm going to have to bid you *kwaheri*.'

George watched him negotiate the whitewashed iron ladder on the side of the boat. The expensive camera was now secured in a padded shoulder bag slung across his broad back. The Boss Man tottered unsteadily on the leading rail before sitting down and easing himself into the bobbing speedboat. He turned and smiled at the bemused crewman.

'Hope you don't mind – but I'm sure you know how to drive, don't you, George? It'll be a little treat for you. And you know that bloody reef like the back of your hand.'

George nodded dumbly.

'Nearly forgot.' The Boss Man rummaged in the pocket of his shorts and flung George a ten-dollar bill. 'You'll get the rest back on dry land.' He grinned. 'Then you can buy me a beer, eh? Maybe some girls. Lots of pretty *manyanga* for Georgie-boy, eh?'

Then the Boss Man said something to the man in the speedboat, and the craft's mighty engines coughed into life. George watched as it moved away from *Martha B* in a lazy arc, and saw its stern bite into the churning water as the turbos kicked in and fired it towards the distant mainland.

George shrugged. *Five hundred dollars and no questions asked.* He stared at the ten-dollar bill in his hand, then put it under his cap and shinned up the ladder to the flying bridge. He'd been on the flying bridge of one of these game boats before, of course. But always at the shoulder of the skipper. Bait boys weren't allowed near the wheel or the controls, not unless they were trusted.

When he'd been a bait boy, George reflected bitterly, he'd never been trusted.

He had watched though. He knew how to steer, how to ease forward the throttles and make the engines throb – and, although he wasn't sure how the compass worked, he knew every last inlet of the coast. George settled himself in the cushioned pilot's chair and sighed contentedly.

*Five hundred dollars*. Yes, he would soon be like Mr Kili in Mombasa. Maybe one day he would have his own boat. Yes, that would be good. Little Benjamin would like that.

He reached forward and jabbed the starter button.

A mile away now, the Boss Man winced in his seat in the rear of the scudding speedboat as *Martha B* disintegrated in a ball of flame. Splinters of wood and debris rose on the back of an oily black mushroom cloud, drifted lazily in the air, then fell back to the ocean in a cascade of tiny splashes. Eventually the smoke dissipated into a single thin swathe high above the surface, then vanished altogether. Of the boat, there was no sign.

'*Kwaheri*, George,' the Boss Man muttered as the powerful boat swung round and headed south. '*Kwaheri*.'

# Chapter Two

Ever since the elections of late 2007 and the damn-near civil war that followed, Ernies had been scarce in this part of Kenya. Too many killings. *Too much heavy shit going down*. But scarce did not mean extinct – and thankfully there were always a few gunslingers determined to prove that tribesmen with machetes and cops with batons and semi-automatics couldn't spoil *their* fun.

'Aw – sonofa*bitch*! I've done it *again*!'

Up on the flying bridge of *Yellowfin*, Jake Moore sighed and killed the thirty-footer's twin engines and tried to remember that in these troubled times the Ernies and their money were just about all that kept his boat – and his livelihood – afloat.

'Mr Jake! Mr Jake!'

'OK, Sammy,' he said, wearily swinging his legs from the dashboard and easing himself out of his chair. 'I heard.'

His accent marked him out as an Englishman, and the faint north-east twang betrayed his Northumbrian roots. He certainly had the rugged look of a Cheviot hill farmer – and there were those who said he had the cussedness too. It was a comparison that always amused him, because Jake had never been to the Cheviots in his life. He belonged to the sea. And no matter how many times he tried to escape its grip, he always found himself coming back.

Down in the cockpit, Sammy the bait boy had clambered barefoot on to the stern rail and was peering out at the ocean. Behind him, strapped into the fighting chair, the overweight Ernie in the shop-new bush hat scratched the back of his neck, leaving livid white marks on the red raw skin. He spun round and smiled stupidly as Jake came down the ladder.

'It slipped out of my hands,' he said sheepishly. 'Sorry, man.'

There was a guffaw from the shade of the cabin awning beneath the bridge, where two more Ernies sat in deck chairs and tinked their beer bottles together.

'That piece of kit has got to be worth twelve hundred bucks *at least*,' one of them announced. 'You're a goddamn liability, Ted.'

'I'm real sorry, Jake,' the Ernie in the chair repeated.

'Not to worry,' Jake said evenly, thinking only of the hundred bucks an hour these bozos were each paying for the privilege of dropping his fishing rods in the ocean. 'You see it, Sam?'

'I see it, Mr Jake,' the boy said, his eyes never leaving the water as he stripped off his sun-bleached T-shirt.

'OK.'

He nodded to Sammy. Without hesitation, the boy launched himself from the back of the boat and arrowed into the fizzling remains of its wake. The Ernies under the awning levered themselves from their deck chairs and lumbered unsteadily to the stern rail, beers clutched to their bare chests.

'This I *got* to see,' one of them said, resting a broad buttock on the gunwale. The four men watched as

Sammy moved smoothly and rapidly through the water, tacking left and then right like a porpoise to take account of the swell.

The Ernie in the fighting chair shook his head in admiration. 'I'll be damned. You train him to do that?'

'I guess it's just a talent he was born with, Ted,' Jake said.

The Ernie, gawping out at the ocean, did not register the sarcasm in his voice.

Fifty yards out, Sammy suddenly disappeared under the water. When he resurfaced a few moments later, a twelve-foot fishing rod was clasped in his hand and a huge smile split his face.

'Sonofa*bitch*!' exclaimed Ted. He said something else, but the whooping and high-fives of his buddies drowned out his words.

Jake permitted himself a self-satisfied smile as Sammy returned to the boat. He reached down and retrieved the rod, then hauled the bait boy over the rail and into the cockpit.

'You oughtta get that kid on TV!' one of the Ernies exclaimed. 'I know a guy who's pretty high up in CBS. You're talking big money contracts, man—'

'Sammy's not for sale, pal,' Jake said, clambering back up to the flying bridge.

*Although he had to admit the money would come in mighty handy.*

The sun was setting by the time Jake cracked open his first Tusker of the day. The Ernies, lobster red and worse the wear for drink, had been deposited at their hotel marina, and Sammy, having cleared up after them, had dived overboard at Jalawi Inlet to swim back to the shack on the edge of the jungle he shared with his mother and younger brother. Now, as he steered *Yellowfin* through the narrowing channel of Flamingo Creek towards the boatyard a mile upriver, Jake took a long luxurious pull on the ice-cold beer. The first mouthful tasted of the sea salt caked on his lips, and he wished – as he always wished at this time of the day – that he still smoked. Packets of nicotine gum were no substitute for the harsh impact of Marlboro smoke on the back of the throat. Once the pharmaceuticals companies could replicate that sensation, tobacco's days would be truly numbered.

After anchoring the boat, he jumped into a motor launch moored in the shallows. He ramped up the outboard and directed the craft towards a row of bare lightbulbs strung along the length of the jetty. The jetty led to the workshop, a large breezeblock and corrugated-iron structure on the south bank of the river. From one corner of the building came the low thrum of a generator. In another corner, barely insulated by three large panes of clear plastic, was the office of Britannia Fishing Trips Ltd. Inside, looking for something in a pile of dog-eared papers stacked on a battered metal filing cabinet behind the desk, was Jake's business partner.

'Evening, Harry,' Jake said.

Harry Philliskirk grunted and wafted a hand in greeting, but did not turn.

'What have you lost?'

'I can't remember,' Harry said. 'But I will when I find it.'

'Good luck,' Jake said.

As far as he could see, it was a miracle that Harry could ever find anything in his self-imposed chaos of paperwork. But Harry – as Harry kept reminding him – had a *system*. 'Don't ask me to explain it, old man,' he would say, 'but it works.'

He was forty-two years old, but age meant nothing to the tall Londoner with the crisp Home Counties accent. As far as Harry was concerned, he simply *existed* – and, if you wanted to demarcate that existence into years, that was your concern. In any case, Harry was one of those people who defied any sort of pigeonholing. He stood six feet four inches in his sandals – Harry rarely wore shoes – and the shapeless clothes that hung from it exaggerated his spare frame. His usual choice of attire was a grubby vest and ancient army camouflage pants, a combination which was not helped by the grimy lime-green I RAN THE 1ST LONDON MARATHON baseball cap that he had worn with pride for over a quarter of a century. Unruly sprigs of greying greasy hair sprouted from under the cap, framing a narrow, almost morose face dominated by a large bony nose.

'There you are, you see!' Harry exclaimed triumphantly. 'Always trust in the system!'

He waved a piece of paper between his forefinger and thumb like Chamberlain returning from Munich.

'What is it?'

'An invoice for seventeen thousand dollars' worth of diesel fuel.'

Jake felt a knot tighten in his stomach. 'What about it?'

'I told the Arab that we had paid it. He said we hadn't. This would appear to prove that he was right and I was wrong.'

'Oh shit.'

'Hmm,' Harry said. He sat down on the corner of the desk and stared out of the office's single exterior window at the twinkling lights of the smart new marina complex that had been built on the other side of the creek. 'Still – not to worry.'

'We don't even have seventeen *hundred* dollars, Harry,' Jake reminded him.

'No.' Harry grinned, wagging his finger. 'But we've got the Arab's fuel.'

'Yes. And the Arab has got associates with guns.'

'Don't you worry about the Arab, old boy,' Harry said. 'Business will pick up. I can feel it in my water.'

Jake drained his beer and tossed the bottle through the office door and into an old oil drum in the workshop. 'Jesus Christ, Harry.'

He went to the window. Through the thickening gloom, it was still possible to make out the crisp modern angles of the brick and smoked-glass boathouses, clubs and diving schools which had sprung up seemingly overnight on the opposite bank. Their own premises were like an outhouse by comparison. Jake could imagine the blazered clubmen and their wives staring across from the veranda of the Flamingo Creek Yacht Club and wondering when the developers' bulldozers were scheduled to obliterate the squalor that gave such a sour taste to their gin and tonics.

'How were the Ernies?' Harry asked breezily. 'They were from Detroit, weren't they?'

It was Harry who had coined the term 'Ernies' to describe the pale-skinned tourists who came to Kenya in search of big fish. Jake didn't pretend to know about literature, but Harry assured him that every one of them, whether from the USA or the Ukraine, imagined themselves to be Ernest Hemingway, and that every puny baitfish they heaved aboard would have become a two-hundred-pound marlin by the time they returned home. Jake wasn't about to argue. Harry was an educated man. As long as the Ernies paid, Jake didn't care what he called them.

He reached into a pocket of his shorts and dropped a wad of bills on the desk. 'They paid up in full and in cash.'

Harry rubbed his hands and placed the cash in a tin box. 'God bless America.'

He put the box in a floor safe, then stood and rubbed the base of his crackling spine. Jake watched him closely. Ever since he'd got back, there'd been something about his partner that didn't seem quite right. The good humour and the bravado were in place, but then those were Harry's default settings. Jake had known Harry long enough to tell when he was hiding something.

'What is it, Harry?'

'Eh?'

'Out with it.'

There was a moment when Harry debated keeping up the pretence, but then it passed and his long face fell into an expression of weary resignation. 'Oh, Christ, Jake. I was hoping you might have already heard.'

'*Harry* . . .' Any number of apocalyptic scenarios suddenly flashed across Jake's mind. Had there been a bombing? Was the country about to erupt into bloodshed once again? Had the government in Nairobi imposed martial law and ordered all foreign nationals to get the hell out?

Harry slumped down behind his desk and removed his cap. 'It's Dennis Bentley.'

Jake almost laughed with relief. 'Dennis? What about him?'

Harry nodded in the direction of a ship-to-shore wireless positioned by the door. 'It's been on the radio all day.'

Jake scowled. 'Well, since *Yellowfin*'s radio is still in

bits, you can assume I'm in the dark. What's happened to Dennis, Harry?'

'Well, that rather does seem to be the point, old man.' Harry shrugged. 'Nobody appears to know.'

# Chapter Three

From the elevated third tee of Monte Julia golf course, Norrie Barclay could see for more than thirty miles beyond the scalped, arid foothills of the Sierra de Ronda mountains to the hazy blue smudge of the Mediterranean sea. On a clear day, it was possible to see even further to the jutting black tooth of Gibraltar nearly fifty miles to the south.

Norrie couldn't care less. The only view that concerned him was down into the steep-sided ravine that separated the tee from the handkerchief-sized green 219 yards away. This unforgiving bastard had already swallowed three top-of-the-range Titleists and wrecked his scorecard. Anyone else would have cut their losses and walked away – but not Norrie Barclay. There was the small matter of pride to consider. After careful deliberation, he selected a six iron from his golf bag, removed another gleaming Titleist from the ball sleeve and approached the tee-box.

'Come on, Norrie! This time!'

Norrie turned and smiled grimly at his playing partner lounging in the shade of the golf buggy.

'I'm going to whip its arse, mate,' he said confidently.

His playing partner swigged from a bottle of San Miguel he had plucked from an ice-box attached to the back of the buggy. He was slim built, and Norrie guessed maybe in his early thirties. He wore pressed slacks and a maroon golf shirt. Norrie Barclay knew him as Whitestone, but what he didn't know was that Whitestone had many names.

'Here's to fourth time lucky,' Whitestone said, and raised the bottle in a toast.

*Arrogant prick*, Norrie thought as he dug the point of his tee into the bone-hard earth. Just because his guest had fluked a drive to within five feet of the pin he thought he was Tiger fucking Woods. But just as quickly Norrie reprimanded himself. There was no need to be like that. All in all Whitestone was a decent bloke. Strange fellow, admittedly. A bit *intense* at times – and even now Norrie still couldn't place that accent of his. Was it European? Was there a touch of Kraut in there? It was hard to tell. Anyway, it didn't matter where he was from. What mattered was they'd done some good business since he'd flown in this morning. They could do with a few more like him on the Costa. And, it had to be said, Whitestone's merchandise was top class. Everyone thought so – which was why Norrie was making a healthy little earner for himself by reselling Whitestone's goods to his associates in the Balkans. All right, it wasn't strictly kosher business protocol, but you got nowhere in this world unless you were prepared to bend a few rules.

'Nice and easy, Norrie,' Whitestone said.

Norrie took a deep breath, exhaled slowly. *Backswing, hold, downswing ... Thwapp!* The contact was fat and healthy and echoed satisfyingly from the steep sides of the ravine.

'You're the man!'

With mounting excitement, Norrie shaded his eyes from the sun and attempted to get a bead on his ball. There! A speck of iridescent white against the blue sky, soaring high and handsome and on a perfect trajectory. Christ – maybe he *was* the man! The ball pitched ten yards on to the green, bounced once and then—

'Hold up! Hold up!' Norrie wailed. '*Nooo!*'

The ball bit into the turf and spun backwards, gathering speed as it approached the lip of the ravine. For a moment it seemed as if it might catch on the unruly tuft of marron grass that fringed the green, but instead the ball bobbled once and dropped over the edge, bouncing crazily on the rocky outcrops as it plunged into the abyss.

'Bad luck, Norrie,' said Whitestone, as he stepped from the buggy and made his way to the tee-box.

Norrie leaned on his golf club like a bent old man. 'I do not fucking believe what I have just seen. I *never* get backspin. *Never!*'

'Of course, it could be worse,' Whitestone said.

'I don't see how.' Norrie shrugged, staring balefully down into the crevasse.

In a single fluid movement that would have graced anybody's golf game, Whitestone swung a Big Bertha War Bird with nine-degree loft into the side of Norrie's head. Norrie staggered across the tee-box, blood pumping from a two-inch gash, then fell on his backside on the artificial grass.

'What did I tell you about business etiquette, Norrie?' Whitestone said calmly, the club resting on his shoulder like a parasol. 'About doing deals behind my back with *my* merchandise?'

'*Wha—*' Norrie said, his eyes spinning in their sockets.

'Now maybe you people here think it's acceptable to do that. Maybe you think it's all part of the rough and tumble. But it's not how I do business, Norrie. So as of now our arrangement is terminated. Do you hear me?'

Norrie attempted to swipe the blood from his eyes but succeeded only in overbalancing and slumping over on to his side.

'*Terminated.*'

Whitestone broadened his stance and drove the club head into Norrie's face. Three more swings, and what was left of the Englishman's skull had turned to pulp.

Whitestone scooped up the inert body with a single easy movement and dumped it behind the wheel of the golf buggy. After wiping the blood from the clubface with a towel, he replaced it in the bag tied to the rear of the buggy and then jammed the gear lever into the forward position. By standing on the running board, Whitestone was able to direct the vehicle to the lip of the ravine. As its fat front wheels went over the edge, and the buggy and its single passenger plunged two hundred feet on to the unforgiving rocks below, he noted with irritation that there was a single spot of fresh blood on his brand-new $300 golf shoes.

# Chapter Four

Suki Lo's skull-face cracked open as Jake and Harry walked into the bar and her Nike-tick eyes all but disappeared in the harsh creases of skin.

'Hey, boys – how you doin'?' she called out in a shrill voice that some of her regulars said could cut through fog better than the siren at Galana Point.

'A bottle of Mr Daniel's finest, Suki, my pet,' Harry said. 'And two large glasses.'

Suki smiled again. Her teeth were mottled and crooked; as long as they'd known her, she'd insisted that one day she was going back to Malaysia to get them replaced because dental work across there was dirt cheap compared to Kenya, and a million times safer. She claimed to know a dentist in Penang who would, for just one hundred US dollars, pull those rotten pegs right out of her head and replace them with gleaming white porcelain tombstones. Jake didn't know how gleaming white porcelain tombstones would look in her mouth. Suki Lo had the kind of lived-in face that suited the teeth she'd got.

She placed a bottle of bourbon on the bar and skimmed across two half-pint glasses.

'God bless you, my darling,' Harry said, tipping two large measures into the glasses.

Suki Lo's bar was three hundred yards along the dirt track from the boatyard and blended in perfectly with the rest of the ramshackle buildings on the south side of the creek. It was a rudimentary drinking den with nicotine-brown walls and bare wooden floors eroded by cigarette butts and spilled liquor. Along the length of the bar, shallow grooves and nicks had been carved by the elbows and gutting knives of Suki's regulars, mostly game-boat skippers and mechanics, a few of whom now sat in dark corners hunched protectively over their bottles of hooch. Normally they talked about money and women. Tonight they were talking about one thing and one thing only.

'Terrible 'bout Dennis,' Suki said in a low voice. 'Fuckin' uh-believable.'

'We heard,' Harry said, nodding. 'Shocking business.'

'Fuckin' uh-believable.' She shook her head and, muttering to herself, wandered into the kitchen.

Yes, Jake thought, sucking back a mouthful of bourbon. *Fuckin' uh-believable* just about summed it up.

Dennis Bentley was a white Kenyan who ran a game boat called *Martha B* out of a yard up near the mouth of the creek. He had a reputation as a loner and a cantankerous bastard, but then who didn't round here? Like most of the longtime independent operators in this part of Kenya, Dennis was more concerned with keeping his shoestring outfit solvent than affecting pleasantries. Jake remembered him as a tall, rugged-looking man in his mid-fifties who occasionally dropped into Suki's for a shot of rum.

According to Harry, Dennis had set out shortly before dawn that morning to pick up some Ernies from one of the all-inclusive hotels at Watamu beach, thirty miles to the north of Flamingo Creek. It was a routine job – the punters wanted to see some humpbacked whales – but *Martha B* had never arrived. After an hour waiting for him to show, the Ernies predictably kicked up hell; and it was this, rather than any concern for Dennis's welfare, that had persuaded the hotel owner to contact the coastguard. By then, however, a sugar freighter bound for Mombasa had already sighted oil and debris on the water around twelve miles east of Watamu. Fishing boats in the area had picked up the chatter on their radios and immediately switched course – but after six hours trawling the open sea they had found nothing.

*And all the while* Yellowfin *had been blithely chugging along with a boatload of Ernies and a radio that didn't work.*

'You OK, Jake?' Harry asked.

He nodded, but in reality he felt sick to his stomach – because as far as he was concerned there was an extra repugnant twist to Dennis Bentley's apparent demise. The Kenyan skipper's bait boy was a thirteen-year-old kid called Tigi Eruwa who lived with his mother and his elder brother Sammy at Jalawi Inlet.

The same Sammy who that afternoon had been amusing the Ernies with his swimming prowess, unaware that his kid brother was missing, presumed dead.

'Fuckin' hell,' Suki said, lighting a menthol cigarette and blowing the smoke in the direction of a long-defunct ceiling fan. 'How the hell does a boat just *blow up*?'

Harry shrugged. 'Who knows?'

'We don't know for sure that's what happened,' Jake said, but his words were greeted by a harsh cackle of cynical laughter from the other end of the bar.

A man in a khaki shirt and a greasy Peugeot cycling cap sat nursing an open rum bottle.

'*Martha B* was a fine boat – but she was fifty years old,'

the man said in clipped South African tones.

'Good evening, Tug,' Harry said without conviction. 'Are you well?'

'As well as can be expected, Harry,' the man said, splashing three fingers of liquor into his glass and raising it in salute. 'To absent friends, eh? Absent fucking friends.'

Tug Viljoen could have been anywhere between forty and sixty, but his deeply etched, leathered face made it difficult to tell. Behind his back Suki's regulars reckoned he looked like one of the mouldy old crocodiles he kept in his reptile park up near the Mombasa highway, but he always reminded Jake of the Tasmanian Devil cartoon character of his youth – a squat, powerful torso supported by unfeasibly spindly legs, and with a similarly wild look in his eyes.

'Yeah, *Martha B* was a bloody fine boat in her day,' Viljoen growled. 'But, when Dennis bought her, she was rotting away in a dry dock. I kept telling him he should get a new boat, but he treated her like a vintage car.' He drained the glass and immediately refilled it. 'Trouble is, vintage cars aren't as robust as new ones. *Martha B* was designed for rich piss-artists to go cruising up and down the coast, not for belting the shit out of for fifteen, twenty hours a day chasing marlin. The parts get old, they get worn. Pipes can start to leak. All it takes is a spark, or some drunken fuck to drop his cigarette end between the boards and . . . *kaboom!*'

'Aren't you a ray of fucking sunshine?' Jake said.

Viljoen swiped his mouth with the back of his hand, revealing an ugly stitchwork of scar tissue on the underside of his arm.

'Just being realistic, son,' he said. 'Used to happen

regular round here. Long before you pair of English *conquistadors* arrived. Speaking of which, how old is that bucket of yours?'

'Fifteen years.'

'Hah! Then you want to think about getting a new one before it's too late.'

'We'd need to think about robbing a bank first,' Harry admitted.

Viljoen stared at him for a moment, then laughed gruffly and turned back to the already half-empty rum bottle.

'Anyway,' Harry continued, 'as Jake said, we still don't know what's happened to Dennis. And, knowing that old bastard, there's still every chance he might be found drifting on a plank of wood.'

'You really think that?' Viljoen said sceptically.

'Always look on the bright side, Tug.'

'Bright side?' Viljoen said. 'I don't recall seeing one of them round here recently.'

**Do you love crime fiction?**

**Want the chance to hear news about your favourite authors (and the chance to win free books)?**

Kate Brady
Frances Brody
Nick Brownlee
Kate Ellis
Shamini Flint
Linda Howard
Julie Kramer
Kathleen McCaul
J. D. Robb
Jeffrey Siger

**Then visit the Piatkus website and blog**

www.piatkus.co.uk | www.piatkusbooks.net

**And follow us on Facebook and Twitter**

www.facebook.com/piatkusfiction | www.twitter.com/piatkusbooks